MONEY, POWER & SEX

A Love Story

NORIAN LOVE

This is a work of fiction. Names, characters business, organizations, places, events and incidents either are the product of the author's imagination or used factiously. Any resemblance to actual persons, living or dead, events or locales is entirely coincidental.

ISBN-13: 978-0692664780

ISBN-10: 0692664785

www.norianlove.com

Dedicated to my father's confidence ♡
My mother's love
My siblings support
And all of my T's, who spend their days inadvertently creating a better version of me
NL

WHY I WROTE THIS BOOK:

This book was inspired by fear, the fear that paralyzes us all. When I wrote the first chapter, doubt set in, asking me who I was to think I could do something this bold. What gave me the audacity to think I could tell a story from start to finish? There is a lot of cynicism in the world, sometimes your mind echoes the voices of those cynics and repeats those thoughts. Who you are meant to be gets muffled and you go quietly back into your routine, hoping to blend with society, and never be criticized. My mind told me this was foolish. And fear told me to do nothing.

But my heart, the one thing when at all possible we should try to listen to, told me to write chapter two. And so I bundled up those would-be future doubts and the thoughts of my would-be critics and kept stroking the keyboard. In short I wrote this book to let fear know that it won't dictate my time on this earth. I wrote it to challenge myself and I wrote it to leave something behind once my time on this beautiful planet of ours is done. If you are reading this, I thank you from the bottom of my heart. You validate the late nights, the early mornings, and the occasional interruption from my toddler for a diaper change. My one note directly to you, outside of my undying gratitude would be this: Spend the time you have on this earth making some contribution to it in a way that means something special to you and your creator. A higher power gave us each something remarkable. You owe it to yourself to find out what that gift is, and then share the beautiful uniqueness that is you. It's an exciting time to be alive because you're here.

Blessings always

No

www.norianlove.com

Twitter: @norianlove

Facebook: https://www.facebook.com/NorianFLove/

Amazon Author Page: amazon.com/author/Norian

CHAPTER 1
THE RESPONSE

It was 6:30 in the evening. Lucas was just getting home from a long day's work and was ready to unwind for the evening. Before he walked in the house, he let his dogs out of the garage. The weather had been dreadful the past week—every day below thirty, which was odd for Texas, but particularly Houston.

The weatherman's forecast had been for about twenty degrees warmer than it actually was, but Lucas, being a native of the city, wasn't really surprised that the forecast had been that far off.

AccuWeather, my ass, he thought as he petted his oldest dog, a full-blooded black lab named Nightcrawler. He'd taken a liking to the dog because of his jet-black coat when he found him as a pup at a shelter. Lucas, being 5'11" with a comparable dark-chocolate complexion, found the dog similar in nature to himself—compassionate, playful, and intelligent. He knew they'd get along once he named him Nightcrawler after *The X-Men* comic book character, and he wasn't wrong. The two had been great companions ever since.

On the other hand, Mika, his newest dog, had been abused by her previous owner before Lucas found her at the same shelter. Lucas had yet to win Mika's affection, but decided to leave her to her own devices until she finally came around in her own time.

As he slipped his key into the lock, his cellphone rang. Looking at the caller ID brought a big smile to his face. "Hey, you! How you doing?"

A soft, sensual voice on the other end responded, "Hey, baby! You home already?"

The world around him became warmer the moment Lucas heard Nichelle's voice. "Yeah, I'm home. How was work today?"

"You won't believe what happened," Nichelle replied. "You know that crazy lady I'm always telling you about? Well, you won't believe what she had the nerve to say to me today!"

Smiling on his way to the kitchen, Lucas said, "Oh, boy! I can't even begin to imagine what Ms. Patrice has going on."

Lucas took off his coat and turned on the kitchen light as Nichelle dove into her story—one Lucas knew all too well. Ms. Patrice had been working on Nichelle's nerves for the past year or so. She complained about everything from the other employees to why she wouldn't eat cantaloupe, but Patrice's current focus was on the recently ended review process—and Patrice was pissed. Not only was she upset, but she wanted everyone to know, especially Nichelle.

Nichelle continued. "So Patrice was just leaving my desk, and our coworker, James, was behind her as they walked into the kitchen, right? Now, you'd *think* the woman would hold the door open for him because he had both hands full, but this heifer slams the door in his face! When I asked her why, she was like, 'I'm a lady, so he should always open doors for me!'"

Nichelle was laughing so hard she sounded on the verge of tears as she continued her story. Lucas was laughing just as hard as he cut up the onions, the final ingredient for his entrée. He was making baked chicken stuffed with bits of turkey bacon, cheese, green onions, mushrooms, and a hint of garlic—prepared specifically for Nichelle.

"I don't mean to interrupt, baby, but how far are you from my house?" Lucas asked.

Nichelle replied, "Probably about thirty minutes with all this traffic. You know people don't know how to drive down here when it's cold, and they *sure* don't know how to drive when it's raining—and today it's cold *and* raining... so make it forty-five."

"Perfect," Lucas said.

The chicken would need thirty minutes to cook, and his sides of sweet potatoes and a broccoli and cheese casserole would need twenty minutes. He wanted to make sure the sweet potatoes were soft and the casserole cooled to the right temperature.

As they continued their conversation, Lucas went outside to get some firewood. He had acquired a stockpile of large- and medium-sized wood after he helped in the relief effort following Hurricane Patricia. He had anticipated burning the wood, but Nichelle called him crazy for doing it, considering the weather in Houston hardly ever got really cold. He decided to use this opportunity not only to heat the house and set the mood, but to make an "I told you so" point.

As Nichelle continued telling him about her day, Lucas interjected affectionately, "I miss you."

His heartfelt remark paused the conversation. It was filled with all the potency and weight of his meaning—and Nichelle understood his words perfectly. He couldn't wait to get his arms around her and draw her into one of those passionate kisses they shared so frequently. It was as if time lost all meaning when their lips met.

Some people throw their words around like Frisbees, but Lucas wasn't one of them. He was meticulous about his words to deliver his precise meaning. Nichelle admired the way he used his words.

In return, she filled her own words with fervor. However simple they might be, they were equal to his in value. "Baby, I miss you too."

At that moment, the silence was so dense that their individual thoughts carried them to the same place. The moment could've gone on for hours as they thought about what each wanted to do with the other. How they'd kiss, enjoy each other's scent, and touch each other tenderly.

As those thoughts snowballed, something unusual took place in the city of Houston. It began to snow, which brought both of them back to reality.

"Lucas, it's snowing out here!" Nichelle screamed.

"That's insane!" Lucas responded, still outside, loading his arms with firewood. "Hurry home. I've got a little something planned. In fact, I'm going to get off the phone right now so I can make the final preparations."

"Well, go ahead, Mr. Man. I don't want to hold you."

"Nichelle, before you go," Lucas added, "do you remember the question you asked me the other day? Well, I have an answer for you. I'll tell you when I see you."

As Nichelle tapped her phone off, she searched her memory for the question Lucas mentioned—and it made her giggle. Two days earlier, they'd been at Mike and Divia's house playing team Scrabble when Lucas ended up getting the winning word—a word she'd been having a hard time finding: value.

Beating the other couple prompted Nichelle to ask Lucas, "You bring so much value to my life, boo. What do I bring to yours?"

In response, Lucas said half-jokingly, "Let me think about it."

She should've known he was being literal—it was just his style. He was a man who stood behind his words. A good man—tall, dark, handsome, sexy, funny, smart—and he was all hers.

As she came up with more adjectives to describe Lucas, Nichelle's fingers slowly slid down to her crotch, and she almost lost sight of the road in front of her. The mere thought of that man turned her on. She could only imagine what he had in store for her when she got to his house. He was always full of surprises. She wanted him inside her, and the closer she got to his home, the more she wanted him.

Her panties began to grow moist the moment they first got on the phone, and she was finding it hard to concentrate. It seemed that no matter how cold it was outside, it was heating up inside the car. By the time she made it to the subdivision, she had worked herself up to the point where she was eager to practice her cowgirl skills.

After she parked her black Audi A5 in the driveway, she checked herself out in the rearview mirror and applied a fresh coat of her favorite lip gloss, *Petal,* by Bobbi Brown. She then adjusted her C-cup bra and took a deep breath. For the last forty-five minutes, the moisture that had been building in her panties had developed into a borderline gush. She was aching to get inside, peel off her clothes, and be pounded into submission.

She was so wet that it was hard to walk as her thighs glided from lubrication. There was no doubt in her mind that when she opened the door, Lucas would claw at her in an urgent attempt to get her into her birthday suit.

She scurried through the gate and fiddled with her keys to open the back door. Before she could slide her key into the lock, the door opened, startling her slightly, since the back hallway light wasn't on.

Lucas was at the door. Nichelle dropped her B. Makowsky purse in the hallway, slammed the door behind her, and kissed Lucas furiously, as if his lips were water in a dry desert. Lucas explosively returned the kiss, embracing her and pressing his body firmly against hers.

That kiss was only the beginning of what Nichelle had in mind. She could feel every inch of Lucas's manhood rising in his pants, so it startled her when he suddenly pulled away.

"What are you doing, baby?" she asked with concern and slight irritation.

"We have to wait," Lucas responded halfheartedly.

"Lucas, I'm in no mood to play," Nichelle said as she rubbed her hand over his erection.

"Believe me, baby, I don't want to play either," Lucas said, "but I told you I have something planned, and we—"

"I know, baby, but could you just fuck me really hard first, and then do what you have planned?"

It was an offer that Lucas didn't want to turn down, but he knew that as kinky as having sex in the hallway might be, they had all night, and eventually they could fuck their way back to that spot. "Nichelle, baby, I promise I'll make up for it," he said. "Please, come with me."

"Fine," she responded, her voice dripping with disappointment.

Only then did she realize that not only were the hallway lights off, but the only light she could see looked like candlelight glittering in the dimness of the dining room. As she wrestled her horniness into a corner, she smelled the scent of cinnamon-baked sweet potatoes, turning her grumpiness into curiosity. Her mood elevated even more when she realized there was a delicate trail of pink, red, and white rose petals leading to the kitchen.

Lucas led her by the hand, and as they entered the dining room, she saw a candlelit table containing a bottle of Yamhill-Carlton, one of her favorite pinot noir wines, and a three-course meal. The dinner looked and smelled as if it were prepared by Aida Mollenkamp herself, and her glass of wine sat poured and waiting.

“Surprise,” Lucas said softly. “If you’re ready, baby, let’s eat.”

Unable to speak, all Nichelle could do was sit, eat, and be astonished. She knew he had been planning something, but she never anticipated this.

The food was perfect; the ambiance heightened by what seemed to be a never-ending stream of her favorite songs—everything from *Let It Snow* by Boyz II Men and Brian McKnight to *Love TKO* by Teddy Pendergrass. By the time Ray Charles’s *Baby, It’s Cold Outside* came on, the only meat Nichelle wanted in her mouth was the one in Lucas’s pants. It was a double-edged sword. Lucas could turn her on, but Nichelle was so impatient once she got going that she didn’t want to wait—ever. His self-control was an enigma to her.

"Lucas, I want you—now!" Nichelle said breathlessly.

“Baby, you know I want you, too, but before we go there—and I *promise* we'll go there—I have one more thing I want to give to you.”

“Is it in your pants?" Nichelle asked with a wink.

Lucas smiled and replied, “Not just yet.”

“Lucas—” Nichelle said impatiently. She was excited to see what he had in store for her, but she was horny as a toad and didn’t know how much longer she could deny her inner freak.

Lucas smiled again at her impatience and said, “But it *does* require you to take off your clothes, so if you wouldn’t mind, I need you to strip.”

That last word couldn’t have sounded sexier at that moment, and Nichelle was instantly down with the idea of getting naked, yet she still wondered why he needed her to be naked while not mentioning anything about making love. Whatever it was really didn’t matter. She began to take off her clothes, since it was definitely a step in the right direction.

As Nichelle unbuttoned her crème-colored Ralph Lauren blouse and slid out of her charcoal Jones of New York slacks, she heard Lucas whisper, "Oh, damn."

Looking at Nichelle's 5-foot-3, silky-smooth caramel frame enclosed in a black satin Victoria's Secret bra-and-panty set, Lucas wondered why he'd been torturing himself for so long. The candlelight flickered on her skin, as if conforming to her natural shapeliness. Her body would have made a goddess feel inadequate, and "Oh, damn" was all he could muster at the moment.

She teased him slightly as she removed her bra, and in spite of himself, the way her breast popped out reminded him of a jack-in-the-box. Her breasts were so firm and perky that the bra was really just for show—and he couldn't wait to lick them.

As she slid off her black satin thong, Lucas was rock hard again, staring at the buildup of wetness clinging to her panties. He wanted to lick her where her moisture lived. He extended his hand to her now fully naked body and led her into the bedroom.

As he opened the door, she noticed the smirk on his face when she glanced at the fireplace next to the large window and saw an unspoken "I told you so." Lucas wasn't the type of brotha to let it go unmentioned, so Nichelle decided to beat him to the punch.

"So you got to use some of your firewood," she said with a sly smile. "Con—"

The word would've been *Congratulations* if the cat hadn't gotten her tongue at that moment. Sitting in front of her was a massage table and what appeared to be one of the most inclusive masseuse tool kits she'd ever seen.

"Okay, baby, just lay on the table and relax," Lucas said softly.

He was definitely in control of the evening, and she instantly understood his plan. His mission was to give her the full-service treatment, which she often referred to as the three F's: Feeding, Foreplay, and Fucking.

"I want you to just relax and enjoy this," Lucas said.

She did what he suggested, and then Lucas poured a mint oil extract onto her body to open her pores. Her muscles, tense from her sex drive, yielded to his will as he rubbed the oil onto her body. By the time he applied the butter crème wax, she had nearly orgasmed from sheer pleasure. He had mentioned this before, but she never had the pleasure of having wax applied to her body. It was warm as he applied it generously—the most marvelous thing she had ever felt.

The crème began to harden around the tense areas of her body, though it was still soft enough for his fingers to apply added pressure to her muscles. The only thing she could do was moan with pleasure as his hands worked her entire body, from her shoulder blades to her spine, from her waist to her plump bottom, from her thighs to her calves, and all the way back to her shoulders again.

"Lucas, baby," she said dreamily.

She didn't have to finish her request. Lucas knew it was time to give her what she'd been wanting all night. What they both wanted—each other.

"You ready for me, baby?" he whispered gently in her ear.

Nichelle could scarcely make out what he said. She had been so consumed with pleasure that she felt drugged. He'd brought her to the height of ecstasy without ever going inside her. She struggled to regain control of her senses as he pulled the hardened wax off her body. Only then did she realize that he was completely naked, too. He must've taken his clothes off at some point during the massage, but his hands felt so good she couldn't remember when.

Lucas had been waiting for this moment since he'd left her side the night before. He picked her up and laid her gently on the bed, then kissed her navel, working his way down her right thigh, picking up intensity as he moved into the center of her legs. Her clitoris was fully exposed and firm. He began to write the alphabet with his tongue, as if her clit were his notepad.

"A, B, C..."

Nichelle's inner freak had met its match, and Lucas wasn't playing around.

"G, H, I..."

His tongue bounced her clit around like a speed bag by time he got to "O," which ironically was when her body began to shake with an intense orgasm.

"Now let's set it off," Lucas said as he climbed on top of her.

She looked into his light-brown eyes and welcomed his body into hers. She'd been waiting for hours for him to give her his massive rod, and now it was finally going to happen.

For Lucas, it was like entering a temple. He had already been on his knees in worship; now he was about to enter the sanctuary.

Nichelle couldn't believe what she was feeling. Each thrust filled her with a completely new sensation. He was so firm, so thick, and so intense that her pussy felt as if it were being stretched each time he stroked in and out of her body.

His penis continued to rub against her G-spot, and like the massage, it broke down her tension, sending Nichelle's body into a stream of multiple orgasms. He plunged so deep inside her with each thrust that she gasped with pleasure, as if breathing for both of them.

The lovemaking lasted for hours. Nichelle came so many times that she could no longer recall when or how many times they switched positions. Each time she tried to put it on him, Lucas returned the favor by bringing her to another climax. When she found herself in the middle of one of the most mind-bending orgasms she'd ever experienced, Lucas finally reached his own climax. Her nails dug deep into his skin, but she couldn't have cared less as he moaned savagely, filling her vagina with a massive dose of his sweet, sticky semen.

His eyes then glazed over, letting her know he could go no more. He was as satisfied as she was—but a dozen times over. As they lay together in the darkness, Nichelle put her head on Lucas's chest, feeling his solid physique. She wiped away a final tear of pleasure, then sighed deeply, as if trying to catch her breath for the first time in hours.

"Happiness," Lucas whispered.

"Huh?" Nichelle asked, not sure if she heard him correctly.

"Happiness," Lucas whispered again. "The value you bring to my life is happiness. It's my pleasure to *serve* you."

She looked up at him and found serenity in his eyes. The entire night had been about catering to *her* needs. He took joy in pleasing her.

Laying silently in his loving arms, Nichelle wondered if there was any limit to Lucas's amazingness. She even wondered if he had somehow managed to make it snow, just to make the night more memorable. He knew she loved snow, even though it never snowed in Houston. Had he somehow worked a miracle? She wouldn't have put it past him. Not at this moment. After all, this cold winter night had been nothing short of perfect.

CHAPTER 2
RETRIBUTION

It was after midnight, deep in the month of November, as Donovan Brown waited for a cab. The night was overcast and only a degree or two above freezing.

Donovan, wearing only an olive-drab jacket over a black T-shirt and his favorite pair of Levi's 501 blue jeans, wasn't concerned about the weather, though. He itched for a smoke. It had been too long since he'd had one, and he wasn't sure what time the stores closed where he was going.

His wait finally ended when a Liberty cab pulled up to the curb. As Donovan put his duffle bag in the back seat, the driver asked, "Where to, fella?"

Donovan paused. After all the waiting, he wasn't entirely sure how to answer that question. To be honest, he hadn't really thought far beyond grabbing the pack of cigarettes.

"Hey, fella," the cabbie repeated, "where to?"

"6631 Apple Grove Lane."

It was the first address that came to Donovan's mind, and whether he admitted it to himself or not, it was where he'd been going all along—the only place he could go, really. He'd actually been waiting for that cab for the last thirty-seven months. Simply put, he'd been waiting to resume his life, starting with 6631 Apple Grove Lane. The only thing he wasn't sure of was if there would be a life there for him to resume.

As of late, his luck had been looking up. He'd been released from federal prison four years early for good behavior. Sighing deeply, Donovan thought about the last few years. He had been sentenced to ten years, but a plea bargain knocked three years off his term. With good behavior, his seven-year sentence had been shortened to three. It felt like a miracle, but he asked no questions about it while on the inside. On the outside, however, there were dozens of questions to ask —and he intended to start asking tonight.

The one thing prison had taught him was to keep his head down and his mouth shut, but now he was on the outside.

If there had been any advantage to being locked up, it was time. Time to work out, time to read, but mainly time to think. But too much thought could be a dangerous thing. Thoughts could play tricks on a man's mind—and Donovan had been spending a huge amount of time thinking about *her*.

He wondered what she looked like now. Would she be happy to see him? What had she been doing? Mostly he wondered why in the hell she stopped writing, visiting, or accepting his phone calls. In spite of himself, he brooded about who she was sleeping with. He'd been gone more than three years and she was an attractive woman, but the thought of her with someone else made his blood boil with silent rage —the same rage that got him locked up in the first place.

One thing he knew for certain: No matter what happened, he didn't want to go back to jail. As bad as he wanted answers, he had resolved to control his temper.

"Who are you talking about?" the cabbie suddenly asked.

"What did you say?" said Donovan, snapping out of his reverie. "Are you talking to me?"

The cabbie responded, "No, fella, you were talking to me. You just said, 'I hope she isn't pregnant,' so I asked who you were talking about."

"Oh," Donovan stammered. "Sorry. I was just rambling, I guess." After collecting himself, he added, "How far do we have to go?"

"About fifteen minutes," the cabbie responded flatly.

Donovan sighed. The mind really *was* a dangerous thing.

He decided to clear his head and focus on his freedom. The first thing he had promised himself when he got out the joint was a pack of Camels. He began smoking fourteen years ago, when he was just seventeen, and had developed a taste for the mesquite flavor of Camels.

He smoked in prison, but no one liked Camels, so he took what he could get—mainly Newports. But after a few months, he decided to quit smoking altogether. He believed that if a man had any control in this old world, it should start with his brand of cigarettes. In Donovan's mind, Newports were synonymous with incarceration, and so it had been two years since he had last smoked a cigarette of any kind. It was his small way of not becoming a part of the system.

"Is there a corner store on the way there?" he asked the cabbie.

"The closest one is about six blocks away."

"Okay, take me there."

"You got it, fella."

As he looked out the window, Donovan saw nothing familiar about this part of town. The area had been undergoing gentrification when he was sent to prison. There had been protests regarding the changes, and even State Representative Sheila Jackson Lee advocated leaving the historical parts of the neighborhood unchanged. It looked like she had lost that battle.

As the cab pulled up to the corner store, Donovan was surprised to see that the entire neighborhood had turned into something out of an IKEA catalog. Every building was *neo* this or *post-modern* that, and for a moment, Donovan wasn't sure he was in the right place.

As he reached for the door handle, he asked the cabbie, "Is this Third Ward?"

"Yes, my friend," the cabbie responded with a smile. "Just go six blocks down the street you're on and turn right. That'll be the street you're looking for."

"Wow, it looks like gentrification won," Donovan said, shaking his head.

"Huh?"

"Never mind."

The cab fare was $22.31, so Donovan gave the cabbie thirty dollars, grabbed his duffle bag, and stepped out. He took his time walking into the store, trying to acclimate to his new surroundings. It seemed impossible that things could have changed so much in such a short amount of time. He only wanted two things: a bottle of rubbing alcohol and a pack of Camels—and though he tried to maintain his cool, he found himself a bit edgy. He was actually uncomfortable in such a trendy convenience store. Just three short years ago this store would have been one of several, run-down stores that reeked of too much Pine Sol, no doubt to cover the scent of decaying rodent corpses. Today, it was nothing like that. It was clean and organized and lit very well. There was no glass shield to protect the cashier in case of a robbery, and the security cameras were optimal. It even had Wi-Fi. Ironically, the safety precautions made him uncomfortable.

"That will be $18.31, sir," the young teller said to him, She was an Asian girl with glasses and hair pulled back into a bun, no doubt a college student at the nearby university. Another rarity for the neighborhood he remembered. Young women did not work in places like this at night. He paid for the cigarettes and alcohol with his last twenty dollars, along with a box of matches before stepping back outside.

He opened the box of Camels slowly, savoring the moment. He pulled out two cigarettes, put one behind his left ear and the other in his mouth. He lit the first one and had every intention of smoking the second one before he got to 6631 Apple Grove Lane.

He took a long, deep drag, and as the smoke filled his lungs, he relished the moment, holding the smoke longer than normal. Then he let the smoke out in one long, calm breath.

After the smoke had been completely exhaled, he said softly, "Babygirl."

That was the second thing on his list: find his Babygirl. He picked up his duffle bag and walked off toward 6631 Apple Grove Lane. As he walked, he thought about the last time they were together—and how many times he fucked her that night after she realized he was going away.

He had a lot of explaining to do that night, but he'd never really been good with words. As wrong as he'd been, he truly wanted her to wait for him. He had taken her virginity, and since that time, he felt that she always belonged to him, mind and body.

Part of the reason he planned to show up unannounced in the middle of the night was because he knew she had been reading the letters he'd been sending, even if she never responded. She had to know he was on his way.

After three blocks, Donovan lit the second cigarette, still amazed at how much the neighborhood had changed. He didn't even feel like he was in Houston. Every building was either brand new or totally remodeled. Things had certainly gone on fine without him. He was hoping *she* hadn't done the same.

It was 1:35 A.M. when Donovan finally reached the front of the condo, edgy and uncertain. He'd been waiting for this day for so long, yet had no idea what was about to happen next.

Finally, he took a deep breath and told himself, "Cool it, D. Just be cool."

He rang the doorbell. He didn't want to wake up the neighbors by knocking. Besides, he'd always used a distinct knock when calling on her so she'd know it was him as soon as she heard it—and he wanted his sudden appearance now to be a surprise.

As soon as he rang the doorbell, he heard rustling from inside the condo, which was a surprise. She was a sound sleeper, and one ring shouldn't have been enough to wake her. As he waited, a dead space grew in the pit of his stomach. He was close to a quiet panic when the lock finally turned and the door cracked open

"Donovan!" she said in surprise.

"Babygirl!" he replied with a grin.

"What in the hell are you doing here?"

"You didn't know? Today is my lucky day!" Donovan responded. "'Course, if you had read my letters, this wouldn't have been so surprising."

She met his words with silence as he stood in front of the door. She was obviously at a loss for words, but he was determined to ask the questions that had haunted him for so long.

"So," he said as nonchalantly as possible, "who's the man in your life?"

"What?" she asked defensively.

"You've always been a heavy sleeper, Babygirl. There's no way you'd wake up after just one ring. You also didn't check the peephole before you opened the door. That means you were expecting somebody to pop up like this in the middle of the night. So I'm just asking who he is."

She ignored his accusation and asked more forcefully, "What in the hell are you doing here?"

Three years earlier, they would have been halfway toward tearing each other's clothes off, but here she was standing in the doorway offering him no invitation to come in.

Donovan knew he had to play it cool. "It's good to see you, Babygirl," he said softly. "You mind if I come in?"

"I... um..." she stammered, as if speaking to a ghost who suddenly appeared to open wounds she had been trying hard to heal.

"Babygirl," Donovan said after an uncomfortable silence, "your neighbors are gonna start wondering."

She opened the door wider, sighed, and said, "Come in, Donovan."

As he walked into the condo, Donovan was taken by the polished hardwood floors, the hand-woven burgundy-and-gold rug, the pastel-white crown molding, and the summer-teal paint in the hallway. Babygirl had apparently done pretty well for herself in his absence. She must have dug into architecture or fine arts to make her condo so impressive, although he knew that teal was one of her favorite colors.

"You did good for yourself, Babygirl," he said, nodding his head in appreciation. "You did real good."

After a long pause, she tried again. "Donovan, please tell me what you're doing here. Did you escape from prison?"

"Early release for good behavior," he said with a sly smile. Then he added, "What's the matter? Ain't you glad to see your man?"

"Donovan, don't go there," she said firmly.

"What you talking about, Babygirl?"

"I'm saying don't go there!"

He knew where this was going, but he also knew he had nowhere to stay and was hoping to sleep next to a warm body. Her warm body. He hadn't gotten any since he'd gone in, and even if they weren't going to stay together, he was determined to at least try to break her off once more.

"Donovan, you're a convict and a liar, and I'm not comfortable having you in my home," she said, her tone making it clear she meant business.

"Is that how you talk to your first love nowadays?" he responded. "Damn, things sure are different since the last time I seen the world."

When she made no reply, he sighed, then continued, "Look, Babygirl, we both know I did some bad things, and I'm really not trying to pick up where we left off. I just don't have many options right now. I know you don't wanna hear what I gotta say, and that's cool, but the only thing I'm asking for is a place to lay my head tonight and a warm shower. Could you at least do that for me—for old time's sake?"

Donovan knew she wouldn't be able to resist—it was his trump card, even though he was disappointed he had to use it so soon. She had really grown in his absence, and deep in his heart, he knew that nothing but another man could make a woman change that fast.

Part of him remained stunned at the way she was treating him, but he really shouldn't have been surprised. An attractive woman like her would never be alone too long.

After a long pause, she finally said, "Okay, but just for the night."

"Cool!" Donovan said. "If you'll point me to the shower, I'll clean the jail off of me. Then I'll answer any questions you've got, okay?"

"It's down the hall and to the left," she said, obviously uncertain of her decision.

When Donovan opened the bathroom door, he was again impressed by his Babygirl's flair for interior design. There was a rustic sink and bathtub, combined with off-white contemporary cabinets. The room itself was a baby-soft yellow, accented with off-white crown molding, and a décor that matched the teal hallway. It was all topped off with a light-brown accent on the bath towels.

He turned on the shower, elated to know he could have the perfect temperature of water hitting his skin for the first time in three years. Even when the hot water in the prison was working, he couldn't control the temperature—and it never got hot enough for him.

Donovan took off his clothes, then put his hand in the water to see if it was just right. It was. He stepped into the shower, thinking about his Babygirl as he lathered his body with soap. She'd cut her ponytail into a short bob and carried herself with a new sense of confidence. She was nothing like the girl he left—the one who couldn't make a decision without his say-so.

Moreover, she hadn't even given him so much as a hug in greeting, and he could tell from her body language that she was clearly defensive. There was definitely a man in the picture somewhere. As he was thinking, he heard her voice from the hallway, but he couldn't make out what she was saying.

"What?" he called, but he still couldn't understand her response. "Babygirl," he called again, "if you're talking to me, I can't hear you. Open the door and say what you gotta say."

The door opened slightly, and he heard her say, "I was just saying that there are washcloths and bath towels in the—"

She stopped mid-sentence as she caught sight of his dark, naked body. His chest was rock solid, the result of 400 pushups a day, and his torso was perfectly chiseled, complementing his well-endowed manhood—which had brought her to many orgasms during their time together.

Finally, she realized that she'd been staring and said, "Sorry. There are washcloths and bath towels in the cabinet." She then turned to leave.

"I'm sorry if I embarrassed you, Babygirl," he said, "but you've seen me naked before. Could you do me a favor and hand me that rubbing alcohol on the sink?"

She paused a moment, then handed him the alcohol, keeping her head slightly bowed. As she again turned to leave, Donovan said, "Babygirl, I'm gonna need some clothes to wear when I get out of the shower. Do you think you could find something your man wouldn't mind me throwing on?"

"Donovan," she said defensively, "do *not* presume to know me! I'll see if I can find something for you to wear."

"Thanks, Babygirl," Donovan said as she closed the door behind her. Then he began applying the rubbing alcohol to wash the stench of jail away from his body.

Donovan's father, Clive, had also been a con, and he frequently saw his father use rubbing alcohol to clean off the germs from his frequent prison stretches. More than anything, it was a psychological celebration of his release from incarceration. Although his father had never learned his lesson, Donovan was determined that this would be his first and *last* alcohol bath.

When he was done showering, he grabbed a towel out of a cabinet and was drying himself off when he heard a knock. He opened the door and asked, "Are these for me?"

"Yeah," she said. "Some sweatpants and one of your old T-shirts."

He grinned at the thought that she'd held on to some of his clothes. "Cool. Thanks."

He took his time getting dressed, imagining his Babygirl pacing the hallway trying to gather her thoughts, just as he was gathering his. Had he been delusional in thinking they were still in a relationship when he'd gone away? He wasn't one for a lot of talk, but tonight was going to be an exception.

As he opened the door, he found her sitting on the living room sofa, a glass of merlot in her right hand, her legs crossed, staring blankly into the distance. He walked toward a matching couch, where a glass of Jack Daniels sat on a coaster on the glass coffee table.

He sat down, picked up the glass, and took a drink. As he put the glass down, he let out a sigh. It was clear she had a lot to say, but there was apparently no way she was going to start the conversation. And so he waited and sipped his Jack, then poured himself another glass. She might not be the girl he left, but some things never change. She'd crack—and then he could talk to her without a fight.

It worked. Finally, she asked once more, "What the hell are you doing here, Donovan?"

"Look, Babygirl—" he began, but she cut him off.

"I wish you wouldn't call me that."

He leaned forward and said, "Now wait a damn minute. I know three years is a long time, but don't you think you should watch the way you talk to me? I didn't do anything to you, *Babygirl!*"

Her eyes narrowed as she responded, "Oh, really? Donovan, you shouldn't even *be* here! I've been watching the news while you were in the shower just to find out how you escaped from prison."

Donovan shook his head in disbelief, then leaned back and said calmly, "Babygirl, that dick he's givin' you must be mighty good."

She ignored his words, firing back, "How did you get out of jail for murder and robbing a bank in just three years?"

Donovan's composure buckled under her question, and he struggled to control his rising anger. "Hey, look! I ain't no damned con. They got me on manslaughter, true enough, but they couldn't pin that bank shit on me. I did my time and I got out—that's all!"

"They may not have found you guilty for the robbery, but that doesn't mean you didn't do it," she said firmly. "You were sentenced to seven years for manslaughter in the second degree. So why are you out in half that time?"

"Hell if I know, Babygirl," Donovan replied honestly. "The man said I'd been a good boy, and I ain't got no priors." He paused, then asked for the answer he really wanted to hear. "All I wanna know is how long you been fuckin' around on me?"

"What are you talking about?" she said protectively.

"Well, the last I checked, you and I had something goin' on," said Donovan.

Her temper flared as she responded, "Fuckin' around on you? You went to jail for robbing a bank and killing a man! I think anyone would have the right to decide it was over after something like that!"

"Is that right?" Donovan said calmly.

"Yeah, that's right, Donovan!"

He tried to maintain his composure and let her speak her mind, but her raw words hurt like an open wound doused with salt. He downed the rest of the Jack Daniels, then said, "Well, excuse the fuck outta me, Miss High and Mighty. I gotta admit I was expecting you to be mad, but I never thought you'd come at me like this."

When she didn't respond, he continued, "But since we're putting all our cards on the table, I might as well lay mine out. The last three years I've been holding onto just one thing—and that was the thought of me and you holdin' each other like we used to. Well, it don't look like I'm knee-deep in pussy right now, does it? The only thing you owe me is the name of the mothafucka who's been in my cookie jar since I've been gone."

With that, Donovan stood. His 6-foot-3, 240-pound body was intimidating even when he *wasn't* mad, and it was easy to see the fear in her eyes as he took a step toward her. "Babygirl, this can be easy or it can be hard, but I will get an answer. So I'm gonna ask you one more time: who in the fuck has been in my cookie jar?"

Her body was trembling as she looked up at Donovan's face. "L—Lu—"

Donovan stared down at her and demanded, "Tell me his name, Nichelle."

A tear rolled down her right cheek as she responded, "Lucas. Lucas Kimble."

CHAPTER 3
RONNIE

"I'll take it in red." Ronnie reached into her purse, pulled out her American Express Centurion card, and handed it to the clerk to pay for the Lise Charmel bra-and-panty set she had just finished trying on. "Better yet, I'll take one in red and one in black."

It was the end of the fiscal quarter and she was treating herself to something sexy, and when she found something she liked, she didn't mind buying two. As she waited for the clerk to bag her purchase, she got an incoming text message: "R we still on 4 2nite?" She didn't respond. She just slipped the phone back into her purse and glanced over to see how much longer the clerk would be.

There was no one word to describe Ronnie Duvalle. The court of public opinion had labeled her everything from a deity to a whore during her twenty-eight years of life. She had never liked labels, particularly ones imposed by other people, and that fact, more than any other, made Ronnie enjoy manipulating people's perceptions of her.

She carried herself with the confidence of a living fantasy. She was what every woman envied and what every man desired. Whatever the case, she was anything but *normal*, which was both a solace and a dilemma. Everyone who knew Ronnie, including Ronnie herself, understood that she was never meant to settle down. She'd never been interested in long-term relationships. In fact, the very thought of such a thing bored her. Because of that, she invested a great deal of time and energy into the thing that pleased her most—career success.

Physically, it was easy to understand why she attracted so much attention. Ronnie was 5'6" with forest-green eyes, auburn hair, and her golden, slightly bronze tone or "high yella" as the fellas called it, frequently drew comparisons to Michael Michele, which annoyed Ronnie. It was also the reason she worked so hard to differentiate herself from that woman. Although Ronnie was confident that her 36C bra and 38-inch posterior put her in a different league, it irked her that people still made the comparison.

Ronnie enjoyed finding new words to shock those who compared her to Michael Michele. Her other favorite was, "Let's put it this way —if we were both in the same room, which one of us would you want to fuck more?"

That not only ended the conversation, it established her as the alpha female—something Ronnie enjoyed because she loved being in command.

As physically stunning as she was, Ronnie was also mentally intimidating. A tiger in the boardroom, she was the youngest vice president in Burrows Industries' marketing division. While her looks certainly didn't hurt her rapid rise, no one challenged her knowledge or ability to succeed. She commanded respect, and she spent endless hours working on new ways to market, streamline, and understand the company's products. She took nothing for granted and never let anyone make her feel as if she didn't deserve every bit of success she achieved.

"Thank you, miss. Have a nice day," the clerk said as she handed Ronnie her bag and credit card.

Ronnie responded, "I plan to. You do the same."

As she walked out of the store her cellphone vibrated again. She pulled the phone out of her purse and saw another text message: "Ronnie, are we still on for tonight?"

She sighed and again slid the phone back into her purse. Once outside, she headed toward her platinum BMW X5 series SUV parked directly in front of the store. She opened the car door and sat in the driver's seat, placing her new trinkets in the passenger seat. When she turned on the engine, she glanced at the time: 7:56.

"He'll wait," she said with a smirk on her face.

As she put the car in reverse, the phone vibrated again. She leaned over, sifted through the purse, found the phone, and saw that the call wasn't from the man she'd been avoiding.

She answered, "Hey, girl, what's up?"

The voice on the other end was soft-spoken and refined. "Ronnie, did I scare you just now?"

Ignoring the question, Ronnie said, "Hey, Kendra! What's going on, girl? I thought you were someone else."

"Oh, really? Don't tell me you're dating now."

"Something like that. Girl, are you okay?"

The question was met with a pause, and then a labored, "Yeah... I'm—"

Ronnie interrupted, "Where are you right now?"

"At The Guadalajara having a drink."

"I'm not that far from you. I'll meet you there."

"Ronnie, you don't have to do that. I don't want to bother you."

"Kendra, if something's wrong, I've got time for you. You know that. I'll be there in five minutes, okay?"

"Okay."

The Guadalajara was within walking distance of the store Ronnie just left. Many Burrows' staff members frequented the restaurant after work, but by now, most employees were at home with their families, leaving the place fairly empty.

Ronnie grabbed her purse and walked toward the restaurant. She'd only taken a few steps when her phone vibrated again. She didn't even bother looking at the caller ID. She just powered down the phone to avoid any further distractions.

Within minutes she was opening the door to The Guadalajara and entering a contemporary décor she'd seen many times. The dimly lit room had mahogany furniture and crème-colored walls. Granite countertops and marble floors added to the ultramodern feel, offset by nineteen-foot double-glass windows, which gave the room a sense of transparency. It was a cozy spot to hang out or seek seclusion.

A server greeted her as she scanned the room for Kendra, but Ronnie said, "Thanks, I see my party."

Kendra looked sullen and deflated. Ronnie had known her for eight months, but it was the first time she'd ever seen her looking so disheveled. She'd obviously been crying, and there were napkins scattered about the table. Considering Kendra was borderline obsessive/compulsive, this was unusual.

Ronnie gave Kendra a hug and sat down across from her.

"Okay, girl, spill it," Ronnie demanded. "What did he do this time?"

Kendra responded, "Girl, Marcus is the least of my worries. Hell, I wish it *was* just Marcus. At least he would be a devil I'm used to."

Ronnie listened, then asked a more focused question. "Okay, if Marcus isn't the issue, what is?"

Kendra took a sip of her fourth glass of chardonnay before letting out a long sigh, "Do you remember when I first got here from Virginia? You and I didn't exactly get off on the right foot."

Ronnie smiled and replied, "Uh, if I remember correctly, your first words were something to the effect of, 'Look, bitch, stay out of my way.' That was only five minutes after you got your ID card."

Kendra couldn't help but chuckle. Taking another sip of wine, she continued. "I'd been warned about you by many people, so my defenses were up. You know how hard it is for a sista to excel at this level. Girl, it wasn't anything you did. I was just so focused on getting the senior vice presidency that I tried to show my authority. We were both competing for the job, and I knew you wouldn't have gotten as far as you did without being a fighter. So I brought my A game."

Ronnie leaned back and said, "I knew you were in a tough situation—new to the scene, and had to prove yourself. I didn't want to get into the back-and-forth of being the only two women executives at the firm—"

"Let me finish." Kendra interrupted. "I treated you like a subordinate instead of a peer because we were competing for the same job. It was wrong of me, and I'm sorry. You were always diligent about your work and willing to help out and, unlike me, never brought your personal life to the office."

"Kendra, you've had a lot to drink," Ronnie said. "Just tell me, what's all this about?"

A tear rolled down Kendra's cheek before she could catch it with a napkin. "I just want to apologize for ever being a bitch to you, that's all. I thought I was fighting against you, but you turned out to be my *only* friend through all this. You were just trying to be supportive."

"Kendra, you don't have to apologize," Ronnie said softly. "We barely knew each other. I mean, coming down here to a new city, revamping the entire marketing division, and then constantly being put in a position to compete for the very job you were hired to do—not to even mention Marcus. Like I said, you've been through a lot, so it's all understandable. I just wanted to be a team player."

"No, Ronnie. I really do need to apologize. You've *always* been a team player. I just couldn't see it. Behind my own bullshit and Marcus ... well, don't even get me started on his ass. He's the reason I'm in this situation in the first place."

"Girlfriend, what situation are you talking about?" Ronnie said forcefully. "Are you going to talk to me, or should I just start ordering shots of Patrón for both of us?"

"I'm being transferred."

Ronnie was stunned. At this level, it was unofficially a demotion, an indication that Kendra wasn't competent. For a woman, it was akin to career suicide. Poor performance would have resulted in being assigned to less significant projects or time out of the spotlight, but a transfer indicated lack of confidence by senior management—and that was nearly impossible to recover from.

Ronnie understood the full implications of what Kendra said. She sighed, flagged down a waiter, and said, "Two double shots of Patrón, please."

They sat in silence until the Patrón arrived. Then, with no hesitation, they downed their shots.

Ronnie broke the silence. "Where?"

"Back to Virginia."

Ronnie grabbed the waiter as he passed again. "Keep the shots coming, please." Struggling to find anything supportive to say, she told

Kendra, "The important thing is you're going to be near your family, and—"

"I don't want to hear that shit, Ronnie!" Kendra interjected, her voice dripping with frustration. "I busted my ass to get out of Virginia. I just needed some time to get my life together. I can't believe this is happening."

Another round of shots arrived, and after Ronnie downed hers, she looked deep into Kendra's eyes and said, "Kendra, I wouldn't be a good friend if I wasn't honest with you. You sacrificed a lot to get to Houston, and you sacrificed a lot for Marcus—but when you two started having a rough time, sweetheart, you chose him over your job."

Kendra sobbed, "I know I made mistakes. I thought he was cheating, but I couldn't prove a damn thing! It was too much to deal with at one time. He was coming home later and later, and then there were the phone calls at odd hours of the night. Hell, I even dragged you along to follow him. We didn't find anything, but I know he was there to meet someone. You tried to cover for me at work, and I have to admit that I thought you were being opportunistic at first, but in the end, you were the one who kept me sane. You could have gone after my neck because of the way I treated you when we first met, but you didn't. I've been a wreck lately, but you've always been right there. You get such a bad rap, and I wish I could be here to help prove everyone wrong about you, but I'm not. Needless to say, the promotion's yours. They're going to announce it next week."

"Girl, I'm not worried about that," Ronnie said reassuringly. "And as far as people's perceptions, people will think what they want. It never bothers me. I know most men are intimidated by a woman who thinks for herself. It's just something we have to deal with."

Kendra paused, took a sip of the latest round of Patrón, and said, "You know what bothers me most? Marcus and I had a great relationship before we moved to Houston. I never worried that he couldn't support himself or buy me nice things. He was *good* to me. I worked more hours in Virginia than in Houston, so it couldn't have been the hours. I think it was the city that changed him ... that changed us."

Ronnie leaned forward and gently stroked her friend's hand. "It happens, girlfriend. Let's be real. You were made for a city like

Houston or New York, but Marcus might be a bit simpler. I've never met him, but from the way you talk, he sounds like he's overwhelmed by everything Houston has to offer. Maybe he's insecure about all the men downtown who can buy you all the nice things he can't."

"I understand what you're saying," Kendra said, wiping away a tear with a napkin, "but I just feel it, you know? I can't put my finger on it, but something isn't right."

"Hell, men are too complicated," Ronnie sniffed. "That's why I stay single."

They were working on their fourth shot when Ronnie signaled to the waiter that they'd had enough. For the first time in eight months, Kendra looked beaten and unsure of herself, totally different from the woman who came to Houston to compete with her for the coveted senior position. Kendra had appeared strong, even overconfident, when they first met, but her ongoing troubles with Marcus eventually knocked her out of the race for the job.

"So what are you going to do?" Ronnie finally asked.

"Find out if Marcus is cheating on me," Kendra said with a sigh. "My career is in shambles, and I have no peace of mind. I need to—"

"You need to relax," Ronnie interrupted. "Listen to me: Marcus sounds like a good man. There isn't a lot you can do at work right now, so before you truly lose everything, go home and work on getting your relationship back on track. You've been chasing ghosts for some time now, but you haven't come up with anything. I think Houston has taken its toll on both of you. You were happier in Virginia, right? Well, it's time to find that happiness again. Then the relationship will work itself out."

Kendra sipped the last of her initial glass of wine as she thought about Ronnie's advice. After wiping her eyes, she took both of Ronnie's hands in hers. "The best thing that ever happened to me was making friends with you. You're right. I love Marcus. He was my rock. With him at home, I could take on everything that came my way. The moment I lost that connection, I lost my strength. I don't hate him for acting the way he's been acting—I just don't want to lose him."

"Then *don't* lose him, girl," Ronnie said, looking Kendra straight in the eyes. "Fight for your man! Don't ask what or why things have changed. Just go back home and love each other."

The waiter placed the bill on the table, and Ronnie placed a credit card inside the holder, not looking at the total. Then she looked at Kendra, a mere shell of the woman she'd been eight months before. She extended her hand, helped Kendra to her feet, and embraced her as tears streamed down Kendra's face.

"Take some time off and focus on putting it all back together, one step at a time," Ronnie said softly.

"Oh, Ronnie, thank you," Kendra sobbed. "I wish I had let you into my life sooner. Maybe things would've turned out differently. If there's ever anything I can do for you—"

"Girl, the past is gone," Ronnie interrupted. "Let sleeping dogs lie."

Ronnie signed the receipt, and then the two women walked outside, arm in arm.

"When do you start in Virginia?"

"Next Monday. I'll be gone by the end of the week, so there won't be any chaos when they make the announcement. I'm sorry I've been so worked up that I didn't congratulate you on the position. You do know I'm jealous, right?" Kendra said, smiling through her tears. "But right now I have bigger things to sort out."

"Kendra, work is the last thing we need to talk about!" Ronnie countered. "You just get better. If I don't hear from you until you get to Virginia, don't worry about it. We'll catch up soon enough, and one day I'd like to actually meet this Marcus character so I can give him my two cents worth."

"I'd like that," Kendra said with a smile. "Goodbye, Ronnie."

They gave each other a final hug, then turned and walked toward their vehicles. Ronnie got into her car, turned on Maxwell's *BLACKsummers'night*, and pulled out of her parking space. The title track, *Bad Habits*, made her start to move her hips in the seat as she drove home. By the time *Fistful of Tears* came on, she was all but dancing as she pulled into her condo parking space. She waited until the end of the song before turning off the engine.

As she got out of the car, she powered up her cellphone and saw that her inbox was full. She rolled her eyes and walked up the stairs to her second-floor condo, her keys and purse in one hand, her shopping bag in the other.

When she got inside, she walked into her bedroom and ran the water for a nice long bubble bath. The music was still playing in her head as she got undressed, slipping out of her four-inch Christian Louboutin shoes and her two-button Jones New York red top/black bottom suit.

She was in her bra and panties when her mind snapped back to the set she bought earlier. She pranced into the front room, sorted through the bag for the black set, then pulled it out and lifted it into the air in delight. Keeping it hoisted above her head, she waltzed back into the bedroom, imaging how sexy it would look on her body. She laid it at the edge of the king-sized bed and then went to stop the bathwater. She dipped her left foot into the water to gauge the temperature.

"Perfect. Now where is that lighter?"

It was never far from the bathtub since she enjoyed soaking in her bubble baths. She found it on the counter, next to her toothbrush. She lit two Love Spell candles she bought at Victoria's Secret sitting on the edge of the tub.

She was about to take off her panties when there was a heavy-handed knock at the front door. She grabbed her eggshell-satin robe from the back of the bathroom door and went to the living room to peer through the peep hole.

When she saw who it was, she rolled her eyes, unlocked the door, swung it open, and asked, "What do you want?"

"Ronnie, did I do something wrong?" the gentleman said as he walked into the condo.

"Yes, actually, you did."

"What was it, baby? Why haven't you answered my calls? I've been calling you all day."

"Clearly," Ronnie said sarcastically. "I could tell from the full inbox on my phone. Let's be clear about something: first, I don't have to answer your calls—ever. Second, I'm being courteous by letting you in my home, and third, the only thing you've done was outlive your usefulness."

"What in the hell are you talking about?" the man asked with increasing agitation. "I mean, we were just rolling around in your bedroom yesterday! Hell, you asked me to come over tonight, and now you're saying you don't want to be with me? If it's guilt, I mean—"

"Guilt?" Ronnie interjected, chuckling slightly, "There's no guilt on my part, but let me paint you a picture. You're about to go home and work things out with your girlfriend because she just found out she's being transferred back to Virginia and she *needs* you. Your services are no longer required. To be perfectly clear, it's over, Marcus!"

"What? I mean, what about what we have? If it's about Kendra, I was going to leave her for you, I swear!" Marcus responded, stunned by Ronnie's words.

"And why on earth would you do that? Wait ... you don't *actually* think I'm the type of sista who would support your non-working ass for the rest of your life, do you? To think, with all Kendra's strengths at work, her one weakness was your sorry ass. What you and I had was a business arrangement. We fucked, and it was alright—but now it's over. Am I making myself clear enough for you?"

Marcus's six-foot-one ginger-brown frame tensed with anger, and the veins in his neck bulged with resentment as he growled, "You evil bitch! Are you saying you deliberately set out to ruin us?"

"No, not at all," Ronnie responded coldly. "I set out to ruin Kendra. You were just ... collateral damage. But what are you so upset about? Like I said, the sex was okay, and Kendra doesn't know a thing about your cheating ass. I've been covering your tracks, because Lord knows she's been suspicious."

"Well, what if I decide to come clean and tell her the whole thing?" Marcus said, his eyes narrowing. "What if I tell her how you came over to our place one afternoon, knocked on the door, and then fucked the shit out of me when I didn't even know who you were? What if I tell her how you kept saying you wanted me?"

Ronnie's eyes were cold as marble as she responded, "Marcus, you can tell her whatever the fuck you want. It won't stop her from getting transferred, and it won't make a damn bit of difference to me—but where will you be? She'll be devastated—broken by that 'good man' she keeps bragging about, the one that cleans up so nice for corporate functions. I don't want you, and you'll find your sorry ass out on the street after that little revelation—and Kendra will be the laughingstock of the firm, even worse than she already is. Of course, you could do the smart thing. You could go home and *beg* for forgiveness, chalking it up to the pressure of the big city. Then you could give her some of that long dick of yours, pack your bags, go back to Virginia, and pretend the last three months never happened. It's your choice. I don't really care what you do."

Marcus glared at Ronnie, stunned at what he'd just learned about the true nature of the woman he'd been sleeping with for the past three months. He glanced around the room, then turned his attention back to Ronnie. The thought of hurting Kendra further was overwhelming, and he knew his own stability would be in jeopardy if she learned the truth. As much as he hated Ronnie, there were no other options.

"Well, what's it going to be, Marrrrrcus?" Ronnie said mockingly.

"You stay the hell away from us," Marcus said as he opened the front door. As he stepped outside, he turned back and repeated, "Just ... stay the hell away from us."

Ronnie's face showed no emotion as she shut the door and locked it again. Her mood quickly returned to delight as she waltzed back into the bedroom, picked up her phone, placed it on the Bose docking station in the bathroom, and pressed *play*.

She dropped her robe and slid off her panties as Sade's *Is It a Crime* began playing. She stepped into the warm water, unfastened her bra, and dropped it on the floor before slipping her body into the tub.

As the warmth of the water relaxed her, she thought about her day and smiled.

"Senior Vice President Veronica Duvalle," she said softly. "I like the sound of that."

What if they pick a man and don't give it to her? All hell will break loose!

CHAPTER 4
RESTRAINT

"Mr. Kimble, they're ready to see you now," the receptionist said politely.

"Thank you," Lucas responded as he placed his IPhone back in its holster.

Slightly agitated, he picked up his presentation folder and his laptop bag and walked into the conference room. It had been a couple of days since he heard from Nichelle, which was unlike her—unlike either of them, really, over the past few months. Every night, one or the other would stay over, or at the very least call—but it had been forty-eight hours with no communication. For now, he had to put all that aside. He was finalizing an Air Liquide financial audit and had to tell them what needed to be done to comply with government regulations.

The meeting lasted more than four hours, and Lucas found his thoughts wandering off, wondering if he could somehow wrap up the meeting early and drive by Nichelle's workplace to see if she was okay.

Well into the fourth hour, he was still more concerned about his lover than his job, but not once did Lucas let it show. He had an analytical mind and every detail was covered, every loose end tied, long before giving a presentation. He often spent hours with each member of the management team to gather as much information as possible before going on to the next phase. His system was so neat and efficient that the presentation itself was a mere formality, but Lucas prided himself on precision. He wanted to feel like he'd left a lasting impression on anything he touched, especially his work. No detail was expendable.

He believed that even if ninety-nine percent of his work was done perfectly, if the handoff wasn't just as seamless, it was a failure. However, he wanted this particular meeting to end early. There was a dread growing in the pit of his stomach that wondered if Nichelle had ignored his messages. His mind was consumed with how to leave the meeting as soon as possible without appearing to be in a rush. He was relieved when the group finally reached the last page of his presentation.

"As you can tell, we have taken the liberty of making sure all of the firm's funds were allocated to the proper places, saving you twenty percent going forward."

"How did we get to twenty percent?" one of the executives asked. *Were you not listening to a fucking word I said over the last hour?* Lucas thought to himself.

"We examined your wasteful areas of purchase and your technology areas and found places we could upgrade your systems and reduce spending." he replied as politely as he could.

"Where is that on the document I'm holding?" the same executive asked.

"The main points are on the final page." Lucas responded

"Oh, I see it now. Thanks."

"Not a problem," Lucas said aloud. *You fucking moron,* he thought to himself.

He tried to anticipate any questions from the other side of the table, carefully crafting his closing statement to keep questions to a minimum.

But there were questions, enough to require an entirely separate meeting. It agitated him to his core that he had to see this through. The one executive, the fucking moron, wanted to go in depth about the numbers because he was older and hardly ever showed up to these things. He had a vested interest today, even though Lucas did not have time for this. Every moment here was a moment away from Nichelle.

"Why can't we just lay people off like in the good old days?" the executive asked.

"Your company is running at optimal levels. Cutting staff could hurt morale and production. The technology we're recommending will allow you to cut waste while meeting your needs at peak production times. And best of all, your executives get brand new operating systems to play with," Lucas responded.

While several members in the meeting chuckled, the moron persisted. "I—I'm too busy to learn anything new. Why don't we just look at laying off employees to cover our expenses?"

I don't have time for this, asshole, Lucas thought to himself.

"John, the numbers are better than we expected. You're just afraid of change," another executive chimed in.

Thank God, Lucas thought, knowing an ally in the boardroom would allow him to end this pointless meeting early. "If the numbers work for you, John, I will personally address any outstanding issues you have once the transitions are made."

"Okay, but I'm only talking directly to you. I don't want to deal with anyone who doesn't know what they're doing."

"You have my word," Lucas responded. He shook hands and left cards with each of the senior partners, who were all impressed by his presentation. With the good-byes said, he briskly walked into the hallway and headed toward the front door.

Once he reached the parking lot, he hurried toward his black Mercedes CLK. As he opened the door, he checked his phone one more time to see if there were any missed calls, but there weren't any.

He put his laptop bag in the passenger seat, thinking, *I've never actually been in the building where she works. I don't want to look like I'm hounding her, but I can't help wondering what's up with all this. I thought everything was good between us. Maybe I should just chill, but what if something's wrong with her?*

"Fuck it, I'm going!" he said aloud as he started the car.

During the thirty-five-minute drive, he thought about their last few days together, trying to remember anything he could have said or done to create this uncomfortable situation. He thought about the last morning they talked. Nichelle had said she was going to work late and would be going home that night. Nothing in her tone indicated anything was out of the ordinary.

Maybe he was smothering her. He enjoyed every moment of her company, but maybe she didn't feel the same, which was reasonable because of the sheer volume of time they spent together.

Hell, we have been going pretty strong. Maybe she just needs a break and doesn't know how to tell me.

Every mile he drove seemed to bring a different scenario to light, each more dire than its predecessor. He tried to calm himself by remembering that he was imagining worst-case scenarios. The reality would probably be far less dramatic. Still, the last three months with Nichelle had been some of the best of his life, and he just knew he wasn't alone in that sentiment. Not if their passionate nights were any indication.

No, something had to be wrong.

Lucas decided that if he couldn't locate Nichelle at work, he'd head for her condo. As he exited the freeway, he looked for her office building. He was only a few blocks away from the answers to the questions that had been nagging him for hours.

He parked half a block away, fed the parking meter two dollars in coins, locked his car, and dialed Nichelle's number one last time as he walked toward the front door.

As usual, there was no answer, so he left one final voicemail. "Nichelle, it's Lucas. Baby, I'm sorry to do this, but I'm worried about you. If it's something I've done, I'd like to talk about it, but if you don't want to talk, I'm willing to wait. Right now I'm in the downstairs lobby of your building, and I'm headed to your office to make sure you're okay. If you're not there, I'm going to head over to your place, and if you're not there, I'm going to call the police and file a missing person's report. I'm sorry if you think I'm overreacting, but I'm worried about you, baby. Give me a call."

As Lucas entered the building, he looked at the security desk. He hesitated before deciding to proceed with purpose. He approached the guard sitting behind the security console.

"Excuse me. I'm here to see Nichelle Myers."

"And you are?"

"Lucas Kimble."

"Have you been in our building before?"

"No, it's my first time."

"Then you'll need to fill out this form. What's the purpose of your visit?"

"A form? Is that necessary? I'm a friend, and we were supposed to have lunch together. I just want to know if she's here today."

Lucas, agitated by the guard's words, picked up his phone again to call Nichelle. There was no answer.

The guard turned toward his computer screen. "How do you spell the name?"

"Her last name is MYERS. M-Y-E-R-S."

Unfucking believable, Lucas thought. The guard was obviously hassling him, and he was in no mood for this today. He picked up the phone and dialed Nichelle's number for a third time, pacing back and forth but not breaking eye contact with the security guard.

"Nichelle, it's Lucas again. I'm standing in the lobby of your building, and your rent-a-cop is giving me a hard time. Give me a call."

Lucas was so engrossed in his call that he didn't realize he was blocking the door until he heard a woman's voice from behind him say, "Excuse me, sir."

Lucas turned around and said, "I'm sorry. I was somewhere else."

"Well, yes, I can see that," the woman replied, "and I couldn't help overhearing your conversation. Are you looking for Nichelle Myers?"

Lucas was surprised. "Yes. Do you work here? Do you know her?"

The lady smiled and responded, "Yes, on both counts. She's actually in my department, but I haven't seen her today. I'm sorry, but who are you?"

"My name is Lucas. This is awkward, but ... we're dating and I haven't heard from her in a while, so I wanted to make sure everything was alright. I don't want to involve you or anyone at work in this, but I'm concerned."

"It's not a big deal," the woman said. "I'll double-check if she's here today because, as you've probably figured out, security gives non-employees the runaround."

"No kidding. Thank you. That would mean a lot to me, Miss—?"

"Veronica," the woman said, reaching out to shake his hand. "But everyone calls me Ronnie. Ronnie Duvalle."

"Lucas Kimble. It's nice to meet you."

Ronnie reached into her purse and called one of her co-workers. "Hey, Mia, it's Ronnie. Did Nichelle come into work today?"

Lucas waited expectantly, but could tell by Ronnie's eyes that he wasn't going to like the answer.

"Okay, thanks, girl. I'm on my way up. I'll see you in a minute." Ronnie hung up the phone and said, "Sorry, Lucas, but she's not in."

Just then Lucas' phone rang. He looked at the caller ID as Nichelle's picture popped up. Holding up a finger to ask Ronnie to wait, he said, "Nichelle, baby, are you alright?"

"Hi, Lucas," Nichelle responded gingerly.

Lucas took a couple steps back, but Ronnie followed him as the conversation continued.

"Baby, where have you been?" Lucas asked. "I tried to call and email. Hell, I'm standing in your building right now. What's wrong, baby?"

"Nothing's wrong ... I ... um... just needed to think about some stuff."

"Baby, did I do something? Whatever it is, we can talk about it."

"No!" Nichelle said emphatically. "You've been perfect, baby, and you haven't done anything wrong. I'm ... I'm just going through some stuff, and I need you to give me some space while I figure it out."

"Baby, tell me what's wrong," Lucas pleaded. "Are you home? I'm on my way over."

"No! Please don't come over!" Nichelle countered. "Please just respect my space and give me time. I promise I'll talk to you about it later. I have to go now. I'll call you later. Just ... just go home."

With that, the phone disconnected.

Ronnie, observing from a few paces away, knew the conversation hadn't gone the way Lucas hoped. She had heard how sincere Lucas was, and it impressed her. She wasn't displeased by his appearance, either. All 5'11" of his chocolate physique, housed in a two-piece charcoal Oscar De La Renta suit, brought the term "eye candy" to mind.

"How is everything?" Ronnie asked softly.

After taking a second to compose himself, Lucas said, "She's ... um ... she's okay, I guess."

"I don't mean to pry, but how are you?"

"I'm ... fine."

Ronnie moved in closer, "Listen, Lucas, it's none of my business, but I can tell when someone gets bad news. I know you don't know me, but you seem like a good guy having a bad day. Why don't we walk across the street and grab a cup of coffee? My treat."

"Veronica, I appreciate what you're trying to do, but right now—"

"It'll be my treat, and I'm not taking no for an answer." Ronnie interrupted, interlocking her arm with his.

She led Lucas toward the Panera Bread bistro directly across the street. At that time of day there was little traffic at the bistro—just a few stragglers from the work crowd. Lucas walked in a daze, his emotions focused on the conversation with Nichelle.

"No! Please don't come over!" Nichelle's plea played over and over as he blindly let Ronnie lead him across the street. The words kept scratching through his mind like nails on a chalkboard. It made no sense.

As they walked into the bistro, Lucas decided that maybe his self-imposed chaperone was right. He could use a distraction, even if only for a few minutes, just to clear his head.

"Two chocolate mocha lattes, please," Ronnie said as she handed ten dollars to a girl behind a counter. Then, scanning the room, she escorted Lucas to a booth by the window while their lattes were prepared. As they waited, she asked, "So, Lucas, what do you do for a living?"

"I'm a consultant. Audits mainly."

"Really? What firm?"

"RainHouse & Arms," he responded blankly. "Actually, we have a bid in for Burrows' marketing arm right now."

"Is that so?" Ronnie replied as the waitress arrived with their coffee.

"Yeah, but there's a good chance we won't get it," Lucas added. "Word on the street says Price Waterhouse is a shoo-in to get the account."

"Why do you say that?"

"Well, it's no secret that Burrows Industries has been looking for a good auditor since the collapse of Arthur Andersen, and they've done more work with Price Waterhouse than any other firm. Besides, we've had a bid in for three weeks now and haven't heard a thing, so, no offense, but it's probably sitting on some blowhard's desk who hasn't taken the time to look at it."

"No offense taken," Ronnie responded with a smile. "I'm sure everything will work out in everyone's best interest."

"What about you? Do you work with Neecie ... I mean Nichelle... directly?"

Ronnie laughed. "Is that what you call her? Neecie? That's cute." Lucas was clearly uncomfortable that he let his nickname for her slip, but Ronnie continued, "Well, I don't work with *Neecie* on a daily basis, but we do work in the same area, so I'm familiar with a lot of her projects. I must say she's done a good job hiding *you,* though."

"What do you mean?"

"Well, there are a few women around the office who can't seem to keep their personal and professional lives separate, and with a nice-looking man such as yourself, most women would parade him up and down in front of the whole office."

Now it was Lucas's turn to smile. "Oh, is that right?"

"That's right, and about six months later, they either lose him or start complaining about how miserable he's making their lives. It's a common thing, really." Lucas chuckled, softening the concern on his face and prompting Ronnie to add, "So, you can laugh! That's a good sign."

Lucas took a sip of his coffee and responded, "I guess I didn't make a very good first impression. I'm sorry we had to meet like this."

"Lucas, I'm just messing with you," Ronnie said as she leaned in.

"There's nothing to apologize for. You've just had a long, hard day. Our meeting was a healthy distraction. After all, it gave you a few minutes just to breathe."

"No argument there," Lucas responded. "I'm a little embarra—"

Ronnie interrupted, "Matters of the heart are never an easy thing, and we all respond differently. But if you want my unsolicited advice ... if you go looking for something, you're usually going to find it. Give it time."

There was a brief pause as Ronnie gathered up her belongings. "I'll tell you what. Let's not bring it up, and if we ever meet again and you see me upset about something, you can buy *me* a cup of coffee. Deal?"

"It's a deal," Lucas said, taking a final sip of his coffee and standing as Ronnie grabbed her purse and stood to leave. When they got outside, Lucas turned toward his car, then turned back, shook Ronnie's hand, and said, "Thank you for everything, Veronica. It was very nice to meet you."

Ronnie smiled and replied, "It was nice meeting you, too."

The two parted, Ronnie returning to her job and Lucas to his vehicle.

As he sat in the Mercedes, Lucas told himself, "Chill, Lucas. She's right. Just play it cool and go home." For a few moments, his fingers tapped nervously on the steering wheel as a tornado of thoughts swirled inside him.

"Fuck this!" he said as he turned the key and darted into traffic.

From where she was standing, Ronnie could see the CLK pull away. She had passed the security checkpoint, but slowed her pace. As she watched Lucas disappear, she reached into her purse and pulled out her phone. She scrolled through her contact list and stopped at the name Doug Villarreal—Burrows Industries. She dialed the number to his desk phone.

A male voice answered, "Burrows Industries, this is Doug."

"Douglass, hi! It's Ronnie."

"Hi, Ronnie. How are you doing?"

"I'm fine. Listen, Douglass, what was the difference between the bids from PWC and RainHouse & Arms?"

"Well, RainHouse & Arms came in about seven percent lower overall, but I thought you decided to go with PWC like we always do."

Ronnie smiled and replied, "It's a woman's prerogative to change her mind, isn't it? Let's change things up. I think we should try RainHouse & Arms for the next year so we can make some comparisons and see if it makes more business sense."

"Are you sure? They came in lower than Price Waterhouse in the past, but—"

"Yes, I'm sure," Ronnie said. "In these times, we need to cut costs wherever we can, and I think we'll be pleasantly surprised with the talent RainHouse & Arms has to offer."

"Okay," Doug said. "I'll make it happen."

"You do that. You make it happen." Ronnie smiled as she slipped her phone back into her purse, stepped into the elevator, and pressed twenty-one. "You make it happen, indeed."

CHAPTER 5
THE RESOLUTION

Lucas parked his car in front of Nichelle's condo. As he stepped out of the vehicle, Ronnie's words echoed through his mind: "If you go looking for something, you're usually going to find it."

He knew something was wrong, and he was determined to find out what. He looked around the neighborhood, one he rarely saw in the afternoon. School had just let out and children scurried across the crosswalk directly in front of Nichelle's condo.

As he walked up the cement stairs, his stomach churned with apprehension. His legs felt as if they were pulling themselves out of the cement with each step. It was intuition. Every sense told him something on the other side of the door was out of order. He wanted to be wrong and tried to convince himself he was, but his nagging fear wouldn't go away.

He hesitated before ringing the doorbell to cool his internal dialogue. When he finally rang the doorbell, he listened for any unusual activity from the other side of the door. He heard no indication that anyone was home.

He waited, his instincts battling his poise. He knew Nichelle had to be home. It took her hours just to get ready to go to the grocery store, so it was impossible she could have left in the time it took him to drive here.

"Chill, Luke," he murmured as he pressed the doorbell again.

There was a lot of activity going on outside, but he kept a laser focus on Nichelle's door—and the silence on the other side echoed louder in his mind than all the outside hustle and bustle of the afternoon.

Just as he was reaching to ring the doorbell a third time, the lock shifted. The door swung open and there was Nichelle, standing in the doorway in a blue silk robe. A wave of relief rushed over Lucas as he looked at her. She appeared to be unharmed, but he was disappointed she didn't seem happy to see him.

"What are you doing here?" she said flatly. "I told you not to come over." The words were foreign to him, a far cry from the woman who had always been glad to see him in the past.

"I—I just wanted to make sure everything was okay," Lucas stammered as he walked into the condo, closing the door behind him. "Are you alright?"

"Everything's fine," Nichelle responded defensively. "Thanks for checking. You can leave now."

"Leave? Then why did you bother to let me in?" Lucas said, flustered and confused. "Nichelle, baby, what's wrong?"

The woman standing in front of him physically resembled Nichelle, but the similarity ended there. The fact she didn't seem to want him there was completely out of character. He wanted answers, and thought he deserved them.

Nichelle sensed Lucas's frustration and softened her tone. "There's nothing wrong, baby. I'm ... I've just got a lot on my mind right now, and it's stressing me out. I need to take a few mental health days."

Lucas continued looking at her, trying to understand. In all their time together she had never lied to him, as far as he knew, but now her eyes were telling a very different story. He wasn't sure why, but he knew he wasn't going to get a direct answer. That didn't mean he would let it go.

He hesitated, then asked, "Is there anything I can do to help?"

Nichelle could tell Lucas was hurting, but she didn't know what to say. As much as she wanted to, she couldn't be honest. She also knew that Lucas had to go before a bad situation became even worse.

"Baby," she said, finding it hard to look him directly in the eye, "I have a major project to turn in by the end of the quarter, and it's stressing me out. That's all that's going on. I'm sorry for being so short with you, but I'm tired and I need to clear my head and get some sleep."

With each word Nichelle said, Lucas felt more cracks developing in his heart. She had never hidden the truth from him before, so why now? Something was obviously wrong. Since the time he entered the condo, they hadn't left the hallway or made any attempt to go into the living room. For the last day or so he felt unwanted, and standing in the hallway further confirmed those feelings.

He sighed deeply as he resigned himself to the situation. "Okay," he said, shaking his head, "I'll get out of your way. I'm sorry—"

Before he could finish, Nichelle interrupted, "Baby, everything's going to be fine. I'm just ... well, I'll be fine ... *we* are fine."

He couldn't be sure if she was telling him that to console him or if she actually believed it. In either case, he could tell she wasn't being honest. He reached into his pocket for his car keys, looked into her face, and said, "Okay. Call me when you're ready to talk."

He leaned in and kissed her on her cheek. Nichelle closed her eyes as his lips pressed against her face, partly because she couldn't look at him directly and partly because she was fighting the tears building up inside her. Instinctively, her arms wrapped around him. He clutched her in response, and they stood in each other's arms for a long moment.

Then Lucas released her and turned toward the door. "Okay ... I better go."

"'K..."

"I'll ... talk to you soon," Lucas said uncertainly.

He didn't wait for a response. He opened the door and walked out, then made his way downstairs, climbed into his Mercedes, and drove away, never looking back.

Nichelle closed the door and pressed her back against it, tears flowing down her cheeks. She had never wanted to lie to Lucas, but she had no other choice. She walked into the kitchen to pour herself a glass of wine, wiping away the tears.

As she took a sip, the sound of the doorbell called her back to the front door. She put the glass down and went to answer it, hoping it was Lucas so she could tell him the real story—from the very beginning. He'd always been so understanding, and she hated to see the pained look on his face as he walked out the door. She wanted to apologize.

She unlocked the door, surprised and disappointed to see Donovan Brown waiting outside. "Babygirl, what's wrong with you?" Donovan asked. "You look like you just seen a ghost."

"I have, and he keeps haunting me," Nichelle said, turning around and leaving the door open.

As he followed her inside, Donovan said, "Oh, you got jokes, right?"

Donovan sat on the couch as Nichelle went into the kitchen to retrieve her glass of wine. As she returned to the living room, she took a giant gulp to calm her nerves. Donovan pulled out a cigarette, but Nichelle aggressively snatched it out of his hand.

"Oh, damn!" Donovan said unconvincingly. "I forgot I can't smoke in here."

Nichelle rolled her eyes as she sat on the arm of the couch, seething with resentment. "Donovan, you gotta go. I got something good going and I don't want to mess it up." she said, her voice trembling.

Donovan leaned forward and said, "Word? So I guess I'm supposed to mess it up for you, huh? Always the victim, aren't you?"

"Look, I ... I don't want any trouble from you. Hell, I'm letting you stay here out of respect for what we had, but I'm happy right now."

"With Lucas, right?" Donovan said, his agitation unhidden. "That had to be the cat I just saw climb into that Mercedes. Nice car." Nichelle's jaw dropped, but before she could respond, Donovan continued, "Yeah, Babygirl, I saw him leave. I mean, how long do you think it takes to buy a pack of Camels?"

"Look, all I'm saying is that what we had is over. It's over! You need to make some other arrangements."

Donovan stood and walked toward Nichelle. "So you happy now, huh?" he said, his tone dripping with sarcasm. "And I need to make new arrangements."

"Yeah, that's right," Nichelle said, trying not to be intimidated by his approach.

Donovan walked behind her, then leaned in and whispered gruffly, "Babygirl, I thought we were past all that, but looks like you need a little reminder of what happiness is."

He grabbed her by the neck before she could speak and pushed her down over the arm of the couch. He then reached under her robe and pulled down her panties.

Still holding her by the neck, he pulled down his sweatpants and entered her forcefully, saying, "Oh, I see you was expecting me."

"I hate you!" she screamed.

"Really? Say it again," he said, stroking in and out of her body. Her body shivered and she repeated the phrase, but with only a fraction of her previous defiance.

"You what?" he said, sliding even deeper inside her as she moaned and tried to catch her breath. He pulled most of his cock out, leaving only the tip inside, asking again, "You what?"

"I ... I ... want it," she moaned quietly.

Donovan smiled and said, "Well, then, I'm gonna give it to you, Babygirl."

As he thrust his ten-inch shaft deep inside her torso, Nichelle's eyes rolled to the back of her head. She arched her body higher to receive all of him, and he slid in and out rhythmically, pushing as deep as he could into her core.

"He ain't been hitting it right, huh?" Donovan said firmly. "You creamin', Babygirl."

She didn't reply. She just continued to push her body back toward him, her body begging for more of him. Her fluids trickled down her legs as he roughly dove in and out of her in that way she had missed so much. Lucas was a passionate lover, but what they were doing at that moment wasn't lovemaking. Donovan was fucking her—and fucking her well!

Donovan placed his hands around her buttocks and gripped them tightly, pulling her toward him with brute force as he thrust his pelvis forward violently. Nichelle felt as if he was touching her spine. He'd always been able to reach her G-spot this way. He was bringing her to an orgasm, and he was in full thrust when she came the first time.

As she moaned, Donovan growled, "Is this what you want, Babygirl?"

She moaned again and breathed huskily, "Daddy, I missed it!"

He turned her over and climbed onto her, lying on the couch and never making eye contact. Starting slowly to regain the trust of her body, he pushed into her. He picked up speed as he masterfully drilled the insides of her vagina. He taught her what to like many years ago, and it was as if his penis was the key to her body, unlocking the gates of pure ecstasy.

"Oh, Donovan," she moaned, pushing up to meet every thrust, wrapping her arms around his waist to pull him even deeper inside her as she came again, even more intensely than before.

As he felt her body trembling beneath him, Donovan pulled Nichelle to the floor and entered her again. As he moved his hips, he looked her in the eyes for the first time since they began and whispered in her ear, "You got one more in you, Babygirl?"

Nichelle spread her legs as wide as she could and gasped as he continued massaging her G-spot with his shaft. She clutched his back as he grunted, the sweat dripping from his face onto her robe, exciting her so much that another orgasm instantly seized her body. She dug her nails into his back as she came, with Donovan close behind, his body trembling as he released his load deep into her body.

Almost instantly, he pulled out and lifted himself back onto the couch. He reached into his sweatpants, which he hadn't even bothered to fully remove, and pulled out a Camel. Looking defiantly at Nichelle's trembling body, he lit the cigarette and deliberately blew the smoke toward Nichelle still lying on the floor.

After a long pause, he said gruffly, "So, this Lucas cat—how 'bout you take care of that?"

Nichelle's eyes again filled with tears. She had just betrayed her lover in the worst imaginable way. More importantly, she knew Donovan wasn't going anywhere anytime soon now that he'd had his way with her again. She didn't know if she even wanted him to go anywhere. She hadn't felt this good in so long that she could hardly process her thoughts. Her body still shook with the physical ecstasy she had just experienced.

"Babygirl," Donovan said firmly, "you heard what I said?"

"I heard you."

"So what you gonna do?"

Nichelle rolled onto her side and turned her back toward Donovan, her mind drifting to the last hug she shared with the best man she had ever known before he walked out the door.

She wiped the tears from her cheeks and softly said, "I'll end things with Lucas."

CHAPTER 6
REMEMBERING

"Morning, baby. Did you sleep well?"

With her eyes still closed, Nichelle groggily responded, "I slept like a baby thanks to you, daddy. You know you know how to put it on me."

He responded, "You know how I do, baby. Would you like some coffee?"

"Ooh, that sounds nice," she said as she pulled herself closer to his warm body next to hers.

"It does, doesn't it? So why don't you get your ass up and fix me a cup, too?" The words hit her frame as hard as her reality did. The man sleeping next to her was not her lover, Lucas Kimble, but Donovan Brown, her recently paroled ex-boyfriend. The ex she spent so much time, energy, and money trying to escape. The self-serving ex she couldn't stand. The ex she had been sleeping with every night for the past week. She turned over and opened her eyes, hoping that the past seven days were somehow a nightmare she had awakened from, but Donovan was laying in her bed. She did not hide her disappointment as her face confirmed her sad reality.

"Babygirl, you gonna get up and get that coffee?" the bronze-skinned rogue interjected, roughly interrupting her thoughts.

"Damn it, Donovan, get your own damn coffee! Matter of fact, get your own damn life and leave mine alone!" Nichelle lashed out as she sat up in the bed to grab her robe and cover her naked, caramel physique.

"But Babygirl, you are my life," he responded mockingly. "Is that what old boy would tell you right now?" Donovan's words dripped with sarcasm.

"Don't go there, Donovan. You know what—when are you leaving? This situation wasn't supposed to be forever. It's well past time you get your shit together and keep moving."

"Is that right?" Donovan responded with slight agitation.

"That's right. I'm not taking care of you. You needed a place to get on your feet, and I've gone above and beyond to help an old friend, but now it's time for you to get on with your life. *Your* life, not *ours*."

Donovan got out of the bed, grabbed his black sweatpants, and slid them on a leg at a time. He grabbed his cigarettes and lighter off the nightstand, took one in his hand, and lit it. Taking a deep puff, he exhaled like a dragon, his fiery glare extinguished by Nichelle's icy gaze.

"So you not gonna take care of me, huh? Did I ever ask you to take care of me? What about all them years I took care of yo' ass, huh?" He walked in closer. "What about all them times you was buying purses and shoes and whatever the hell else you wanted—and don't give me that shit about you didn't know what I was up to because not once did you ever ask where the money came from. You didn't seem to have a problem when I was holding things down. But now not even one week out of jail, all of a sudden you too good for me? Well, too good for anything but my *dick*. I guess that the one thing you haven't been able to replace in your new man. Isn't that right?"

The words sliced into the harsh truth she'd been trying to ignore, and she responded with all the growing frustration and confusion she'd built up over the past week. "Donovan, you don't know anything about me. It's been *three years*. I don't owe you anything."

"Nah, you wrong, see. I know *everything* about you. I know you ain't told that dude it's over yet, and that's for a reason. I know you ain't over fucking me yet, and that's for a reason, too. And what's the reason, Nichelle? You want the best of both worlds, 'cause that's who you've always been. It's the only way you know how to be. You like reaping the benefits, but turn a blind eye to anything you don't want to deal with. So you can sit there and front like you've changed so fucking much since I've been gone, with your nice job and your new condo, but we both know what this is. You're the same old selfish-ass Babygirl, just a different wig."

He was putting his cigarette in the ashtray when she swung her fist full force and made contact with his left shoulder blade. He grabbed her arm painfully as she tried to attack him with her other hand, but he captured it just as easily and forced her backwards onto the white goose-down cover laying on top of the bed. Her temper flared as she screamed, "Let me go!"

Donovan smirked, drew her in closer, and condescendingly said, "Same old Babygirl." He shoved her onto the center of the bed and pulled down his sweatpants, his shaft at full attention. There was fight in her eyes, but her hands were busily unfastening her robe to unveil her enticing frame. He wasted no time with the formality of foreplay as he slid himself inside her. She reacted like a heroin addict, rolling her eyes into the back of her head and arching her back to receive him fully. He was the man she gave her virginity to so many years ago; the man who taught her how to first make love, then how to fuck, and then how to do what they were doing now. There was no real name for it—it could only be described as a vicious symphony of sexual expression. She wrapped her hands around his neck and gazed deeply into his eyes. He responded with the same intensity, pulsating inside her the way he did the night before. There was a fierce aggression to their intimacy. Nichelle hated Donovan for the hold he had long held over her, but she also missed him. He understood a piece of her that she couldn't share with the world. Donovan may have disliked how easily he had been discarded over the past three years, but his heart, however cold, had never left Nichelle, his Babygirl. This ferocity was demonstrated repeatedly during their lovemaking. She would slap him as he thrust into her; he would wrap his hand around her neck as she bit him. And he never waited to make sure she was satisfied. No, he fucked her as if his orgasm was the only thing that mattered, and to her body, it was. The more punishment he doled out during their encounters, the more she would cum, reaching her own explosive peak during his violent eruption. This was a bond only the two of them truly could appreciate. After all, he was her mentor in love. She was able to help bring herself to a nice orgasm with other men, but her orgasms with Donovan were beyond her control. He would consistently make her cum multiple times in their sessions. When the sex was over, she felt immensely satisfied, panting, quivering, and gasping for air. He, too, was satisfied, but he never stayed around long enough to cuddle or hold her; never showed her any affection beyond a slight gaze. The only way he signified his pleasure was by smoking a cigarette immediately afterward, however cliché.

As Nichelle slowly regained her breath, Donovan reached for his lighter. She had been riddled with guilt since she had all but stopped communicating with Lucas, but the more time she spent with Donovan, the easier it became to deal with hurting Lucas. She had suppressed her true freak nature for too long and needed this volatile release. She wouldn't have to see Lucas until she was ready. She wasn't strong enough to deal with her issues, and at the moment, had no cure for her addiction to Donovan. She examined the fresh wounds on his back from her acrylic nails, impressed by how little they seemed to bother him as he grabbed his black T-shirt and put it over his strapping frame.

"Where are you going?" she asked halfheartedly.

"It's like you said, Babygirl, I don't owe you anything."

Nichelle scowled at him. She knew this feeling all too well. She was falling in love with him again. Donovan could make a woman—any woman—feel like she was alive for the very first time, and then, in an instant, take it all away. He was what was known as a plumber; a master of dick-o-logy. She came more intensely, more frequently with him than anyone she had ever been with, which was odd since he was so selfish in bed. It was never his intent to please her, his strong, almost violent strokes merely an endgame to his own climax. But his endurance, his girth, and his control always guaranteed the multiple "O." Nichelle had no control over their sexual escapades. He gave it to her how he wanted, when he wanted, for as long as he wanted. She was just along for the ride, which, she realized, was the thing she liked most about fucking him. She was so often in control at work or in her day-to-day life that she needed to be fucked into submission. Lucas was a gentle and attentive lover, but she missed being fucked into compliance. She missed Donovan's dominance.

Slipping out of bed and walking into the bathroom, she turned on the shower. She then looked back toward the white goose-down cover that blanketed the bed. Donovan, in his ruggedness, was still a handsome man, and she always found it appealing how his muscles contracted after sex. His skin clung tightly to his flesh; every motion of his body telegraphed by his flexing muscles. Any guilt she had for her infidelity was slowly being replaced by the assertion that she had, in fact, never broken it off with Donovan. The heat from the water washed away any notion she had to tell Lucas about him. She didn't want to feel this way, but seeing him, touching him—and being touched by him—brought everything back. In the good old days, he would pick her up from design school and take her to Frenchie's for lunch and tell her how she was going to *blow up*. Donovan believed in her far more than he believed in himself. That belief gave her the confidence to finish school at the top of her class and quickly climb the corporate ladder. She threw herself into her work to forget the pain and embarrassment it caused having her boyfriend jailed for robbery and manslaughter. Now she was here, where she always dreamed of being, and there seemed to be no place for him. Yet here he was, carving out a place for himself in her home, her life, her bedroom.

Work came rushing back to the forefront. She had taken several personal days since this fiasco began, and now it was time to go back to the office. She had been following the events of the week via email. For the most part, things were quiet, though that could change at the mandatory office meeting. Any news of importance was always shared at that meeting. There were meetings for all kinds of reasons, but the mandatory ones introduced major changes. Whatever the case, she looked forward to the change of pace. Going back to work would be a healthy distraction from her life. As she got fully dressed, she looked for Donovan, but he had, as expected, left without saying a word. She saw him through the window walking down the street and momentarily considered calling out to him to give him a ride wherever he was heading, but decided against it. She could leave without saying a word to him, too. She picked up her keys and headed off to work. A quick trip down 288, and she was in the heart of downtown Houston, not far from the Allen Center. She typically had time to put on the radio and listen to about four songs before parking her car, but today she chose to drive in silence. Left alone and with no distractions, she let her mind go blank as she re-entered the work world. She didn't want to think about Donovan, and she definitely didn't want to think about Lucas. All she wanted right now was to be the manager of the marketing arm and deal with whatever the mandatory meeting presented.

There was a science to determining if the meeting would be good or not. There was always a catered breakfast, but if the meeting was positive, the company brought in Panera Bread. If the meeting was negative, then doughnuts and kolaches were ordered from the nearest bakery. Today, there was Panera, so today would be good. As she made her way toward the conference room on the 21st floor, she heard Ms. Patrice cackle. Her good mood meant she was either trying to make an impression, or she had taken the right dosage of her medication. The running office joke said she was on medication because she was always so nice when you first met her, only to become a ball of drama after the first month. Normally, Nichelle would steer clear of Ms. Patrice and her antics, but having been out of work for several days, she decided to let curiosity get the better of her and find out the name of her latest victim. Nothing could have prepared her for who she was talking to.

"Oh, there she is! Nichelle, we were just talking about you!" A cocktail of surprise and sullenness bled into her system as Ms. Patrice stood next to Lucas. "What's wrong, Nichelle?" Ms. Patrice said aloud, far louder than normal, making the awkward scenario even more uncomfortable.

"Huh? I—nothing..." she stammered, blatantly lying.

"Ms. Patrice, could you give us a moment?" Lucas said, coming to his mate's assistance. "Well, I wanted to tell you about ..."

"We'll be back, Ms. Patrice. I promise," Lucas insisted as he grabbed Nichelle by the hand and led her toward an empty conference room, not bothering to wait for Ms. Patrice to respond. They walked into the conference room, where he closed the door firmly behind them.

As Lucas was about to speak, she cut him off, her agitation apparent. "Lucas, what are you doing here? I thought I made it abundantly clear that I need time, and you take that as an invitation to come to my job and talk to my coworkers? Not cool, Lucas. Not cool in the least!"

"Nichelle, calm down."

"No, I will not calm down. You show up to my home unexpected; now you're at my job? This is a little Michael Ealy of you, don't you think?" she said, referencing the actor who played a stalker in *The Perfect Guy*.

Lucas, stunned by the accusation, decided enough was enough. "Look, Nichelle, I'm here because ..."

"I don't care why you're here—this is my *job!* You need to go now!" Not hearing another word, she opened the door and was startled to find a slender, six-foot-two, handsome Caucasian man in a blue, Ralph Lauren custom-tailored suit standing in the hallway.

"Ah, Lucas, I was just looking for you. Ms. Myers? Welcome back. Do you two know each other?" Milton Burrows, the president of the company, asked. Nichelle was at a loss for words—not because of his sandy brown hair or deep, ocean-blue eyes, but because she had no idea why he was looking for her mate.

"We're old friends," Lucas said, saving his lover for the second time today. "Is the meeting about to begin?"

"Yes. Conference Room B."

Lucas turned to a still speechless Nichelle and said, "It was great seeing you again. We'll catch up later."

His quick thinking helped her collect her derailed train of thought. Nodding in agreement, her curiosity consumed her. As the trio made their way to the conference room, Nichelle wondered how Milton Burrows knew Lucas, and why her partner was part of the meeting. She glanced at him to gauge his reaction, but he was stone-faced. The conference room was almost full as they walked in with the president of the company and took seats at the very front of the room. Milton crossed over to the podium, leaving the two of them next to each other. She took advantage of the moment to whisper the first question bubbling about in her forehead. "What in the hell is going on?"

"Shhh, your president is talking. Besides, you seem to have all the answers, don't you?" he said matter-of-factly, without ever looking at her.

CHAPTER 7
RIGHT OR WRONG

Milton stood at the podium as the rank-and-file executives took their usual seats in the brightly lit conference room before the door closed. Lucas, agitated by Nichelle's behavior of late, made sure he gave her a condemning glance. He wasn't sure why he was the recipient of her disdain. Their relationship until this point had been perfect. Even though it was rewarding to see her doing well, it did not make him feel easy. The lifespan of their relationship seemed to hang in the balance, fully at the mercy of this new persona she had adopted. Something was certainly going on, but whatever it was would have to wait for another place and time. Milton proceeded with his speech. It was the typical speech Lucas heard from countless CEOs and company presidents—calling on a company like his to examine the books before the final quarter to evaluate employee performance and show that the executives had squeezed maximum profit from the firm's revenue stream. The running joke at Lucas's firm was that this was "Yacht season" for the higher-ups. While it was tongue in cheek, it was not too far off from reality. After all, Lucas was well aware his primary function was to make sure the top executives' bonus payouts were as large as possible, even if that meant recommending mass layoffs. While layoffs always left a bad taste in his mouth, it was a cost-effective strategy for ensuring his own continued employment. His mother had been laid off from her own job his senior year in high school, and he saw firsthand the devastating effects of downsizing. She struggled for years to get back on her feet, and he struggled to pay for college. He made it, but not everyone did. He couldn't let that happen if at all possible.

The sound of Milton's voice mentioning a familiar name brought his focus back to the meeting.

"...Ms. Duvalle has brought in RainHouse & Arms to ensure we are on task. Right now, it is my pleasure to introduce Mr. Lucas Kimble. He'll be the senior auditor for the next six months to make sure we are right where we need to be."

Lucas stood up and glanced at Nichelle, whose eyes displayed embarrassment following her accusations. He waved to the employees in attendance and nodded to Ronnie siting further down the row next to her lackey, Douglass. Lucas then sat down to allow Milton to proceed with his presentation.

"I also want to announce a major promotion in this department. By now, I'm sure you're all aware that Kendra Daniels has decided to go to our Virginia office to head things up there. With that said, the board looked at several options carefully and, in the end, concluded there was only one candidate to fill her shoes; the kind of employee that will continue to bring the originality and progressiveness we are known for here at Burrows Industries. I'd like you all to join me as I announce, effective immediately, the promotion of Nichelle Myers from senior manager to vice president."

Lucas looked at Nichelle, who was visibly stunned. He stood up to clap along with everyone else, thinking to himself, *Maybe this is why she's been so distant.* It made sense that she needed to put in extra effort with such a big jump in responsibilities looming. He conceded that he may not have been as understanding as he should have been. He leaned over to tell her "Congratulations" while everyone else applauded. Her genuine excitement for the promotion further convinced him his concerns were in his head. Her corporate culture was unforgiving and demanding. Pressure could make anyone distant or distracted. The smile she showed at that moment was the one he fell in love with. He decided to eliminate any of his concerns until they had a chance to talk. While he continued to celebrate with the crowd, he noticed Ronnie Duvalle

seemed to be the least enthused person in the room.

Milton proceeded to close his speech. "I think that's all I have, ladies and gentlemen. I will be sending out a correspondence to recap this meeting later in the day. Feel free to email me with any questions or concerns, and thank you all for the work you do for us here at Burrows Industries."

As the meeting dispersed, Lucas walked over to Nichelle and congratulated her again, this time placing his hand on her shoulder. She turned to him. "Thank you. I'm—I can't believe it."

"If anyone deserves it, it's you," he said with an honest smile. "Look, now that you're a big-time VP and all, maybe we can celebrate later?"

He noticed his words made her uncomfortable. "Honestly, Lucas, I'll probably be busy getting up to speed. Excuse me for a moment. I have to catch Mr. Burrows before he leaves." Once again she was short with him, bringing back his apprehension like a festering wound. Something was certainly off, but they couldn't discuss it right now. It wasn't the time or place to express how everything had been turned on its head. How quickly it went from passion to frost, as if their love had a light switch attached to it. He would have to deal with that later, for both their sakes. He turned to locate Ronnie, who was already heading his way with purpose. "Veronica, I was hoping we could get together later on today and begin creating the framework for what we need to examine—"

"Not right now, Lucas," she said. While she gave him the courtesy of stopping, she made no eye contact with him as he spoke. Instead, her eyes were fixated on Milton as he and Nichelle walked out the door. Unsure of what was going on, Lucas decided to remain on task and continue pitching Ronnie.

"Based on preliminary data, it appears that your company would be happy with ten to twelve percent of revenue saved. I think we need to—"

"That sounds great," Ronnie said before he could recommend his strategy. She was anywhere but there with him, and so he decided it was best to get out of her way.

"I'll let you go where you need to be, Veronica."

"Fantastic job. Now, if you'll excuse me, I have an elevator to catch."

And with that, Veronica Duvalle, passed-over senior vice president, chased after the company's president.

CHAPTER 8
ROLLING HEADS (SON OF A BITCH)

Ronnie hastily walked toward the elevator desperate to reach the steel doors before they closed. As Milton pressed the closed button, she slipped a hand between the rubber bumpers a split second before they met, stopping the elevator from moving.

"Milton, do you mind telling me what the hell is going on?"

"I'm sorry?" he said, pretending to be unaware of her gripe.

"You know goddamn good and well what I'm talking about! Are you telling me I need to compete for a job that's already mine again?"

Milton looked at his administrative assistant, who pretended to be busy making arrangements as the elevator opened on the first floor. Ronnie could care less if the woman was in the elevator at all. She demanded answers for Nichelle's promotion, and Milton didn't feel like he owed her one. "You know as well as I do there are no guarantees in business."

"Are you fucking kidding me?" she screeched, venom secreting from her voice.

"Ronnie—"

"Don't tell me to calm down, Milton! I worked too damn hard to get leapfrogged by some novice. I've gone the extra mile too many times for you to make this woman, or anyone else, my peer."

Ronnie looked at his crotch as she finished speaking. Milton pulled Ronnie to the side of the elevator bank, away from prying eyes. "And I appreciate your ... ahem ... efforts tremendously, but the board feels we need to have a larger sample size."

"The board? Fuck the board! I'm the one over here making this company money. While everyone sits on their ass and screws their mistresses and girlfriends, I'm the one working my ass off so their kids can go to boarding school and equestrian classes. This is bullshit! I should be senior vice president, yet you promote someone else to vice president and I get nothing? After the year I had? Bottom line is you *owe* me, Milton, or is one chocolate treat not enough for you?"

Milton looked at his assistant, agitated by the direction this conversation was taking. "Angela, could you give us a moment?"

"I'll confirm that your car is brought around, Mr. Burrows," she responded softly.

As Angela walked away, Milton adjusted his tie and his coat and leaned in closer. "Now you listen to me. I'm the goddamn president of this company! You do not talk to me like that in front of people! That kind of attitude is the very reason we didn't give you the promotion."

"We?" she said with animosity.

"Yes, we."

"And I thought you were the goddamn president of this company," she replied sarcastically.

He took a deep breath and held it before exhaling, the scent of Irish crème lingering on his breath from the coffee he drank during the meeting. He put his right arm on her shoulder. "I don't make these choices on my own, Ronnie. Believe me, if I could, I would have already done so just to stop your ceaseless whining about it. Every decision is reviewed by the entire board, including my father. Look, your work is incredible, second to none, but you are a wild card that doesn't always fit into the deck. You don't play nice with others. That doesn't inspire confidence in matters of the billions." Ronnie looked at him, annoyed by his honest assessment. "Nichelle is a hard worker and a great coworker, and with the vacuum Kendra left when she moved to Virginia, we needed to fill a vice presidency. And even you have to admit there was no better person to fill the job."

Ronnie's eyes flared at the statement. By removing one adversary, she accidently created a new one. *Son of a bitch,* she thought to herself as Milton removed his hand from her shoulder and put it in his pocket.

"You still unofficially run the department, and if we hit our target numbers after the next two quarters, it will demonstrate you are a great leader that works well in a team environment. I will publicly sing your praises, and this little unpleasantness will be an afterthought."

Ronnie leaned in and whispered in his ear. "You want me to be a team player? Okay, fine. I'll play your little game, but in six months, you better sing my praises to the high fucking heavens. You think you're the only one who can make threats? Just remember that while you're sitting on top of your father's empire worried about image and perception, I literally have you by the fucking balls."

She discreetly but firmly grabbed his testicles to drive home her point. As he doubled over, she walked away, her heels clicking on the marble floor as if crushing his balls beneath them. "Son of a bitch," she muttered to herself as she got back on the elevator. She hit the button to go back to the 21st floor. As soon as the steel doors closed, she banged her hand against the wall. "Son of a bitch!" she yelled repeatedly as she hit the wall over and over. She couldn't believe she created this vacuum by running Kendra out of town. Ronnie anticipated that she would be promoted to oversee the whole department since there would be no one else to do the job—a battlefield promotion, of sorts. She misestimated the fact they would promote someone else to fill the void. "Son of a bitch!" she screamed one final time before the elevator doors opened. She composed herself, straightening her olive Kobi Halperin blouse and walking out as if nothing had occurred. She then made her way toward the common area on the floor, a place most people would go to talk by the water cooler after a big meeting. She was certain Nichelle would be there because, unlike herself, Nichelle was adored at the company. Everyone would be happy that "one of their own" had been promoted to the executive level. To her surprise, though, Nichelle was not there. Instead, she found her hard at work outside her new office—Kendra's old office—placing her personal items where she wanted them. *Son of a bitch!* Ronnie thought to herself as she entered the room.

"I see you wasted no time getting acclimated to Kendra's—I mean your new title," Ronnie said, a snarl behind her tone.

Nichelle was beaming from ear to ear when she turned around. "Ronnie, I didn't see you there! And you know what they say—no time like the present. I figured I'd just get started now because I have some ideas I want to go over for the fourth quarter a bit later on."

Ronnie's aggression spilled over. The thought of an amateur—a former subordinate, no less—coordinating meetings was too hard to digest. "Can I talk to you for a second?"

Nichelle smiled innocently. "Sure thing. What's up?"

Ronnie closed the office door behind her. She knew it would be more intimidating to defeat this fake-ass, Sweet Valley High bitch on her own turf. She detested Nichelle's bubbly persona. She knew it had to be a fraud. "I'm not happy with you taking a very dear friend of mine's job."

Nichelle stood her ground in front of her new desk. "Two things: one, I didn't take anyone's job, and two, I didn't think you two liked each other judging by all the negativity in the emails."

They didn't like each other. Kendra was a threat, and Ronnie knew it. She initially let it be known via condescending emails, until she realized Marcus was the key to unraveling her rival. "Things like that were above your paygrade, Nichelle. In fact, this entire job may be over your head, so you best just sit down, be quiet, and let me handle all the heavy lifting."

"Well, it's not above my paygrade anymore."

The words created a dead silence in the room. Ronnie was unprepared for this seemingly nice girl to have a backbone. Nichelle strolled confidently behind her desk and took a seat. "Now, if you don't mind, please leave my office and close the door on your way out. I have some fourth-quarter strategies to work out. I'll be sending you a meeting request in order to discuss them, from one vice president to another."

The words hit Ronnie like a ten-pound bowling ball in the stomach.

"Son... of... a... bitch!" she muttered to herself.

CHAPTER 9
THE RUN-AROUND

It was the middle of the day when Donovan got off the bus in the heart of South Park, his old neighborhood. Third Ward, now called "Midtown," had changed dramatically, but he knew nothing was going to change in here. It was one of the ghettos the city had given up on years before he was even born, and he knew it like the back of his hand. He walked down Bellfort Street toward the old Walgreens not too far from his old high school. He wanted to stop and see if the neighborhood bum was still running his "I just ran out of gas down the road." scam, but didn't really feel like being bothered. The walk was about a quarter-mile to his destination, and along the way he saw a few familiar locations and events that made him feel right at home such as a '96 red Chevy Caprice sitting on 24-inch rims. He'd never been a rim man himself; in fact, he never understood why someone would spend so much money on hubcaps. Still, it felt good to see, knowing it belonged in this neighborhood just like him. He passed by *Tidy's Vacuum Repair Service*, a shop that had been open for twenty-five years. For as long as he could remember, Tidy had that vacuum repair shop. It was obviously a front for selling drugs. Every day several "customers" would walk in, stay for a while and leave, but never did they take or pick up a vacuum. *Good to be home* he thought to himself.

When he got to the house he was heading to, he realized he had not been "in the streets" for three years. People stared at him uncomfortably. Yeah, the streets were always watching, but movement like this usually had something behind it, and they, the streets, wanted to know what he was doing here. He stopped at an unkempt home with gray Hardie planks and black reinforced burglar bars. The fence surrounding the entire home was also black and reinforced. Donovan opened the gate, and a pit bull came running at him across the brownish grass barking. Unafraid, he leaned down to embrace the dog he had known since it was a pup. "Rocky! What you up to, boy?" he said as he petted the dog and it submissively licked him. The pit knew its true master and the one who treated it better than its current owner.

As Donovan played with the dog, a voice cut through the air. "Back from the motherfucking dead, I see."

"Something like that," Donovan replied, eyeing Terrance "Trouble" Woodard. He was a slender man, 6-foot, 2 inches, with a cinnamon-brown complexion.

"What's up, D? Long time," Trouble said as he walked over and embraced him. "You look like you been hitting the weights."

"Nothing to do in jail but wait and lift, so yeah, I got it in."

Trouble looked at the pit bull. "Get out of here." Rocky reluctantly walked away, looking back at Donovan as if to say, *Save me.*

"Still a mini Mike Vick, I see," Donovan said in defense of the animal's demeanor.

"Hey, cuz, like I said before, you can have that mutt when you ready. I only kept him for you."

"Well, I'll probably be getting him soon now that I'm back. Soon as I get what's mine." Trouble looked around, scanning the neighborhood. Several eyes and ears were on the conversation. "Yeah, about that, homie ... Let's go inside and talk."

Donovan, recognizing the same, obliged and headed toward the enforced steel-bar door.

The inside of the house wasn't far from the exterior. Two burgundy couches with floral prints on them were at least twenty years old, and the ceiling fan held four lightbulbs, half of which worked to light the living room. Dominoes, apparently from a game the night before, sat out in the open on a kitchen table at the edge of the living room, and the entire home had a fragrance of vanilla and flower potpourri, no doubt to mask the lingering smell of recently smoked marijuana. Donovan took a seat on one of the floral couches. He looked around and realized that someone else had recently either been here, or was still there. "You have company, Trouble?"

"Oh, yeah, man, I had a couple of freaks over, you know how I do," he replied jokingly. Donovan half grinned at his friend's copious nature when it came to women. "But I'm sure you didn't come all this way to catch up."

"No doubt, T. Where's Rico?"

Trouble looked outside his window, scanning the neighborhood before he sat down on the couch opposite Donovan. "Man, you haven't heard, huh?"

Donovan shook his head. "Been locked up, bruh. Hard to hear behind those walls." Trouble nodded. "Well, Rico got picked up about a year ago, and then he got stabbed in a prison riot. He didn't make it."

Donovan was visibly upset. He had known Rico since high school and would miss his friend, but he also robbed several banks with him and had entrusted him with his small fortune of $437,000 before he began his stint in the federal facility. Trouble pulled a pack of Camel cigarettes out of his green camouflage cargo shorts and lit one. He then handed one to his friend and lit it for him.

"But that's the least of your problems, homeboy," Trouble continued. Trouble took another puff of the cigarette and let out a long trail of exhaust. "See, the word on the street is you got home early because you snitched."

Donovan took a drag on his Camel and laughed as he let the smoke escape his lungs. "So let me get this straight—out of the four of us that hit those banks and went to get this money, I'm the one who snitched? There were no fingerprints, no videotape, nothing to connect us to the crime, but I get picked up three days later. I'm the only one who did time. Federal time. But I'm the one who snitched?"

"That's the word on the street, D."

"So what did the streets have to say when my ass got locked up? I mean, did I go and tell on myself to give up three years of my life?"

Trouble leaned in closer to his friend. "That's just it, homeboy. You did three years on a seven-year bid, fed time. That just don't make a lot of sense, and with Rico getting picked up and

then killed ..."

Donovan took another drag of his cigarette and stood up off the couch. He walked to the window to look outside to see if there was any activity. It all seemed quiet. He turned back to Trouble. "Well, I ain't never been no snitch."

"That goes without saying, bruh. I just wanted you to know what you were up against." Donovan nodded in Trouble's direction as he looked back out the window. "One thing's for damn sure—someone said something, and if it ain't me and it wasn't Rico and it wasn't you, that just leaves K.T."

A gun clicked behind Donovan's head. "What's up, D? Been a long time."

Donovan turned around slowly to find Kelvin "K.T." Terrell pointing a gun at his skull. He was a stocky man, about 5'11" with tattoos covering each of his ginger arms. There was another man with him who Donovan had seen around but didn't know very well. Donovan then looked at Trouble still sitting on the couch as if nothing had happened. He thought about the dominoes on the table and how things seemed out of order when he first walked in. "A couple of freaks over, huh?" He mocked Trouble, who smirked at his statement.

"You know how I do," he replied.

Donovan rolled his eyes and made eye contact with K.T. "You know, I gotta say I'm almost impressed, Kelvin. I mean, if I didn't know you were such a goddamn pussy, I'd almost be concerned right now."

"Shut the fuck up, D! You think I'm playing with you, don't you?"

Donovan ignored the threat and looked at Trouble. "I'm just saying if it were Trouble here holding the gun, I might be worried, but it's just pussy-ass Kelvin. Trouble, you remember how that cop got shot, right? I mean me, you, and Rico ran into those banks, and Kelvin sat outside in the car always ready to leave before the cops came."

K.T. cocked the gun and walked closer to Donovan. "I'm not playing with you, fool!" Donovan continued his monologue. "Till one day we run up in the bank and the cops actually got there ahead of schedule. Me, you, and Rico get outside, and the getaway car done got away. Go figure. So what we have to do then? We have to make a run for it because somebody's pussy ass had already left. Because they are simply not built for jail, so we're running and a cop is in front of us. But it's only one no back up. So what I do? I take one for the team and put slugs in him so *everyone* can get out."

K.T glanced over at Trouble, who was nodding to every word. That was all it took for Donovan to disarm K.T. with a bone-crushing right hook to the jaw. He picked up the gun before anyone could react and pointed it at his former comrades.

"What I tell you, Trouble? Pussy." Donovan kicked K.T. as he lay on the floor holding his broken jaw. Donovan motioned to the third guy to sit down on the couch. "But me, on the other hand, I'm built for jail. See, I just did three years for shooting that cop, which begs the motherfucking question: What do you think I'm willing to do to your Cowardly Lion ass?" Donovan walked over to the guy he didn't know and hit him with the butt of the gun twice, rendering him unconscious. He then sat on the couch across from Trouble, who was now visibly worried as Donovan pointed the gun at him while he sat and rested both feet on K.T. "Here we are, one big happy reunion. I gotta say I'm a little disappointed in you T. I thought you would've known better than to take this route with me."

Trouble lit another cigarette and nervously responded, "Man, like I said, it just didn't make no sense how you got out in three years. You had to be the one ..."

"Is that what K.T. convinced you of? You know what? Fuck you, and fuck this piece of shit right here." Donovan slammed his foot into K.T's jaw, making him scream in agony. "Where's my fucking money?" Trouble looked at Donovan as he aimed the gun at his head. "Choose the next words that come out your mouth carefully."

Beads of sweat started to form around the temple of Trouble's forehead. "D, you know I wouldn't play you like that. The only reason I went along with this is because we thought you had something to do with Rico getting killed. I mean, I was always down. I didn't need the money, man. I'm still living in the hood. All I did was buy that car in the garage and a few pairs of Jordans, and tricked on some hoes once you got locked up. I thought it was too hot to spend, so I sat on mine. I swear to God, homeboy."

Donovan looked around and knew he was telling the truth, but the fact was his share was still missing. "I believe you and all of what you just said, but it ain't got shit to do with my $437,000. So again, somebody need to say something and real quick because it's about to be a triple homicide up in this motherfucker." K.T. mumbled something incomprehensible. Donovan removed his feet, but that was all the mercy he showed him. "Speak up, bitch!"

K.T. held his jaw through the pain as he responded, "Rico wouldn't let us touch your share."

Trouble chimed in. "When you got locked up, Rico took all the money. We weren't sure what he did with yours." Donovan stood up. He pointed the gun at Trouble to indicate he stand up, too. "You didn't spend the money, T? Show me."

Trouble got up and stepped over K.T. to head to the back door. Before they exited into the garage, Donovan turned around. "K.T., if you do anything stupid between now and the time I come back, I'm going to kill you. But before I do that, I'm going to murder all the other pussies in your family, starting with your grandmother, then your mom, and finally your big sister while you stand there and watch. Do you feel me?"

K.T. looked at him and started to sob. "I'm sorry, man," he said through clenched teeth and excruciating pain. "I don't want no problems with you."

"Hey, we cool, homeboy. Just sit your punk ass there, and I'll be back." Donovan nudged the gun into Trouble's back to make him move forward.

The pair walked through the kitchen to a back door that led directly to a garage that mostly contained oil cans, some drug paraphernalia, a standing safe, and a three-year-old, grey, 750 series BMW. Donovan was impressed by the ride's condition considering the rest of the house was slightly above salvage yard. "Damn, boy, you did good for yourself."

"I told you, man, I didn't really spend a whole lot. Rico started spending a whole bunch of time around Carlos's house. He might know where the money is."

"That's a mighty convenient story, Trouble."

"Man, I swear it's the truth," Trouble responded desperately

Donovan looked at the safe. It was a tall and solid safe, and Trouble probably kept a gun on the inside for situations like this. "I'm not gone lie, T. I don't want to kill you, but I will. I just want you to open the safe so I can see you telling the truth about my money. If it ain't in there, then we got no beef. So what I need you to do is to get on your knees and put your hands behind your back and give me the combo to this safe." Donovan could tell his friend was trying to think of a way to get out of his request. He lifted the gun to the back of Trouble's head "I know you're thinking about it, but if you don't do what I say, you won't have a brain to think with. Feel me?"

Trouble got on his knees and complied. Donovan opened the safe and spit. His friend was telling the truth. There was only $148,000 in the safe; not enough to cover his share of the robberies. Donovan took out $25,000 in cash and closed it. Trouble barked at him angrily. "What the fuck, D! You said you wasn't gonna take my money!"

Donovan hit him in the nose with the pistol, breaking it cleanly. "Shut the fuck up! I'm a crook, motherfucker. Haven't you ever heard the saying no honor amongst thieves?" Blood started to gush from his friend's nose. Donovan continued. "This is for trying to set me up. You lucky I left you any bread at all. And I'm gonna need the keys to that car." Trouble pointed his broken nose to the wall where a rack held the key to the BMW. Donovan grabbed the key and looked down at his friend on the ground holding his nose. "Get up, T."

Trouble got up as Donovan handed him a towel sitting on the washing machine in the garage. "You did what you had to do. I respect that. I'm a lot of things, but I'll never be a snitch. Whoever put that dumbass idea in your head, you need to go deal with them. I suspect it's that coward in there holding his broken jaw. At any rate, I'm about to use this car until I figure out where my money at." Still pointing the gun toward his friend, he opened the garage door and then the car door. The last thing he did was call for the pit. "Rocky!" The dog came running full speed as Donovan gestured for the dog to get in the car, never moving the gun off his friend. He then climbed behind the wheel, put the car in reverse, and backed out of the garage, rolling down the window to give Trouble one more warning.

"One last thing—if I don't find my money, you best believe this won't be the last time you see me."

CHAPTER 10
ROBBERY 101

"This fucking dog, Donovan!" Nichelle screamed in disgust as the pit bull found its newest chew toy, one of her plum-colored suede Prada Point toe pumps. "Damn it, this is too far. He's got to go today!" There was no response as she tried to recover what was left of her shoe. "Donovan?" she chimed. Still no answer.

She wrestled the shoe away from the dog she knew since it was a puppy and walked over to the living room area. She located a shirtless Donovan finishing his final set of his daily routine of 400 push-ups, a regimen he hadn't broken since prison. She watched him as he pushed his frame into the sky as he mumbled a barely audible, "375, 376, 377—" He didn't stop. She took a seat at the kitchen table and watched him continue his regimen. "389, 391, 392—" His bare chest excited her, and as his muscles clung to his pulsing flesh, she slowly thought of him thrusting himself in the same manner with her laying underneath him.

"Babygirl!" His gruff voice interrupted her thoughts.

"Huh?"

"What were you saying?"

"I—um, Rocky, he's got to go," she said, dazed slightly, still fantasizing about the push-ups she wanted to participate in.

"Look, Babygirl—"

"I don't want to hear it, D. Look at my damn shoe!" She waved the half-digested shoe in his face. "Prada doesn't grow on trees!"

"You hear yourself? This is that uppity-ass Ms. Myers talking right now, not the Babygirl I knew."

"Whoever you think I'm being, the dog's got to go."

She liked Rocky, but didn't sign up to be a pet owner. This was another intrusion— Donovan's way of coming into someone's life and smashing things like a wrecking ball. While she was under no illusion that she found Donovan intoxicating, the dog was a step too far.

"Alright, Ms. Myers, I will promptly remove the mammal from your premises. God save the queen," Donovan responded.

"Thank you."

"Ms. Myers, might I have a word with Babygirl when she's available?"

Nichelle rolled her eyes. The thought that she was being uppity bothered her, but not as much as Donovan calling her *Ms. Myers*. He knew how to push every single button she had, and as much as it annoyed her, the familiarity was welcome.

"What is it, Donovan?"

"Is this Babygirl?"

"Yes, Donovan."

"Alright, cool. So I'm gonna hop in the shower real quick. You get that fat ass dressed. I'm taking you shopping to replace that shoe you're holding, and we can drop off Rocky together."

Startled, she stood looking at him. *He's taking me shopping? Where did he get the money from? Is he back up to his old tricks?* She needed to know the answer, but only after she got the shoes. After all he was putting her through, it was the least he could do.

With a smile on her face, she walked into the bedroom to put on a soft white and pink sweatsuit. It hugged her body tightly and was comfortably warm, it was a perfect combination of chic and comfort. As she was dressing, she remembered how this was something he used to do all the time. In fact, he bought the first pair of Prada pumps she ever owned in what seemed like a lifetime ago.

Donovan stepped out of the shower and began to get dressed. She looked at Rocky playfully tending to his master.

"Sorry, boy, Ms. Myers wants you gone. No pets allowed at the inn."

The dog playfully laid at Donovan's feet.

"Where are you taking him?"

"I'm taking him to be euthanized."

"What! Donovan you can't."

"What else am I gonna do with him? He can't stay here."

Nichelle was quiet. She looked at the dog, thinking how she also cared for him—maybe as much as she cared for her Prada pumps.

"I'm just fucking with you, Babygirl. One of the benefits of this neighborhood being gentrified is that white folk love their animals. It turns out there's a doggie hotel he can stay at not too far from here. I already made the arrangements because I knew Ms. Myers would have a problem with a dog being at her home, especially a real killa like Rocky." She watched as he started to roughhouse with the dog, and the dog responded playfully, almost knocking over a lamp. "A doggie hotel. Can you believe that shit?"

"How much does it cost?"

"'Bout twenty-five hundred a month. I put down a deposit already. Just gonna pay a couple months up front so I don't have to worry about it anytime soon."

That's at least five thousand dollars! Where is he getting this money? She wanted to ask, but looked at the shoe. From the sound of things, she could get a whole outfit today. Maybe two.

She remained silent as the trio got into the car, Donovan's newly acquired 750 series was a question she certainly didn't want an answer to. He had been driving it since he came back with Rocky, and she assumed he borrowed it from one of his many friends. She didn't know his circle entirely well since he deliberately tried to keep her away from his activities, giving her just a name here and there. Yet, in the pit of her stomach, she knew there was more to the story. Earlier this week, when she was leaving for work, she noticed speckles of what looked like blood across the grill of the car.

Getting to the doggie hotel was a breeze. Nichelle stayed in the car while Donovan said his goodbyes and paid the people. Although she didn't want Rocky chewing on her shoes, she didn't have the heart to look at him as he left her home. When Donovan got back in the car, he was surprisingly upbeat after losing his loyal companion. Nichelle was going to say something, but Donovan beat her to the punch.

"Rocky is going to love this place! They have raw meat treats!"

Nichelle nodded, but stayed silent. *How in the fuck are you paying for all of this?*

"Alright, now it's your turn. Which mall you want to go to? The Galleria?"

"I really would like to go to First Colony. It's a straight shot down 59 from here."

"Cool."

The drive was a quiet one. Donovan put on his oldies music, a fan of Al Green and the Isley Brothers. Nichelle felt the familiarity of this trip—driving to the mall, being spoiled, getting whatever she wanted. She missed that feeling. Lucas probably would have done the same, but it wasn't the nature of their relationship. This was for *Babygirl*.

When they got to the mall, the first thing they did was find the food court. Donovan always wanted something to drink or eat while she shopped, as if it would be hours before he'd have another chance. She figured this would be no different, and she was right. He ordered a large sweet tea from a pizza vendor and then turned to Nichelle. "Alright, you know what to do. Lead the way."

It was music to her ears. She quickly found Nordstrom and ushered him to the shoe area. For the next hour, she compared more than a dozen shoes while Donovan watched her try them on. When she got down to the last four pair she liked, Donovan stood up.

"You like all of these?"

"I can't make up mind. They're all nice. That's why this is so hard!"

"I agree. You know, you should make up your mind, but not now"

Donovan spoke to the attendant who had been helping Nichelle for the last hour.

"She's going to get all four of these. Pack 'em up."

Another fifteen-hundred dollars! He was definitely up to his old tricks. As the teller rang up the shoes and Donovan paid for them in cash, he turned to Nichelle. "Where do you want to go next?"

There was a slight hesitation. She wanted to keep shopping. She loved being spoiled, but in two hours she just saw her ex-boyfriend spend almost eight thousand dollars. She needed to know where the money was coming from before she let him spend another penny.

"All I wanted was the shoes. We can leave now."

"You sure?"

"Yeah, I'm sure."

"We coulda done more shopping if you want. I gotta admit, I wasn't expecting to get off so easy."

"No, I'm good, Donovan. Let's go."

As the pair walked back to the car, Nichelle processed the possible outcomes of their impending conversation. Donovan was back in the game—that much was for sure. But could his lifestyle hurt her?

When they got in the car, she was as silent as if they were leaving the scene of a crime. She allowed him to clear the parking before she spoke up.

"Where's the money coming from, Donovan?"

"It was a gift from a friend."

"Was the friend Chase Bank?"

He chuckled and looked at her. "Damn, that's cold. Nah, it wasn't Chase Bank—it was Bank of America."

"Damnit it, D! You said you weren't going to do that anymore! I can't believe you!"

Donovan laughed out loud "Would you chill out? You see any bank robberies on the news? No, I didn't rob a bank, although the timing of your question is extraordinary. You could've asked me that before we got to the mall."

"You're right. I'm not sure why I didn't ask sooner."

"I do. Because you're a sel— "

"Don't say it, D."

He was going to call her selfish, and maybe she was being selfish, but she figured she deserved this since he'd been causing so much havoc in her life. She did believe him, however— he didn't rob anyone, at least not a bank. That set her at ease and partly made her regret not finishing the shopping spree they had begun earlier.

"So, if you didn't rob the bank, where did the money come from?"

Donovan stopped the car.

"Okay, you want me to be real? I went to a partner's house to look for some money I had waiting for me when I got outside. He didn't have the money, but tried to set me up. That shit didn't work out too good for him. I took 25 g's of his money and this car until I can figure out what's my next move."

He started to drive again. Nichelle was silent, processing his words. The thought of him robbing his friend was actually not a big deal to her. Not in the least, one thief stealing from another, nothing wrong with that. She truly regretted not finishing her shopping spree now.

"So you stole his money?"

"Penalized him for setting me up."

"And you stole his car, too?"

"It's not like that. He loaned it to me."

"Unwillingly."

"He won't ever bother us, Babygirl."

"So let me get this straight—you stole his car, but he won't report it stolen or try to get it back?" Nichelle said in bewilderment as she and Donovan pulled up to a red light.

"Nah, Babygirl, it's not even like that. The car is paid for. My boy just backed the wrong horse in this race, so now as punishment; I'm going to borrow his car until I get things sorted out on my end. He'll get it back."

"You've had this car for over a week now."

"He'll get it back. I didn't say when."

"Why wouldn't he just call the police and have you arrested?"

"Because everyone would know he's a snitch. The streets are watching him just as much as they are me."

"Why wouldn't he just come after you himself?"

Donovan scoffed at the question as the light turned green. "If he had the balls to do that, I never woulda been able to take his car in the first place."

Nichelle rolled her eyes. "Damn it! Why are you like this?" she blurted out, half talking to herself. She hated herself for being attracted to this side of him. He was a man of action through and through; he took what he wanted, when he wanted, never thinking it through. She knew Donovan could sense her frustration, and liked that he could make her feel that way and still have her come back for more.

He pulled into the driveway of a Wendy's fast food restaurant, parked the car, and diverted Nichelle's attention to a bank across the street. "You see that bank over there?"

Nichelle nodded. "Yeah, what about it?"

"Several things. For one, the camera system is unkempt. You can tell from the dangling wires on at least two of the cameras. It was probably done by an amateur getting a big favor from a friend who owns the property. Bank this size should have a sixteen-camera system, at least. But there are only four that are noticeable. Means there are probably a total of eight; all probably as poorly installed as the ones we're looking at. The problem with that is there are at least three entrances to this bank, so there are a lot of blind spots. But let's just start with the most obvious—you see that camera next to the drive-thru window? Birds are nesting around it right now, which tells me one of two things. One: the staff is so used to that view being obstructed they aren't really checking the cameras, or two: the camera isn't working, which is more likely because birds tend to pick at loose wires. Either way, the camera isn't working. It's an entry point into the bank. Then, you have the location. This bank is a credit union, but it's for the city—a well-to-do city next to an upscale mall. They would at least have $300,000 to half a million on hand at all times in case some basketball player or CEO wants to buy a few diamonds for his mistress at the jewelry store sitting right next to the bank. Lastly, there's the escape route. This being a master-planned community, they take traffic into consideration. Here's where it gets fun. While the masterminds who laid the groundwork for this development are getting patted on the back for doing such a spectacular job, they don't realize those same roads are escape routes, so that road right next to the bank can literally take you into the neighborhood and right onto the freeway in under four minutes without ever hitting a light. You asked why I'm like this. Because I'm good at it."

Nichelle was stunned at all the information he was able to gather in a matter of moments. She would've never been able to decipher all that. She was silent as he pulled the car out of the parking lot and drove toward the neighborhood behind the bank. She questioned if he were planning a siege at that moment. Apprehensively she decided to ask her remaining question. "You were able to see all of that from the Wendy's parking lot from across the street?" Donovan smirked at her question and replied, "Babygirl, I never needed to go to the Wendy's. I was able to tell all that at the light. I only pulled in there so you could see it." Nichelle looked at him as she caught herself smiling at his confidence. He was a criminal; a thug. He was everything she was trying to get away from. Yet, at this very moment, she was with him and not Lucas, the man she always said she wanted. She tried to convince herself she didn't intend for any of this to happen; that she was just as much a victim of circumstances as anyone. She rationalized that she didn't owe Lucas an explanation since she had not slept with him since sleeping with Donovan, but the truth was much greater than that. This wasn't happening because Donovan was so incredibly good in bed or because she wasn't able to break it off with Lucas. At this moment, knowing Donovan was being unapologetic in his honest response, she realized she was still in love with him. His voice, his scent, his confidence—the very nature of his presence—was slowly undermining the foundation she worked so hard to build after he left. She didn't want to love him, but with each passing moment he was unraveling her façade with his brutish charm, and she didn't seem to care. At least parts of her didn't. In thirty seconds, he had broken down how he could rob a bank—and the conversation turned her on.

"Pull over," Nichelle said to him. Donovan, who was taking the back road to get to the highway, parked in front of a suburban ranch behind the bank. As the gearshift hit "Park," Nichelle unbuttoned his black jeans. She exposed his underwear enough to see his entire package.

"Damn, Babygirl, what are you doing?"

"Shut up, Donovan."

She leaned over his car seat, pulled his underwear back and kissed the tip of his cock as he reclined the seat. Looking at it starting to firm in her hand, she stroked it and wrapped her lips around the top of the head, circling it with her tongue. He let out a moan as she engulfed his entire package in her mouth, her saliva sliding onto his lap as she continued going up and down, gracefully. Donovan put one hand on the back of her head, which she quickly pushed away. She didn't want

was five minutes away when she realized her cellphone was in one of the bags she left in Donovan's car. "Fuck, I have to turn around." She was going to meet Lucas tonight, and the last thing she needed was him calling and Donovan picking up. She knew she had to end it, but she wanted to do it as gently as possible. It was hard to love two men at the same time, but the more time she spent with Donovan, the less she cared about Lucas. It was a natural tendency—out of sight, out of mind. Yet, sadly, she knew all too well the consequences of getting lost in a man like Donovan. At the end of the day, he was going to do what was best for him. She was sliding downhill on a razorblade, and a river of alcohol waited ahead. Despite this, she kept hope that things would be different this time. Maybe he was sincere about his desire to change. If so, then she'd gladly swim that stinging river to get to the other side. As much as she hated to admit it, she was fully in love with the man again. She just needed to close the chapter on Lucas before he got hurt too badly.

When she got back to her house, she parked the car and began walking up the stairs. She paused in her tracks. A Mercedes CLK sat in the parking spot by the road. Lucas's Mercedes CLK! "Oh, no, he can't be here!" she said aloud. She stopped walking to the house and proceeded toward the car to further inspect it. It was certainly his car, but no one was inside. Nichelle remembered the key she gave him months ago. "Oh, no! No, no, no!" she shrieked as she raced back towards the house. A weakness grew in her body as she felt her biggest fear being realized. Lucas and Donovan were about to meet in a most unfortunate way.

CHAPTER 11
REAL TALK

Donovan walked into the house still exhausted from the orgasm he just experienced. He was heading straight to bed when he heard footsteps moving about in the living room. He paused and the footsteps stopped. He drew the pistol he took from K.T. and pointed it straight ahead as he walked into the living room. Was this Trouble or K.T. looking for a little revenge? Or was it Carlos, the guy his best friend Rico began hanging around? He knew word would get back to Carlos, but he didn't anticipate it so soon. To his knowledge, no one knew exactly where he was staying, but his focus grew as he knew someone was somewhere in the living room lurking and waiting on him. He found the hallway light switch and flipped it on to provide more visibility in the living room area. Still, he couldn't see anyone, and there was no movement. The only way he could find out what was going on was to go in head first. "Fuck it! Let's do this," he said as stormed toward the living room. Quickly he strode in and flipped the light switch on, pointing the gun straight ahead. A wave of relief rushed over him as he recognized the man sitting in the chair. He smiled and holstered his weapon.

"So you're Lucas, the man that's been keeping my woman warm for me."

"Excuse me? Your woman?"

"You're Lucas right?"

"Who in the fuck are you?"

"Hey, cuz, that's a little out of line, don't you think?" Donovan lit a cigarette. "So I suppose you're over here to fight for your woman? Is that what's about to happen here?"

"Look, man, I don't know who you are or what you're doing here. I just need some answers."

Donovan sat back for a moment, examining Lucas he could tell his would be rival had no clue what was going on, the emotion was written on his face. He could do nothing but scoff at the circumstance. "Same old Babygirl."

"What is that supposed to mean? Look, I'm not an idiot. Clearly I can see something is going on, but I'd like to know what." Donovan could tell the man in front of him was sincere. He didn't have a clue, but he was slowly putting together the context clues. It was time to do the dirty work Babygirl couldn't do.

"Lucas, I'll be straight with you, bro. You seem like a good enough dude. Your chick, your girlfriend Nichelle, has been cheating on you."

Lucas stood up, a cocktail of anger, rage and hurt drenching his face. Donovan could tell Lucas wanted to attack him for presenting this bitter reality into his system, a part of him wanted Lucas to be so reckless. The man had been sleeping with his Babygirl and he didn't like it in the least. But fighting was the last thing that needed to happen.

"Now, before you do anything stupid, it's not worth losing your life over." Donovan lifted his shirt and referenced the gun he had in his jeans.

"Let's talk this out like men," he continued.

Donovan poured two glasses of Jack Daniels and offered one to Lucas before sitting across from him. Lucas reluctantly took the drink as he sat again, but refrained from taking a sip.

"See, the thing is, Lucas, this woman is a selfish creature. Where I'm from, we'd call a woman like that a lowdown bitch. She always been that way. I've known her since as long as I can remember. And while she's spent all this time trying to change her style and appearance, and you think she's your girlfriend and all, five-hundred-dollar shoes don't change who you are. So, she might have all of y'all fooled, but at the end of the day, she's still just a lowdown bitch. My lowdown bitch."

Donovan watched Lucas process his words, he was visibly shaken by the gravity of what was said, finally giving in and taking a sip of whiskey. "How do I know any of this is true?"

"You don't have to believe a word of it, homeboy. That's your prerogative. But real talk, deep down, you know something ain't right. It's the reason you're sitting here in the girl's house to begin with. You know something just ain't matching up with how you feel. You need to follow your gut, Lucas. Now, I'm a G about things—that means gentleman for you Harvard types, so I'm going to let this slide. But if I see you around here again, I won't be so pleasant. You feel me?"

Lucas stood up and looked at Donovan. "Am I supposed to be scared of you?"

"Nah, homie, you're a man, I respect that. You shouldn't be scared of another man period, but from what I can tell, you are successful, and with that being said, you have a lot more to lose than me. So you should consider that. You feel me?"

Donovan smiled. He knew Lucas wanted to rip his head off. A part of him wanted the man to attack him so he could justify assaulting him for sleeping with his woman. Yet, at the same time, he knew Lucas was just as much a victim of Nichelle's choices as he was. It wasn't his fault. It was just his circumstance to deal with.

"We both been dealt some shitty cards, Lucas. You gonna be mad at anyone, be mad at the person who dealt the hand."

Donovan put out his cigarette. He heard the door opening,

"Donovan, don't do anything stupid. I have to—"

"Speaking of the devil, what's up, Babygirl? Guess who stopped by to look for you?"

He watched her face shrivel and her eyes widen. The anxiety on her face told the tale of being caught red-handed in a love affair. Donovan was slightly disgusted by the scenario, feeling like a second fiddle when he should be king. Yet he refrained from losing his temper. This was hard on everyone. If prison had taught him anything, it was how to be patient. He took another sip of whiskey and waited for Nichelle to speak.

"D, What did you do?" Nichelle barked at him.

"Is it true?" Lucas said. He was clearly fighting back the pain that comes with betrayal.

"Lucas, I—"

"Answer me, damn it! Is he telling the truth?"

Nichelle fell quiet. She didn't respond to his question, so Donovan chimed in.

"Quiet, huh? You were pretty quiet in the car an hour ago, but your mouth was full that time."

Nichelle looked up with disgust at Donovan. Lucas, picking up on the insinuation, became sullen.

"Thanks, Donovan, I know everything I need to know." Lucas headed for the door.

"Lucas, wait!" Nichelle pleaded as Donovan sat down on the couch and let her chase after him. She'd be back. Adjacent to him was a wrapped box. He picked up the box and read the attached note. *Congratulations Neecie!*

Dumbass nickname, he thought to himself. Nichelle walked back in as he was about to open the box. The container had a sterling silver nameplate that read: *Nichelle Myers, Vice President*

"Dude really cares about you, Nichelle. You may have fucked up."

"Motherfucker! What did you do?" she screamed.

Donovan stood up and walked toward the door. "I made sure no one was in the dark about who you are, *Neecie*. That's a real good dude who just left out of here. If you tell him you want to be with him, he's the kind of motherfucker that will take you back. He left you a gift. That's some thoughtful shit considering your mouth was just wrapped around my d—."

"You ruin everything! I hate you!"

Donovan picked up his keys. "You think you're a field day? You didn't have to let me in that night, but you did, Nichelle. You didn't have to fuck me, but you wanted to fuck me. And nobody made you lie to that dude, so the truth is, Babygirl, you ruin everything. I'm just always here to clean up your shit. But I tell you what—I'm gonna give you some time to think about how you brought all this shit on yourself."

And like that, Donovan was out the door, leaving Nichelle to sink into her misery. After all, the worst place to be was inside her head.

CHAPTER 12
ROSES (THE GATES OF HEAVEN)

"Ronnie, do you mind telling me what the hell you were doing at my house!" Milton exclaimed as they prepared for a meeting.

"I wanted to tell Jenna hello. She's such a pretty woman. A bit ditzy for my taste, but I can see the appeal."

Milton closed the door to the room before things got out of hand. "Ronnie I need you to listen to me. This has gone too far! You stay the hell away from my family!"

"Or what? Are you going to go to HR and tell them about us? Are you going to fire me? I would love to see how that plays out. I can see the headlines now: *CEO of Prestigious Firm Fires Young Black Mistress.* The press would have a field day with that one. How much do you think the stock price would drop in the first hour of that press release? Thirty percent? Fifty? I bet the stock would drop by at least fifty-four dollars, which is about sixty-three percent by my rough calculations."

Milton sat there silently. "What do you want, Ronnie?"

"I want what I've earned!"

"I can't just promote you. The board would never go for it."

"I've already told you I don't give a damn what the board thinks. I've earned the right to be senior vice president. That's what we agreed upon if Kendra didn't work out. Well, she didn't work out. Hiring more competition isn't a step in the right direction!"

"I'm doing everything I can."

"If you were doing everything you could I'd have the fucking title already. Try harder, damn it!" she replied.

Milton sat there quietly frustrated. Ronnie could tell he was upset about being in this situation.

"Relax, Milton, I didn't tell your wife anything, if it makes you feel better. But make no mistake—this is just the beginning. If you don't give me what I've earned, your life will become a living hell."

Milton got up and walked directly toward Ronnie to stand face to face. "I am the goddamn president of this company! You do not threaten me, you do not stalk my family and you do not talk to me that way!"

Ronnie looked at him and smiled. "You see what your problem is, Milton? You think your title gives you control." She circled him as she talked. "Let's examine this, shall we? Your wife—Jenna, is it?—she's a docile creature meant to be pretty and quiet, and you love that about her. She doesn't ask any questions; doesn't challenge your authority... she's not smart enough to understand anything you talk about when you get home, so she just smiles and nods and opens her legs. One day she'll give you a bunch of little Miltons that you can ship off to boarding school in some Eastern European country, but that's not enough. No, you looked around and realized you were bored with her, and so the affairs began, one after another. Some ended organically; some you had to pay, but they went away quietly. Then you met this little black girl in marketing. You always had a touch of the jungle fever —at least that's what the word around the water cooler was—except this one was different. She was powerful, and 'sassy'— reminded you of those ladies at boarding school in those same Eastern European schools I just referenced. What did you call those women who take care of you? Nannies ... no that's not right. Mum? That's it. She, and by she I mean me, would be a great way to sow whatever oats you built up. So you thought you would just tap that ass and be gone like you were with so many others, another notch on the Milton Burrows belt of overcompensation—but what you were not counting on is that when you got inside this pussy you were entering the motherfucking gates of heaven itself. I mean, whoa. I have to admit, the face you made the first time you came was quick and hysterical, and then you made that face over and over. You could not get enough. You begged for it. You pleaded for it. You tried to buy it. You needed this ... pussy... right ... here. In fact, you would like to see it right now, wouldn't you?

Milton's rage had long disappeared. He was compliant now as he nodded in agreement. "On your knees," Ronnie commanded still circling him like a bird of prey to a wounded animal. He willingly obliged and fell to both knees.

"See, I have a dilemma, Milton. I want to show you this glorious vagina, but you're being a pain in my ass, and not in that literal way I allow you to be sometimes when I've been drinking. But a metaphorical pain—in—my—ass. I mean, why should you see heaven when you're putting me through hell?"

"P... p ... please," he begged. Ronnie noticed his erection through his navy suit pants. She leaned against her desk and called for him with her index finger. He crawled to her until she stopped him with her foot.

"Remove my shoe, Milton."

Milton unbuckled her navy Jimmy Choo, exposing the crimson polish on her freshly pedicured toes that matched her fingernails. Ronnie slid her foot to his cheek and onto his lips. She gently pressed her large toe against his mouth, and he willingly let her in as he massaged his erection over his pants.

"Would you like to see the gates of heaven now?"

"Yes."

"Yes what?"

"Yes, mum," Milton mumbled. Ronnie removed her foot from his mouth. She slowly lifted up her skirt to reveal her crimson, red-laced panties. Milton began to drool with anticipation. She slid the panties to the side and beckoned him closer. "Take a whiff of heaven, Milton."

He crawled closer and pressed his nose against her clitoris and inhaled her essence. "You smell like roses," he replied with a moan.

"Do you like that?" she asked.

"I love it, mum."

"Do you want it?"

"Yes, mum."

"Do you need it?"

"Yes, mum."

Ronnie pushed his face away from her vagina. She then lowered her skirt and looked down at him. "I want you to take a good mental picture. Until you get me what I've earned, you won't see, smell, taste, or touch the gates of heaven ever again! Now, if I'm not mistaken, we have a meeting in five minutes." She began to walk out of the office then stopped and looked back to see the man still on his knees, looking pitiful as he nursed his erection. "I'll leave you two alone. There is lotion on my desk if you need it. Just make sure you clean up your own mess for once." She then walked out of her office, closing the door behind her.

As she entered the conference room, she could hear yelling through the door. The voice sounded like Lucas's. She gently opened the door hoping to hear more while giving the impression she was being considerate.

"Ahem ... I hope I'm not disturbing anything." She knew Lucas had clearly been arguing with the only other person in the room—Nichelle.

"No, you didn't interrupt. We were just going over notes," Nichelle responded.

Ronnie recognized this as a lie, but proceeded to act aloof. "Do we have all the preliminary data compiled, Lucas?"

"I'm actually still putting it together. Some issues came up, and I'd like some time to scrub the numbers a bit more thoroughly."

"So we're unprepared for the meeting?" There was silence from both of them.

Nichelle finally responded. "There was just more work than anticipated."

"More work than anticipated is what we do at this level, Ms. Myers. If you can't handle that, then please let me know so I can make sure you go back to your old job where the work is manageable."

"I'm fine, Ronnie. Thanks."

"It was all my fault, honestly," Lucas interjected. "I can have the numbers this afternoon."

The executive committee filed into the conference room one by one as everyone took their seats. Milton came in and sat in the center of the room making little eye contact with Ronnie.

"We'll deal with this later," she told the two of them as she turned to greet the incoming traffic. Ronnie had no hard data to go on, but she had spades of charm. When the meeting began, she decided to talk the entire duration, though the thought of hanging Nichelle out to dry had crossed her mind. Still, *play nice* was her directive. She knew, on some level, that Nichelle's success was directly tied to her own, and it was too soon to bury the knife between her blades. For now, she would work through this meeting and live to fight another day.

The meeting was long and uneventful. She had accomplished all she had to do in order not to make her team look unprepared. Whenever a question came up regarding actual process, she reminded everyone how this was just a preliminary hearing and that RainHouse & Arms did things a little differently than her firm was accustomed. Her excuse seemed acceptable. When the meeting was over, she made sure everyone left with the impression that they were in good hands. She observed how Lucas seemed totally disinterested in talking to Nichelle, who lingered after the meeting in hopes of renewing the conversation. But Lucas ignored her, engaging instead with several of the other executives. Eventually Nichelle left. Ronnie continued to talk with the remaining executives until the conference room was cleared and she and Lucas were the only ones remaining.

"Can I have a word, Veronica?" Lucas asked as she headed toward the door.

"Sure. What's on your mind?"

"I just want to personally apologize to you about today."

"Can I be honest? That was rhetorical. I don't care about your lovers' spat or your hurt feelings. From the hours of eight to four I need your head in the game. We clear?"

"Yeah, we're clear. I'm sorry about that. You're right. I'm typically more professional than I've been acting."

Ronnie noticed he was trying to compose himself and decided to show a bit of compassion. "I believe you, but stop telling me and start showing me. I gambled on you to bring your firm in here. The board is going to want an update soon, and I'm not going to get caught with my tail between my legs because you fell in love with a Ratchet-ass chick."

Lucas seemed slightly put off by Ronnie's words, but she continued. "Look at you! Even now you want to defend her when she doesn't give a damn about you. Let me help you out— she cheated on you and is untrustworthy. Let it go and move on."

Lucas remained silent as he packed up his paperwork. Ronnie was about to walk away when he responded. "Wait—how do you know she cheated on me?"

"Honey, I've been a woman my whole life, and I know that men only look the way you look for two reasons. One, he lost his job, or two, he found out his woman is giving her kitty away to someone else. And since you're still gainfully employed, we can rule out number one."

He chuckled and nodded, and after a brief pause replied, "You are a pretty insightful woman, Veronica."

Ronnie nodded, then looked him over. Finally, she asked, "What are you doing after work?" Lucas was about to respond when Ronnie continued. "Again, rhetorical. Meet me at Guadalajara at six for drinks."

"I appreciate what you're trying to do, Veronica, but I don't think—"

Ronnie interrupted him. "It wasn't optional. You, the consultant, are going to take me, the client, out for drinks at six p.m. sharp." Ronnie smiled at Lucas, who started to cheer up slightly.

"Six p.m. it is," he said.

"Excuse me, Lucas, can I talk to you for a moment?"

Ronnie looked back to the front door of the conference room to find Nichelle standing there. "Sounds good, Veronica. I'll see you then." Lucas said, turning to face Nichelle. As Ronnie reached the door, she stared deep into Nichelle's eyes. *Oh, this bitch right here,* Ronnie thought as she passed her out the doorway.

But that didn't stop Nichelle from closing the door, putting herself alone in the room with Lucas.

CHAPTER 13
RIGHT TO KNOW

Nichelle stood at the door as Ronnie passed her. *Oh, this bitch right here!* thought Nichelle as Ronnie left. What were they talking about? Where are they going? All questions she wanted to ask Lucas and was in no position to. She had avoided him for weeks while he agonized over questions she refused to give an audience to. Yet the idea of him and Ronnie spending any time together was like scraping nails against a chalkboard. She gently closed the door to give them some privacy.

"Seems like you two are getting along well," Nichelle said, trying to break the ice.

"What do you want, Nichelle?" Lucas demanded.

"I got the nameplate you left. It's on my desk. It's really nice. Thank you." Although she was trying to soften his attitude, it wasn't working.

"That's what you want to talk to me about? Nameplates?"

Nichelle looked away. "I'm sorry about this. I never, ever meant to hurt you."

Lucas shifted his paperwork and said nothing. She wanted to press the issue, but she could tell it was taking a lot for him to be silent at the moment. She wanted to let him know she still loved him and didn't know why she made the mistakes she made. She wished all of this was just a horrible nightmare, but this was reality, and right now Lucas, the man who cared so much for her, was on the verge of breaking down.

"Will you say something, please?"

"What do you want me to say, Nichelle? What the hell happened? Why would you do this? Who was that guy? You should know damn good and well the questions I want to ask!" Lucas shouted in frustration. The fatigue was apparent in his eyes, as if he had only slept a few hours. She could lie to him no longer. She found a chair next to him, sat in it, and took a deep breath.

"Donovan was my first boyfriend," she confessed. "We were together for a long time— years actually—until he went to prison three years ago. He was supposed to be in jail for seven years, but got released early. He found me, and I—fell into some terrible, old habits."

She sat motionless as Lucas paced the floor, actively listening to her every word. "You make it sound like the time was a factor. As if he served all seven years, this would have never happened. Is that what you think?" She was silent as he went on, "So you've been sleeping with him, and he's been staying there—and that's why you didn't want me over."

Nichelle started to well up as she nodded in agreement. "That's why you rushed me out of the house a few weeks ago?"

She nodded again. Her truth from his lips was horrid. Nichelle could tell he was terribly hurt by her admission, as if he had something rancid in his system. She fully, at long last, realized the extent of her betrayal. "I didn't mean for it to happen. I just made a mistake."

Lucas turned his head back to Nichelle, his eyes red with anger. "You made a mistake?" He walked directly toward her chair and spoke. "Forgetting to put the milk back in the fridge is a mistake. Calling someone 'Steve' when their name is 'Roger' is a mistake. You fucked somebody else repeatedly for the last month! That's not a mistake! That is a choice!"

"I'm sorry, Lucas—I'm so very sorry. We can work this out. You didn't deserve this, I know. I have to live with what I've done to you."

"Did I hear you correctly? Did I hear you say, 'We can work this out'?" His question was dripping with sarcasm as he lowered his tone lest he draw an audience in the workplace. "Let me be perfectly clear, Nichelle—there is *nothing* to work out. You made a choice, and we both have to live with the consequences. As much as it hurts, the one thing I am not is desperate. I'm not the kind of guy to sit here and wait on you to know if what we had was real or not. I was happy with you— you know that, and still you betrayed me in the ultimate way. I will work on this project and treat you with the respect I would any coworker, but that is the extent of our relationship now. Never forget that."

He packed up his things and walked toward the door. With his hand on the knob, he stopped and turned around. "Oh, and one more thing. If it's not work-related, then we have nothing to talk about. Make sure you remember that as you stay the fuck out of my life."

He left the conference room, using every ounce of restraint not to slam the door.

CHAPTER 14
ROUNDS AND RECON

Lucas arrived at Guadalajara emotionally drained. In one fell swoop his entire world came crashing down around him, and just as he was in the middle of the biggest project of his career. These thoughts were never far from his mind as he tried to come to grips with how something so special became toxic in a matter of moments. His emotions were very raw. Even though he had been up the entire night, he had been able to get through a day's worth of meetings without going to sleep. He felt terrible—physically and emotionally spent—and it was only Monday. On top of that, he was about to have a drink with one of the top executives in the company who didn't seem capable of taking "No" for an answer. *Can this day possibly get any worse?* he thought to himself as he scanned the room for Ronnie.

"Lucas, over here," she called out as he slipped his jacket off and loosened his tie. Ronnie was sitting in a booth checking her iPhone. When he reached her, he noticed there were two shots of Patrón sitting on the table, and one empty glass that made it clear Ronnie began before he arrived. He looked at her as she put down her phone, smiling at his presence.

"Veronica," he said as a form of salutation.

"Mr. Kimble, so good of you to join me," she replied, picking up the shot of Patrón in front of her. Ronnie raised the glass as if toasting him, and Lucas, in kind, picked up his glass and they downed their shots together. The liquor went down smooth. Under normal circumstances, he would have no problem drinking with one of his clients, but all he could think about was how to get out of this project. It was a nonstarter of an idea. A client this big almost never came knocking. He had to not only finish this but do it well. The second thought he had was how could he get out of working with Nichelle. Although he prided himself on being a professional, he was certain this qualified as an extenuating circumstance. "Earth to Lucas," Ronnie chimed in, interrupting his train of thought.

"I'm sorry, Veronica, I was thinking —"

"Let me take one guess what—or whom—you were thinking about."

Lucas chuckled. "Guilty as charged." He could tell she was examining him, but he didn't really care. The pleasantries were just enough to get through a few drinks so he could call it an early night and get some sleep.

"You know, every time I see you, you're deep in thought about something, and it's typically Nichelle. Now, I don't want to pry into your business, but if you've been deep in thought like this for the last month, it's probably best you find something to take your mind off your issues."

It was an excellent point, but one he was only partially ready to receive, especially from a stranger.

"Let's do this—I won't think about Nichelle, and you won't bring her up. Do we have a deal?"

He could tell that his words were a little sharp for Ronnie's tastes, but she nonetheless nodded in agreement. There was a bit of silence for a moment before she jumped in with another question a moment before their second round of tequila arrived.

"Why do you call me Veronica? Everyone else calls me Ronnie."

"Do you have a problem me calling you by your name?" he asked as the two picked up their shots and threw them back. Lucas wasn't really a heavy drinker, but was making an exception to help move his mind past his circumstances.

"I used to hate the name. I honestly haven't heard it since grade school. At this point,

everyone calls me Ronnie, but I have to say, coming from you, it sounds natural. So, no, I don't have a problem with it. I just wonder why you stick with it." Lucas stretched to unwind. He began to answer her question.

"My first year as a consultant I was sent to New York to work for a law firm. I'm pretty sure they were mob-related because everyone went by a nickname. When I introduced myself, the owner, this guy they called 'Big Ralph', met me and gave me the nickname 'Texas.' Problem was, they already had a guy named Texas working there, so I became Austin, as in the state capital. I was young and full of pride and wanted my respect, so I informed him my name was Lucas Kimble. Ralph turned around and says, 'Austin has a pair of stones on him, don't he?' For the next eight months, I was known as *Austin with the stones.* A few months after my assignment was over, the firm went down for embezzlement. When the feds asked for my books, they were useless. I had a bunch of nicknames in there. Anytime someone was called Texas or Montana, they would just say it was the other guy. The feds couldn't do anything to them, and I almost lost my career before it started. So now I go by full first and last names only. Besides, nicknames are personal. I try to stay away from them unless we have a history together. A nickname is something that is earned, in my opinion."

He sat as Ronnie laughed until tears formed at the ducts of her eyes. "That is an incredible story worth every moment."

"A day in the life of a consultant."

"I see—Austin with the stones."

"You got jokes, don't you?"

"I couldn't help myself. My apologies," Veronica said, still grinning from the story. "So you and *Neecie,* were that close?"

"I thought we said we weren't going to talk about her," he said with a half grin on his face.

"Right. I'm sorry."

"Oh, no, you don't get off that easy. That's a party foul!" Lucas clamored. "Bartender!" The waiter, anticipating the request, walked over with two chilled shots before the order was placed. Lucas then placed an order for a Corona and a glass of White Horse wine for Ronnie. The two worked on their third shot of the evening, and Lucas started to feel like himself again. As his worries and inhibitions slowly melted away, he noticed how attractive Ronnie was. Her green blouse clung closely to her cleavage, and as he eyed the exposed flesh, his curiosity got the better of him. He decided to turn the tables.

"Can I ask a question?"

"Sure," she responded.

"While I appreciate you spending your time with me, and I really do, isn't someone missing your company right now?" As the drinks arrived, Ronnie looked at her glass of wine and placed her neatly manicured fingertip in the center of the glass as she swirled it around. Her green eyes locked onto him.

"That's cute and clever. I guess you're asking me if I have a man or woman at home."

Lucas stammered to respond. The idea that she might be in a same-sex relationship never crossed his mind.

"Well, yeah. I just noticed you're pretty much at work or talking about work or preparing to do work. I was curious if there was someone in your life."

Ronnie took a sip of wine and responded candidly. "No, there's no one waiting on me. I'm a workaholic. Oh, and I'm sure you're curious now, so I'll state for the record I'm heterosexual. Although if Beyoncé was available, I'd reconsider."

Lucas laughed out loud. "You have jokes alright. So why aren't you dating someone?"

"Because I don't do first dates."

"Well, if you never have a first date, how can you ever know if you're going to want to have a second date?"

"I don't have the time. I know what I want and how to go about getting that, and most first dates are just dead ends and who has time for that? Every step I take has to lead somewhere. I don't waste time, hair, or dresses on dead ends."

Lucas sat back, his eyes wide. This was intriguing to him, so he decided to dig a little deeper.

"Then you don't want relationships at all?"

"If they can be avoided, why not?"

"Ouch. Why would you say something like that?"

"I guess if I had to call it ... I don't want to end up looking like a certain auditor I know who's been moping around for the last few weeks." She stared at Lucas as she took another sip of wine. "You have to admit, since I've known you, it's been one long cautionary tale about how relationships suck."

Conceding the point, he nodded and took a sip of his Corona. Two additional shots of tequila arrived.

"I'm assuming they know you here?" he asked.

"One of the most faithful relationships in my life. No pun intended," she responded.

His buzz was strong enough that if he were offended he wouldn't be able to tell. He felt bliss. "It's all good, Veronica." He took his glass and raised it. "To faithfulness," he said, his words beginning to slur.

"To faithfulness," Ronnie repeated.

Lucas loosened his tie even more and unbuttoned the top button of his charcoal Calvin Klein shirt. His filter was completely open, and he knew it was time to leave, but he was enjoying himself. Ronnie had proven herself to be pleasant company, and sitting here drinking with her was the brightest spot of his day thus far.

"Thanks, Veronica, I needed this," he told her.

"Now you owe me two," she responded. Lucas realized she was referencing their first encounter at the coffee shop smiled wearily; he closed his eyes as he sipped on his beer. The exhaustion was setting in, and he struggled to reopen them.

"Do you know how long she was cheating on you?"

"At least a month," he responded. He didn't want to talk about it, but at this point, he didn't care. He felt good and didn't want to bottle it up any longer.

"It was her ex-boyfriend—some convict she met back in the day that came home. I'm sure he's over there right now," Lucas continued.

"Interesting," Ronnie replied. "How did you find out?"

Frustrated and worn out Lucas replied, "He told me himself. He told me about the whole damn thing—I went over there to talk to her, and he was at the house. We had a long talk. I feel like an idiot."

There was a brief silence before Ronnie responded. "If she can't see your value, she's the idiot. Don't beat yourself up about the mistakes a tramp makes." The words irritated Lucas, but Ronnie had a point—none of this was his fault. He looked at his empty glass, now fully feeling the effects of the liquor.

"At least he stopped me before I gave her the Jill Scott tickets. I'm going to have to find someone to sell those to in the next week or two. The concert is about a month away. By the way, what is it with you two? Have you always been this cold toward one another, or is this a byproduct of her promotion?"

Another silence ensued before Ronnie responded. "It's personality types. I'm not very popular because I'm results-driven. I don't need to be friends with you to do the work. I guess I'm not really good at being politically correct. And I don't like skanky women," she said slyly.

"This is going to be the most interesting work assignment I've ever been on."

"Which is why it's imperative that you and I have a close working relationship built on trust. I can't predict how things will go with you and Nichelle, but if history is any indication, it's not going to be easy. As you've already pointed out, she's not inviting me over for her birthday cake, and vice versa. But if you and I stay on the same page, then maybe we can move things along and both come out of this with a profitable resolution."

Lucas tried to focus, but the conversation had taken a tangent he wasn't mentally prepared to deal with being this tired and half drunk.

"All due respect, Veronica, it sounds like you're asking me to choose sides between you and Nichelle."

"And why not? She's clearly chosen sides when it comes to you." Her words were a piercing reminder of the past twenty-four hours. Lucas pulled out his wallet and signaled for the waiter.

"I'm going to call it a night. It's been pleasant. Thank you for everything."

"Just think about what I'm saying, Lucas."

"I'm going to do my job—nothing more, nothing less," he said unwaveringly.

The waiter came over, but did not take the card Lucas had in his hand. Instead, he gave one back to Ronnie. She signed her signature and stood up to walk out with him. "It's all taken care of. I know I told you to take me out, but you looked like you could use a friend, so I covered it all. And as far as work goes, I wouldn't expect anything less from you."

"Thank you for the drinks. That's very nice, and I'm glad we understand each other about work."

"Not a problem. But I was thinking about something else you said."

"Which was?"

"The Jill Scott tickets. It seems a waste that you have to get rid of them with so little notice. I don't doubt you could sell them, but I bet you were looking forward to that concert."

Lucas smirked. "To be honest, I was. She's one of my favorite artists."

"Then you should go!"

"Nah, I'm not nearly that confident— going to a concert by myself. That's a tall order."

"Then go with me," Ronnie interjected. Lucas was silent for a moment, so she continued to make her pitch. "I love Jill, so it's actually a win-win. I'll buy one of the tickets, and you get to see an artist you enjoy."

"You know what? Screw it. Let's go," he responded. "The concert is in about four weeks."

"It's a date," Ronnie said, her green eyes shimmering in the darkness of the restaurant.

The two parted ways, and Lucas got into his car parked a mere half block from the restaurant. He turned on the ignition and thought about Nichelle actively betraying him with Donovan. What would make her do something like that to him? He needed more closure than he got.

He was on 288 when he decided to get off, but he wasn't headed home. In no time, he was at 6631 Apple Grove Lane.

CHAPTER 15
REUNION UNHINGED

The doorbell rang at 11:58 at night, and it just kept ringing. Nichelle, not sure who it was, surmised the only person who would be so disrespectful was Donovan, which meant he must have left his key when he stormed out the other night. Instead of getting up, she laid in bed and didn't say a word. The man ruined her relationship with Lucas, and she wasn't in the mood for an apology. There was a hard knock at the door. *This motherfucker! Doesn't he know I have neighbors!* She got out of bed and stormed toward the front door. "I can't believe you're even—" She was cut off. Lucas stood in the doorway drunk.

"'Sup, Neecie," he said as he stumbled through the doorway. The man could barely stand up and was in no position to go anywhere. "Where's your boyfriend?"

"Lucas, what in the hell happened to you?" she asked, concerned for his safety. "Why are you drunk when the week just started?"

"I been drankin, I been drankin," he sang in response to her question from Beyonce's *Drunk in Love*. Nichelle could smell the tequila coming through his pores. Beads of sweat formed around his neck as she tried to usher him into the living room.

"I'm going to get you some coffee."

"I'm not here for coffee, damn it! I'm here to whoop ass!" he stammered. His words were fully slurred, and he had none of his usual composure.

"How much have you had to drink?"

"I stopped drinking when I felt better, and I was feeling like shit all day, so ... a lot!" He put a hand on the wall to steady himself. "Damn it, Nichelle, didn't we have a good thing? Why did you do this to me? Why did this happen? I love you, but I can't be with someone who isn't honest."

"That's the thing, Lucas. You sit here and judge me for my actions. You think I'm scum because I made a mistake. Well, I'm not perfect, but I'm not scum either."

"I never judged you—you fucking broke my heart! Do you have any idea how that feels? I truly loved you. I still do, and this hurts because I care so damn much for you. When I came over and your... that guy was in here, I kept thinking, there has to be some kind of mistake, Nichelle would never do this, not in a million years. All of the signs pointed in one direction, still I had just a tiny sliver of hope he could be lying. That this somehow just couldn't possibly be true, and then I saw your eyes. It confirmed everything he said and everything I had been feeling. I thought we were building something special, and you just threw it all away and for what? A teenage crush? Because you have a thing for bad boys? A Fuck?"

She remained silent as he asked his questions from a heart bleeding through the alcohol, and though he was drunk and angry and frustrated, this conversation was much more sensitive than the one they had in the office. He looked around the room as if searching for meaning to his own questions. She placed her hand on his neck, which he promptly removed and resumed his interrogation.

"Just tell me this—did I ever really know you? This is all I think about these days. It's like the woman I was with was abducted and replaced by someone else. You couldn't even give me the respect of taking the time and being honest with me. You don't respect me enough to tell me the truth?"

"I was going to—"

"When? At the wedding? You avoided me like the plague! If I didn't come over here, I would've never known." He sat on the floor, his own words making him angry. She knew he was right; they both did. She didn't want to hurt him and he didn't want to be hurt, but this was the world she created for the both of them.

She walked over and hugged him. The tequila-cologne blend formed an unappealing scent, but she stayed by his side nonetheless. He turned toward her and kissed her on her neck. "What are you doing?" she asked, startled by his actions. He said nothing, but kissed her again, more gently this time. She was slightly aroused. The emotional pain released by alcohol and the pleasure created by renewed feelings turned her on. She kissed him as they both rose to their feet, matching the passions rising in both of them. Struggling because of his intoxication, he picked her up and walked toward her bedroom, plopping her on the baby-blue satin sheets.

Unbuckling his belt, she squeezed his not yet fully erect member pressing against his pants. She freed his organ as he descended upon her, removing his shoes and pants in the process. She slid her purple G-string to the side as he entered her gently and stroked her with compassion. It was a welcome change of pace from the sex she had been having lately. He continued to push into her slowly, delicately moving at a rhythmic speed. She arched her hips with each motion, enhancing the pleasure as he slipped one of her breasts out of her nightgown. The moisture of his tongue on her areola, mixed with the cool night temperature, firmed her nipple and generated even more moisture between her legs. He glided in and out of her in such a delicate way that she felt like a queen. The sensual nature of their lovemaking was just that— lovemaking. He always looked into her eyes when they were together. She smiled as the chemistry between them was cemented by her climax. She looked in his eyes, fully satisfied.

"I love you," she said to him as he stroked her hair. Instead of a response, however, his eyes went dull and his face became visceral with rage. He now pushed into her, the gentle lover shoved away by those three little words. He pushed into her with great force, more like Donovan than Lucas. She briefly thought she saw his face as he thrust angrily forward. This wasn't Lucas anymore. He was someone else, something else, willing to hurt her without regard. She grasped onto his back as the pleasure was now intense yet cold. She didn't want to enjoy this, but she didn't want him to stop. She was powerless. She was about to cum again when he bit her nipple, piercingly hard, forcing her to cum when he did, finishing her off with several violent thrusts. He fell on top of her as she gathered her breath. A tear formed in her eye, but she didn't know if it was from pleasure or heartache. The man on top of her was cold and uncaring. He rose and rolled over. Silence filled the air where moaning had been. She wanted to ask a question, anything to understand what just occurred, but she thought she might fear the answer. In all their time together, he had never fucked her like that—uncaringly using her flesh for his pleasure. In one instant, their reunion became unhinged.

"This was a mistake," Lucas finally said, collapsing next to her. The words pierced her heart. She didn't want it to be a mistake, but she knew no matter what happened, things would never be the same.

"I meant what I said, Lucas. I do love you." She hoped that maybe they could salvage some piece of what they had.

"I think you love the idea of me, but you don't actually love me."

"Why would you say that?" Nichelle found it hard to mask her pain.

Lucas sat up on the bed. "The way I see it, the entire time we were kissing and touching each other, that was love. People in love don't lie to one another. You don't love me, Neecie. I don't think you ever did."

She was angry at his words and angry at her actions. There was no arguing this was closure.

"It's over, Nichelle," he said, validating her thought process.

"So you just wanted one goodbye piece of ass, Lucas?"

"No, I just wanted to stop hurting,"

"And so you used me to ease the pain?"

"You're the person who caused my pain, Nichelle. You're the source of all of my pain right now."

"Just get the fuck out, Lucas."

"You want me to leave? Fine I'm gone." He began to dress himself. Nichelle looked at him. This wasn't the man she loved. He would never have walked away so quickly. This entire series of events was a nightmare. She didn't know how to make things better, if it were even possible.

"Please, just listen to me, Lucas. I love you. I know you know that. And you love me no matter what you tell yourself—that's why you came over here. I lost my way, but I'm willing to do whatever it takes to fix what we have."

There was silence as Lucas finished buckling his pants. A silence she couldn't tolerate finally she relented filling the air with her own words "Are you going to say something?"

"I just wonder if you would be telling Donovan the same thing if it were him."

"That's not fair."

"The one thing I've learned in dealing with you is nothing is fair."

"I know I hurt you, but do I deserve your—"

"Did you hear that?" Lucas asked, interrupting her train of thought. Nichelle didn't hear anything, but walked toward the living room anyway. She looked at the door. Her assumption from earlier was wrong. Donovan didn't lose or forget his key; he was using it at this very moment to unlock the door.

"Lucas, baby, listen to me. You have to hide and hide right now."

He looked at her stunned by her words. He could only reply, "Are you fucking serious?"

"Look, we don't have time for this. Donovan is packing at all times. If he catches you in here he will kill the both of us."

The damage her words caused was irremediable. "Like I said before, nothing is fair with you." He proceeded to the front closet hoping to close the door before the front door fully opened.

CHAPTER 16
RECONNECTED

For the past day, Donovan stayed in a motel not too far from Nichelle's home, but it was time to talk about what was going on between them. Although he was certain he did the right thing by telling Lucas about his unwilling participation in a love triangle, enough time had elapsed for him to realize he may have overreacted. He pulled up to her home wearing a white sleeveless tank top, something he packed out of frustration in his haste to leave her home the other night. He knew it was cold, but at this moment it was freezing. He needed to pick up a few more pieces of clothing in order to make it through the remainder of the week, and if their talk didn't go well, maybe longer. Upon arriving, he walked into the home using the key she gave him his second week out of prison. He walked in to see Nichelle sitting on the couch with half a glass of whisky in her cup. She didn't acknowledge him as he entered the living room.

"Step up from your wine, isn't it?" he said, trying to make small talk. It was true. Since he had come home, Nichelle all but stopped drinking wine. Which was fine with him, he never knew her to be a wine drinker to begin with. He loved to point out it was part of her uppity façade, or *Ms. Myers* as he would refer to her when she started to do things out of character. He continued on into the bedroom to find his clothing, unfolded and half in/half out of the dresser, as if she had begun to pack his belongings but reconsidered it. The bedroom in general was mess as if she had a hard time sleeping. He knew she was having the same doubts he was ever since their uneasy reunion. He turned around and walked back into the living room.

"Babygirl, we need to talk."

"Go to hell, Donovan!" Nichelle screamed. "I can't believe you embarrassed me like that."

Donovan pulled her by the arm, but she fought back, refusing to get up from the couch. "Look, I know you mad at me. I should've let you handle things your way. But the dude was sitting in the living room when I got here. It was either talk to him or shoot him."

"Fuck you, D. You were so out of line for what you did."

"Damn it, what was I supposed to do? I've been gone three damn years, and the whole world has been passing me by. When I go into jail, I'm almost rich. I have a girl who I *think* loves me and will stay true to me, so fine, I can do the time. When I get out early —I'm broke, my best friend is dead, and my woman, yes, *my* woman, has moved on. I gotta fight for my place in the world again. You want to know the truth? I don't know how to do anything else but rob people, and I don't want to be that guy anymore. I was out the game with that last job. I was going take that money and open a car wash or something—put you through school, and we'd be happy together. You were happy with me, Babygirl—don't tell me you wasn't. So yeah, I told him the truth because in my eyes you'll always be my woman. I still love you, and I'm gonna fight for you unless you tell me right now you don't want me in your life anymore." He said it as candidly as he could, but Nichelle was silent. He threw up his hands and began to walk away.

"I never looked at it from your point of view." Her words stopped him in his tracks. He turned around and looked at her. Her eyes revealed her heart's true intent.

"That's because you're a selfish-ass woman," he responded as he walked over to her. "But you my woman, and good or bad, you're all I want." He kissed her on the cheek, and she hugged him in return. "Donovan, I'm sorry for everything. I just didn't know how to handle things when you went to jail."

"I'm back now, and if you believe in me, we're going to be fine. I'm going to get this money. It's out there somewhere, and then we're going to live the life you deserve."

"What if you never find the money?" she asked. "Can't you start over? I can't be with you if you're going to do anything to go back to jail."

"Look me in my eyes, Babygirl, I want you to know I'm never going back to jail. You're with me forever." There was a silence in the air. For a moment he was uncertain she wanted what he wanted "You're with me...right?"

"I'm with you, Donovan, I'm with you."

"Then the past is the past. We start fresh from today."

Donovan walked into the kitchen and opened a Bud Light he kept in the fridge. He then joined Nichelle on the couch. "Besides, the money is out there. I know it is, so we don't have to worry about that."

"I don't understand why you keep looking for the money. You're free, we're together, and you don't have any solid leads on where it could be."

Donovan looked at her as if she were from another planet. "I did three years in federal for that money. That's why I keep looking for it. I earned that money, Babygirl. I went to prison and had to fight almost every day. It wasn't easy, but I survived. I just gotta look everywhere Rico would've hidden it. I can't trust anyone in the world, but I trusted him. He wouldn't have spent a dime. But I heard he started hanging with this cat named Carlos. He's bad news. "

Nichelle reached over and stroked the side of his face. "You wanted us to start over, and we're doing that, but part of this whole process is putting the past in the past. Maybe you should let this go. You're a free man, and there is no price you can put on that."

Donovan nodded and stood up, taking her by the arm and gently pulling her from the couch. He hugged his lover for nearly half a minute, then, upon releasing his hug, gripped her by both arms.

"On that note, Babygirl, I need to ask you—is there anything, anything at all, I need to know about. We're starting fresh from here."

"Nothing. I've told you everything. It's just me and you now."

"Cool. Just me and you."

She hugged him as he held her close. He began to kiss her. She returned his passion He pulled her into the bedroom and continued to kiss on her. "Wait, I have to freshen up. D I went to the gym today."

"Well damn girl hurry up you know make up sex is the best sex!"

"Ok baby it's just—"

"What was that?"

"What was what?"

"I could've sworn I heard something."

Boom.

Donovan was sure he heard something. An indistinct sound he couldn't make out, but he knew it was coming from the front of the house. He pulled out his pistol.

"Baby, what are you doing?" Nichelle asked, still trying to hold on to him.

"Girl, chill. It's someone in here."

"No, there isn't. Come to the bedroom."

"Babygirl, sit your ass down now!"

Donovan walked toward the hallway. There were two doors, one to the bathroom he used when he first got out of prison and the other to a closet. He quickly made his way to the bathroom door and opened it, waving the gun in. It was empty. He turned his attention to the closet. He was certain he heard a noise, and whatever it was had to be in there. He redirected his pistol and started walking toward the door.

"Donovan!" Nichelle screamed out.

"Chelle, what the fuck?" he walked backwards, grabbing by her arm forcefully. "Be quiet. Something is going on in here, and you're about to get us killed!"

"Donovan, there is nothing in there. You're hearing things and scaring me with this gun! Put it away now, please!"

"Babygirl, I'm going to say this for the last time—sit your ass down."

He walked back towards the closet. He put his hand on the door and turned the knob.

Boom!

He heard the sound again. It was the front door. He pointed the gun toward it. The door was partially open, being swung back and forth by the night air. Had he forgot to close it on his way in? He looked outside to see if anyone was around. There was no one there. He turned and went back inside, but for good measure, he opened the closet just to make sure. There was nothing there.

Fuck, I must have not closed the door all the way when I walked in. You got to do better, D, especially with Carlos still out there somewhere.

"Donovan!"

"It was nothing, Babygirl. I guess I forgot to close the door, and the wind was pushing it back and forth. My bad."

"So there was nothing in the closet?"

"Nah. I could've sworn I locked the door when I came in though."

"Well, obviously you didn't. I told you you're overreacting. If we're going to start over, that means you really have to play things by the book, D. I'm serious."

He looked at her and looked back at the door. She was right—he was being paranoid. That would have to stop if he were going to have any real shot at a life with her. *I have to get this money and soon*, he thought as he walked over and slapped her on her posterior.

"Where were we?"

Damn that was close!

CHAPTER 17
RELAX, RELATE

Lucas arrived at Ronnie's home to pick her up for the Jill Scott concert. He was still a bit uncomfortable with the suggestion. *Was this a date?* It was certainly unorthodox. It had been over two months since he and Nichelle broke up, and clearly she had moved on with her life, but he wasn't ready to date. He was, however, in need of a good time. The last time he had a *good time,* he ended up in Nichelle's bedroom, a mistake he didn't want to repeat.

He got out the car and brushed off his jet black Michael Kors suit, making sure there was no lint on it or the matching black shirt. He walked toward her condo. Not living far from work, it was easy to find, although he was slightly concerned about running into someone from the office. He prided himself on a certain level of professionalism, and this was definitely crossing all the lines. *Why did I agree to this?* He thought as he rang her doorbell. From the other side, Ronnie called out, "It's open." Lucas walked in and was extremely impressed. Ronnie had spent extensive time making sure her home generated that precise reaction. The scent of lavender and vanilla saturated the air. The hardwood flooring was natural dark mahogany wood, more expensive than laminate. He recognized it right away since he also had natural wood in his house, although he had a feeling Ronnie did not put in the man-hours he did to install it. The walls were natural sandstone with art paintings on each one of them. As he took deep notice of one in particular—a hawk being beheaded by a king—he heard the words, "I'm ready."

He turned around and lost all interest in the artwork. Ronnie stood before him in a blue, form-fitting Chanel dress. Her shoulders exposed, and a black Chanel belt which accessorized her midsection, and her lips were covered with a blue lipstick, no doubt a MAC product. She slipped on her blue Louboutins as the final component. He couldn't help but admire how well put together she looked. It was the first time he had noticed her natural beauty, her cinnamon hair, her full lips, ocean green eyes and this amazing outfit, Kanye's song *Devil in a Blue Dress* came to mind. "You look amazing," he said.

"Well, thank you. You don't look half bad yourself, and I match your tie." She responded by tugging at his tie. Her persona was more bubbly that he had ever seen her. Lucas looked at her dress, the perfect color match for the black and blue pinstripe Kenneth Cole tie he wore.

"Yeah, blue is my favorite color."

"Is that right?" she responded

"I have a feeling you already knew that."

"Not at all. Just lucky, I guess." She was toying with him and he knew it, but it didn't matter. His favorite color looked perfect against her fair skin. How had he not noticed this woman's beauty prior to this moment? She was amazement personified. If this wasn't a date at this moment, a part of him wanted it to be. "You like something you see?" She said interrupting his thoughts.

"Huh? Oh yeah...I noticed your painting on the wall. Genghis Khan right?"

Ronnie paused, looked at him with a heavy gaze then replied. "I have to admit it's not often I'm impressed."

"Yeah, my dad told me that parable about the hawk and its master."

Ronnie smiled, the blue lipstick parting way to her perfect white teeth. "Interesting. What do you recall?"

"Well, Genghis Khan had this hawk he trained to be loyal only to him. One day he stopped to rest before his next conquest. Sitting by the lake, he reached for his cup of water, but as he was about to take a sip, the hawk swooped down and distracted him. It annoyed him greatly, and he fussed at the hawk. As he reached a second time, the hawk swooped down again. He couldn't believe the hawk. It had always been loyal, but today it was disobedient. As he reached for the cup a third time, the hawk flew in, and right as the bird reached the cup, Genghis Khan pulled out his sword and beheaded it. While doing that, he knocked the cup over. Come to find out the hawk wasn't trying to be a pest at all. When Khan knocked over the cup, he found a very poisonous snake had slithered into his cup to sip the water, leaving its venom behind. It would have killed him instantly. Khan beheaded the snake with the same sword after realizing the hawk was trying to save his life."

Ronnie smiled. "Your father taught you well. It's one of my favorite stories. It's about motive and loyalty."

Lucas nodded. "So which one are you?"

"Pardon?"

"Which one are you? Are you the hawk loyal to the death, or the snake with deadly intent?"

Smiling, she looked at him with her green eyes as she walked closer to tell him the answer to his question. "I'm the sword." He was surprised by her answer, yet everything about her was surprising. He was slowly becoming more intrigued by her.

"Before we go, I made us a pre-concert cocktail." Ronnie said as she pointed to the table. There were four drinks sitting there. One shot of 1800 and one shot of Ciroc pineapple for each of them. Lucas scoffed. "What's wrong?" she asked.

"Um, this is more than one drink."

"Okay, two drinks," she replied, smiling.

"It looks like you opened a bar."

She giggled. "Okay, I'm not trying to get you drunk, but the point of this night is for you to loosen up and have a good time. You're overdue."

It was hard to resist someone so stunning. He wanted to comply with almost anything she said, but she had a point. He had been miserable for a while now, and it was starting to show in his work. One night out with a beautiful coworker couldn't hurt. He picked up the shot of 1800 and lifted it in the air. "To a good time."

The two made quick work of both shots and were soon headed to the concert. The

concert hall wasn't far from her home, so the drive would be extremely short. They were halfway there when Ronnie asked, "Something on your mind?"

He paused. He was unusually quiet and was pretty sure Ronnie thought he was thinking about Nichelle. "Yeah, but not what you think."

"Well, that's a first!" she chimed back, confirming what he assumed.

"Is this ... are we on a ..."

"Spit it out, man."

Lucas grinned. He wasn't trying to be shy—he just didn't know how to ask the question. "I know you want to make me feel better and all, but this feels like a date."

Ronnie grinned. She looked at him, but remained silent.

"Well?"

"Well, what?" she responded.

"Is this a date? I only ask because well you spending your time, wearing the hell out of that dress and your hair is on point. And I know you don't do that for dead ends."

"I thought you were too drunk to remember me saying that."

"I'm full of surprises. But you're still dodging the question."

"Which was?"

He smiled. "Is this a date?"

"What this is, Lucas, is two peers having a good time. No label necessary beyond that." Her lips dripped with temptation. She was indeed the sword. He nodded, her elegance on full display. He decided not to press the issue any further.

They arrived at the concert early enough to get a few more drinks in before the opening act went on. By the time Jill Scott took the stage, the crowd was on its feet. Lucas truly got into the energy of the concert, delighted he took his *peer* on an unlabeled good time. The concert began with *A Long Walk*, bringing any stragglers to their feet and setting the tempo for the rest of the night. When Jill transitioned to *The Way,* Lucas slowly accepted the fact he was having a good time with a very beautiful woman. By time she got to *Lyzel in E Flat,* the crowd was going wild, and his inhibition was gone. Ronnie grabbed him by the hand.

"Hold me," she said. Lucas, feeling the energy of this particular song, wrapped his hands around her waist as Ronnie sang every word aloud. Her body was firm, yet tender. She was moving her hips along to the bassline, and he pressed his face against her neck, enticed by her fragrance, no doubt one of the Bond Number 9 series of perfumes. If this wasn't a date, it was rapidly becoming one. He pulled her closer. Her voice, her movement, her dress, her scent—at this very moment, she was living seduction. Ronnie placed her hand on his neck as he stood behind her, holding her. She slowly turned around to make eye contact with him, placing both hands around the back of his neck. Enticed by her green eyes, which looked like emeralds in the darkness of the concert, he listened as she spoke the words along with the artist as the song neared its conclusion:

"You're different and special in every way imaginable —"

He leaned in and kissed her, and she didn't resist. Her arms pulled him by the neck even closer as he kissed her with the passion he had been longing to share with her since he saw the blue lipstick pressed against her caramel skin. The two remained intertwined until the last note of the song, the final song of the concert. The arena went silent as their lips finally separated from one another. Lucas wasn't sure what just happened. He wanted to apologize, but he had enjoyed the kiss. In fact, he had enjoyed the entire night and didn't want this to end anytime soon. As the crowd made its way to the entrance, he held Ronnie's hand and walked her out to the car to drop her off back home.

The car ride was quiet. They drove, never separating hands since the end of the concert as if neither one wanted to undo the chemistry they had discovered. Lucas knew this was unprofessional, but didn't care. It was the best he had felt in some time. After he parked the car, Ronnie looked at him.

"Look, I know tonight has been great, and I know you're getting out of something messy. I want to tell you that I have no expectation but to live in this moment. You are more than welcome to come up for a nightcap."

She released his hand, opened her door, and got out. She closed the door and looked back at him seductively. Lucas sat there for a moment to admire her walk. He admired her from a distance and noticed something—she had slipped out of one shoe, then the next, leaving them on the sidewalk to her condo.

He opened the door and picked up each shoe, wondering why she had done such a thing. Outside her condo door, he found her belt on the doorstep. He picked it up, and with the items in one hand, he opened her door with the other. Her blue dress was on the floor in front of him. He dropped the belt and the shoes and locked the door. Ronnie was nowhere in sight. He walked toward the bedroom and discovered her in a blue *Jean Yu* bra-and-panty set holding two shots of pineapple vodka. He walked over to her, picked up the shot, and drank his as she drank hers. The two resumed the passionate kiss they had exchanged during the concert. He climbed on top of her as she pulled his jacket off his body. He licked her on her neck as she scratched at his shirt to reveal his bare chest. Putting his hand on the small of her back, he worked his way to her bra strap and released her firm breasts from their containment. He put his lips on her left nipple as she rolled her head back, receiving his tongue on her areola.

"Take them off," Ronnie moaned, referring to his pants. He stood up and unbuttoned his pants to reveal his black Ralph Lauren boxers. She slid them off of him and clenched his buttocks from behind, pulling his underwear all the way down. He removed them from his feet as she slid back onto the center of the bed and pulled down her panties, exposing her shaved, naked flesh. He climbed on top of her and kissed her breasts, working his way up to the side of her neck, the lobe of her ear, and finally back to the lips covered in his now, new favorite shade of blue lipstick.

He slid inside her, finding bliss, each stroke confirming how much he wanted this, how much *they* wanted this. This was something they were meant to do. Each stroke made him forget the heartache his last lover caused him. Each stroke made him forget his last lover's name. He was alive and relishing this moment.

"Slap me," she whispered in his ear as he pulsed inside of her. He wasn't entirely sure he heard her right, and he continued to stroke her gracefully.

"Slap me, Lucas."

Her words were unmistakable.

Not your cup of tea...
And she can claim battery in the morning
and take pictures

CHAPTER 18
RELEASE

"What?" he responded, stunned.

"Slap me."

The intensity of their passion began to diminish.

"Slap me, motherfucker!" she insisted.

Lucas stopped. "I can't ... what are you doing?"

Ronnie looked at him. "Oh, you tamed lion. You've never had rough sex, have you?"

"I'm just not into that kind of thing."

"Why not?" she pressed, toying with him.

"I mean I'm just not into it. Is that what you're into? Is that what you want?"

Ronnie pushed Lucas back toward the bed.

"No, Lucas, it's what you want. You just don't know it. We're either trying to take control, or being controlled. See, your problem is you want to go with the flow of life and hope everything works out just fine. That's how you ended up here, in between my legs. Your problem is you don't understand why you lost Nichelle, and yet right here, right now, there's nowhere in the world you'd rather be but here with me. Your problem is you think every woman you meet is a woman you should make love to when the reality is women are far more complex any help in this matter. She was turned on and wanted to please him the way she wanted. Her intensity increased over the next several minutes as she went deeper with each downward thrust until his entire penis touched the back of her throat, his dense rod hardening even more. Her panties started to moisten as her full lips slipped down his shaft to the meet his pelvic bone. Deep throating was something she knew he enjoyed. But over the years she had come to truly love it. He stiffened even harder which she matched with her speed accepting his entire manhood each time she went down.

"Oh, fuck, I'm about to..." Donovan moaned.

That thought was completed inside her mouth as he uncontrollably emitted his sweet seed down the back of her throat. She received all of it as the violent explosion continued until he went limp. His eyes glazed over, indicating he was completely drained. "Fuck that was amazing!" he moaned. She could tell he was losing all of his remaining strength. It made her want to straddle him right there, she was aching for sex at this moment. But she had other plans at the moment.

"I'll drive the rest of the way," Nichelle said as he mustered the energy to adjust the seat. A much more tender version of the man emerged from the car to switch seats with her as she slid into the driver's seat. She started back en route to her home.

The drive didn't take long. The highway was uncharacteristically open for a Saturday evening. By the time they got to Nichelle's place, Donovan was in a full-on slumber. *Good he'll fuck me like a champion when he wakes up*. She thought to herself. As Nichelle parked the car, he became alert, jolting to life when the car stopped moving. "Here are the keys to your stolen vehicle. I'm about to get in my legally paid-for vehicle and leave. Let yourself in. I have a few more errands to run." She kissed him on the cheek as she opened the door. "Babygirl, you know we ain't finished, right?"

"We're just getting started." She winked and walked across the street to climb in her own car.

OK Chelle now on to plan B. She started her car and began to drive. Her destination was about twenty minutes away—a small restaurant called *Bella Fortuna*. It was an Italian restaurant known for their vast wine selection and the delectable spices used in their robust meals. She than that. Women want love sometimes, sex other times, and sometimes they just want to fuck."

Lucas grabbed Ronnie and pressed her against the bed, angrily pushing back inside her, his animalistic thrusts coming with no regard for her body.

"Is this what you want, you dirty bitch?"

Ronnie couldn't respond. Lucas had wrapped both of his hands around her neck, squeezing so tightly that she could barely breathe. She nodded submissively as he repeatedly and violently jabbed her with his manhood.

"You want me to fuck you like this? You want me to hurt this pussy?"

Lucas had entered a place in his mind he didn't know existed. All his pent-up aggression was being released into Ronnie's flesh, and she seemed happy to receive it. He slowly released her neck, and she took a deep gasp of air as if it were the last breath she would ever take. Lucas repeated his question.

"Is this what you want?" Ronnie let out a yelp that sounded like a muffled "Yes." Lucas choked her again, thrusting into her with an intense rage. The bed knocked against the wall as Lucas pounded his way into Ronnie's core. For the first time since he had known her, she was entirely submissive, and she was submitting to him. Lucas, contrarily, felt a sense of power he rarely felt. It was a reclamation of his certainty that had been rocked by his recent breakup with Nichelle. All of the frustration and anger he had not expressed seemed to flow from his body and build up in his penis. "Oh ... I'm ... cumming!"

His orgasm was a lingering sensation similar to a sugar rush leaving his brain through his chest and out through his cock. It felt like a seizure. As he came, his muscles seized then relaxed, draining away all the tension they stored. Ronnie had already taken him to new heights, but for the first time he ejaculated not out of intimacy but recreation. He needed to have sex like this. He needed to fuck. His semen glossed Veronica's golden brown frame as his eyes rolled into the back of his head and sheer ecstasy surged through his body. He collapsed onto her like a sack of potatoes. He could go no further.

"That was ..." He took a deep breath. "That was ..." He looked down at Ronnie's body lying still beneath his. "That was ..." He took another breath, trying to trap the air in his lungs and slow his heart which was about to beat out of his chest. "Veronica?" She lay there motionless. Panic began to set in. He rose and looked into her eyes, green and motionless. "VERONICA!" he yelled, the fear seeping into his tone. Had he gone too far? Did he... was she—

"So if I'm dead, you're just going to lay there and not call anyone?" she finally said. "Damn it, Veronica!" Lucas said.

Ronnie let out a burst of laughter. As she slid over to embrace her newfound playmate, she asked, "Were you worried?"

"Well, yeah. You didn't seem to be breathing. I didn't know if I had—"

She cut him off. "Dandelions."

"What?" he responded, unsure of what she just said. Ronnie went on as if she never said the word.

"Although I know this is rhetorical, I'm going to ask anyway—did you enjoy yourself?" "Hell, yes!" Lucas replied, satisfaction saturating his tone.

"So you're going to want to do this again?" she went on.

He paused, but before he could respond, Ronnie pressed the issue. "Let me rephrase— you *will* want to do this again, no question. With that being said, we need a safe word." Digesting everything that just happened, he decided it was easier to follow this conversation to its conclusion than hang on to any pretense of resistance. "Okay. Which is?"

"Dandelions," she responded. He sat there in silence, processing everything that just occurred. Rough sex, safe words ... was he ready for this? If nothing else, he was curious.

"Why dandelions?" he asked.

"Well that's a very interesting question Mr. Kimble." She said, shifting her body closer to her lover's as she continued "The first day we met, we went to grab coffee. Outside the window of the shop, the groundskeepers were planting dandelions, and I thought to myself, *What an odd flower to plant*. But it only made sense. Here I was having an odd conversation with an unusual man."

"I'm glad you have memories about that day. It was a rough one for me."

"It was obvious."

He nodded halfheartedly, but after a brief pause finally asked, "Why did you stop to talk to me, Veronica?"

"Honestly?"

"No, lie to me. Of course honestly."

Ronnie shifted her body again, looking into Lucas' eyes, her sandy-brown hair resting on her cheek. "You're an attractive man, I won't deny, and I love a good-looking man in a good-looking suit. But, if I had to label it, there was a sadness in your eyes. You looked like a lost puppy—and I'm a sucker for puppies."

"Really? You? Puppies?"

"Lucas, are you inferring something?"

"It's just that with your work schedule and this lavish condo, with all the Boca Do Lobo Furniture and Christian Louboutin shoes, nothing screams *avid pet lover*."

"I will have you know I love animals, *and* it's for that very reason I don't have any," she chuckled. "But that's beside the point. We were talking about why I stopped to talk to you that day."

Lucas chuckled. "What about now?"

"What do you mean?" she responded.

"You said there was a sadness in my eyes. What do you see in them now?"

Ronnie looked in his eyes. When they connected, her jaw slightly hinged open. She saw exactly what he wanted her to see—he was starting to care for her. He was too nice a man to get caught up in her web, yet he was waiting on her to respond.

"Well?" he urged.

"I see... that you want to fuck," she lied. The glimmer in him started to dwindle, put off by her response, but before he could say anything, she grabbed his manhood already at half-mast and kissed him intensely. As she stroked him, she moved her tongue down the side of his neck and back up to his mouth. He was fully erect now. She climbed on top of him and descended upon him in slowly, still moist from their last session. She bounced ever so slightly until he was firmly inside her. He gripped her buttocks and looked into her eyes as she continued to ride him. Any objection he had to their previous conversation was being erased with each downward thrust of her vagina. Desire had taken over, and he rolled her onto her back and stroked deep into her body, kissing her furiously as he pushed himself inside. He had complete control of her body, and she opened her legs wide. His erection hardened even more, and he pushed into her further, his body clapping against hers each time he reached her center. Completely submissive, she moaned noisily, one hand clenching the sheets as the other clutched his lower back, her nails breaking the skin, drawing pricks of blood. She was cumming. "Yes, yes, yes, yes," she panted as he intensified his pace, sweat dripping from his brown skin onto her caramel breasts. She was wrapped around him, clenching his manhood as it fought to push itself deep into her essence. He looked in her eyes with the same passion she exuded. He could tell she was ready. "I want to feel you," she moaned as she started to climax. He nodded as he jabbed her even harder. Her hand dug into his lower torso once more. "Oh, my god, I'm cumming again," she blurted as she released her ecstasy. He was not far behind her as he moaned violently, filling her with the passion they had been working on for the last twenty-five minutes.

As they lay there exhausted, Ronnie by his side, she gathered her thoughts and spoke aloud. "Well, this is some of the best sexual intercourse I've had in a long time."

"Sexual intercourse?" Lucas responded, fatigued but confused by the statement.

"Yes, that's what we just had, right?" Ronny replied as she caught her breath.

Lucas responded. "Well, you could've just said this is the best sex I've had in a long time, or you could've said this is the best lovemaking I've done in a long time, but why the formal words?"

Elation stretched across her face. "We've had a really fun night. We've gotten to know each other very well in—a lot of the right places. I guess we should talk about other things."

"The legal jargon."

She grinned. "Right—the legal jargon." Her body had come down from its euphoric state, leaving facts and distance. "I don't do love."

"Okay, I didn't know we were getting married tonight," he responded, unsure of where this was headed.

"We're not, but for the benefit of full disclosure, I want you to know. Love, the 'happily ever after' kind, it's bullshit to me."

"Oh, yeah, and why is that?" he asked

"The system is just outdated," she responded. "It just doesn't work. I mean, think about it. When's the last time you've met anyone who truly loved anything?"

"Well, in light of my recent situation, on some level, I could agree with you," he said, some humor in his tone, "but I don't. Come on, Veronica, you can't really believe that—parents love their kids, and the right people can find love."

"You think so? I won't even touch the relationship issue, but hell, I think most parents resent their kids for crushing their dreams." Before Lucas could respond, she continued. "If that's the last battlefield for true love, the war is over."

He paused, let out a light chuckle, and glanced in her direction, more focused than before. "But you love your job, and you're happy right?"

"Touché, so let me rephrase. I've earned every shred of so-called happiness I've ever had in my life. The other thing, well—I don't really get how anyone could depend on another person for their happiness. It's human nature to disappoint, so I stopped dealing with those emotions a long time ago."

"Well..." Lucas paused, "that's certainly one of the most morbid things I've ever heard." He placed his hand on her bare thigh and looked into her stunning green eyes. "I have to ask how long has it been since you stopped 'dealing with those emotions?'"

Ronnie shifted in bed to slide closer to him. "Um, I don't know if I've ever been in love," she said matter of factly, "but if you're asking when my last serious relationship was, I'd say—well, I haven't had a serious relationship. Why, do you think all of this should be bottled?"

Lucas examined Ronnie's frame as she placed it on display. He was aroused mentally, but his body could no longer respond.

"I think that confidence looks really good on you," Lucas responded. "I've always wanted the family life. I'm not saying this for your benefit—it's just since we're in a sharing mood, and out of respect for the 'sexual intercourse' we just had, I'll tell you. When I was twelve, my dad taught me how to drive. We went fishing one day, and he stopped the car, got out, and let me get in behind the driver's seat. I had no idea what I was doing, and eventually I ended up crashing the car into a pile of dirt at a nearby construction site. I thought he'd be furious. He just laughed and said, 'Son, I love you. Nothing you could do will ever change that.' His support, and my mom's, always made me believe in myself. And so I've always wanted to be a dad. To see if I could do the job. I sort of feel like when the time is right, it's my calling. To love a family."

Ronnie could see the sincerity in his eyes, and even though she believed in the man, for a brief second she wanted to believe in his words. "Okay, that's enough sharing for one lifetime. Come with me."

Ronnie took Lucas into her bathroom, where she ran the bathwater until the temperature was just perfect. The bubbles clouded all but the candles Ronnie kept near the tub. The air was filled with the scent of her *Amber Romance* candles she had lit before they had left for the concert. As she slid into the water, Lucas said, "You sure it's not going to cause third-degree burns? Looks like a lot of steam."

Ronnie laughed in response. "Lucas, get your ass in this tub."

After he connected his phone to her sound system and slipped into the other end of the tub, Ronnie reached for the remote to her home music console and pressed "play.". *All I Do Is Think of You* began to play.

"Oh, I love this song. Troop was such a classic group. They were so talented."

"Woman, what are you talking about? This isn't Troop. This is the original song."

"The original!?" Ronnie responded with a touch of angst. "I'm not sure if you hit your head earlier on the bed post, but Troop *is* the original. They sang that song first."

She said it with such passion that he responded with tact. "You being an '80s baby, I can see why you'd think that, but listen."

Ronnie heard slight differences in the song, but not enough to convince her she was wrong. After all, this was one of her favorites.

"Lucas, I know my music, and that is Troop."

"Okay," he retorted with confidence. "Put your money where your mouth is—Get my phone. It will give you all the details on that song. If I'm right, you owe me—a movie night."

"And when you're wrong?"

He chuckled. "If I'm wrong, I'll owe you something."

She knew he was wrong, but the longer the song went on, the more doubt set in. As she stood up to grab his phone, the slight inconsistencies in the tone and the music made her only half as sure as when she made the bet.

"The Jackson 5?"

He let out a belt of laughter. "Yes, the greatest R&B group of all times."

"I had no idea," she muttered, easing into the tub again. "Most people our age don't."

"It was actually a B-side to a song by Diana Ross and the Supremes, but my parents loved everything about the Jacksons, so it was hard to get away from them."

She remained silent as he spoke, listening to him with one ear and welcoming into her being this new rendition of the song she loved. She started to emotionally replace the song in her heart with the ballad she was hearing for the first time. Lucas, realizing this, decided to stop speaking and allow her the moment. He watched her as she rhythmically moved, naked in the tub, to the beat and cadence of Michael's voice. He noticed her body as it shifted in the water. He grabbed the bar of soap and a washcloth and began to cleanse himself of the past several hours' intimacy, all the while gazing at her in a musical trance. As he stared, her eyes caught his. She was aware of how he felt at that moment, and he knew he wasn't alone, though he decided not to pursue this emotion. At least not yet. She clearly wasn't prepared for this. Neither of them were. He reached out and rubbed her skin with the soap. As the song ended, he spoke. "The day we met, I didn't realize how beautiful you were."

She didn't know how to respond. She had been called sexy, attractive, hot—even beautiful before—but never with such sincerity. It was as if he was looking through her and finding something inside that had long been buried. He was seeing her innocence. She smiled like a schoolgirl. What was this man doing to her?

"Veronica, I'd like to stay the night. I know that's not protocol for you, but I hope tonight you can make an exception."

She looked at the man sitting at the opposite end of her tub. It wasn't her protocol, but nothing about this night was. "Just tonight, Lucas."

"Okay—just tonight," he replied, realizing that a small victory was still a victory.

CHAPTER 19
RELATIONSHIP (REDUX)

Lucas rolled out of bed bright and early Monday morning and extended his arm to wake his lover. "Baby, wake up, we're going to be late," he said as he reached for his underwear with his other hand. He then realized that no one was next to him. He got up and quickly dressed himself in the clothes he wore Friday night. Ronnie was already dressed and putting on her earrings in a final act to prepare for work.

He smirked, looking at her in a different light than he did before the weekend began.

"Why are you looking at me that way?" she asked.

"I don't know. It's the first time I've seen you in clothes all weekend." The pair laughed while Ronnie came over to his side of the bed to sit next to him. She kissed him passionately.

"This was one of the best weekends I've ever had. Thank you," she whispered in his ear.

"You and me both," he replied, kissing her back and drawing her into the bed again. She shoved him away.

"Now, you know if we get started, we'll be late for work—well, technically you'll be late no matter what. Don't forget, we have a meeting this morning."

"I hate you being right, Veronica" he said.

"Don't you think you know me well enough to call me Ronnie now?"

Lucas grabbed her by the waist and sat her on his leg as he kissed her on the neck. "I like Veronica. It's elegant—like you."

She blushed. "Well, it's flattering coming from you, so I'll allow it. Now, get up, *Austin with the stones.* We have work to do."

"I told you that in confidence!" he joked as she referenced his New York nickname.

"Haven't you heard I'm not to be trusted? Now get that sexy chocolate ass up and get out of here!" she said with a smirk.

"Fine," he muttered. As he put on his suit pants and socks, Ronnie laughed.

"What is it?"

"A man taking the walk of shame—very sexy," she replied. Lucas rolled his eyes in amusement. He continued to partially dress himself in order to leave. When he was ready, she said, "You better take the back road out of here, or people will know what kind of slut you are." She winked as he put his head down jokingly. He gave his lover a final kiss and was out the door. He raced back home in order to change. Downtown Houston had a different buzz this early in the morning. Few people were moving, allowing him to enjoy the scenery.

It took him no time to get home since he was driving against the flow of traffic. But getting back would be another story entirely. The freeway was notoriously busy, and to top it off, a major accident pushed to the side of the road further slowed traffic. When he got home, he showered, picked out a nice gray suit, and was about to leave home when he got a text from Ronnie.

Enjoyed your company this weekend, would love your company tonight - pack a bag and let's finish what you tried to start this morning

He replied *I'll be really late for the meeting*

Don't worry about that I have you covered

The text brought a smile to his face as he went back into the bedroom and packed an overnight bag, as well as another suit. The weekend was exactly what he needed to help his healing process, and tonight would be what he wanted for fun.

The drive on the back roads was much shorter than anticipated since leaving later allowed most of the congestion to clear up. Before he knew it, he was back in the heart of Houston, listening to the radio to catch up on all the sports he missed during his weekend session of lovemaking. The broadcast was interrupted by his phone ringing in via Bluetooth. It was Ronnie's office number.

"This is Lucas."

"Mr. Kimble, it's Ronnie Duvalle and Ms. Myers —we're trying to get an ETA on your arrival for our morning meeting."

"Sorry, I'll be there in the next twenty minutes."

"Sounds good. We'll see you then."

He was actually ten minutes away, but he had plans, He stopped by a nearby flower shop and walked to the counter. A slender, silver-haired, Middle Eastern man wearing glasses stood at the counter.

"How can I help you, sir?" he asked in a heavy Arabian accent.

"Hi. I'd like to send an order of flowers to Burrows Industries today."

"Okay, what kind of flowers would you like to send?"

"I'd like a dozen dandelions delivered to Veronica Duvalle."

"Okay, would you like to fill out a card?"

"No need."

The flowers would do all the talking. Lucas sat back and enjoyed the sounds of the city— the car horns, jackhammers on asphalt, and distant sirens. More than anything, though, he enjoyed the sun penetrating the below-normal temperature hitting the city. A cool day for a typically humid town. Whatever life was going to throw at him would have to wait. For the first time in a while he was happy. Today was a good day. No, today was perfect. Whether the weekend with Ronnie was a fling or the beginning of a great romance didn't matter. His certainty toward life had been restored.

CHAPTER 20
THE REACTION

Nichelle arrived at the office early to prepare for the meeting. She spent the weekend pondering her ex's status. He had been noticeably offbeat over the course of the week. She knew it had to do with the Jill Scott concert. She also wanted to attend, but knew the chances of going were next to impossible since the concert had been sold out for weeks. Now Monday was here and Lucas Kimble was late for work, a very uncommon occurrence. She knew their relationship woes had taken a tougher toll on him than she anticipated. The meeting was just between Ronnie, Nichelle, and Lucas, but his tardiness would leave an impression on Ronnie that would put him in a tough situation later on. Ronnie was not the kind of woman you kept waiting.

"He's normally not late to anything," Nichelle said, feeling a strange need to protect the man she dumped. She had no doubt Ronnie was making a mental note and holding his tardiness against him, but Ronnie was looking out of her window and smiling. Nichelle had never seen her smile before. If she wasn't such a bitch, she might think Ronnie was actually human.

"My apologies for being late. Traffic was terrible this morning," Lucas said, casually strolling through the door. He looked relaxed and in good spirits. Nichelle was relieved to see him finally smile again. It had been a few weeks since she had seen him upbeat.

"As long as this doesn't become a habit, Mr. Kimble, we're fine," Ronnie responded. "Now, do you have the estimate for the quarter?"

"No, I was going to work on that this weekend, but something came up," he responded.

"Was this something more important than your job?"

"Well, no, it's just—"

"So it wasn't more important than your job?"

"Well, it was important, but I had—"

"Well, which one is it, Mr. Kimble? Either your weekend activities were more important than your job, or your work is more important," Ronnie persisted. *This is classic, Ronnie,* Nichelle thought. She knew she didn't want him to get raked over the coals by the woman.

"It was my fault," Nichelle interjected.

Stunned, Ronnie replied, "Really? Do tell."

"I asked Lucas to help me with some work over the weekend, and it took longer than anticipated, which is why he wasn't able to work on the preliminary numbers."

"Nichelle, don't—" Lucas interjected

"It's okay, Lucas. I appreciate you trying to cover for me, but I'll be accountable."

"Nichelle, you really don't have to do this," Lucas pleaded. "Veronica, Nichelle had nothing to do with why I was unable to crunch the numbers this weekend."

"That would be truly incredible if she did."

"You asked me if my work or my weekend was more important, and I want you to know my work is truly important to me. The weekend's events were a surprise, and I should've chosen my words more carefully."

Ronnie sat back in her chair and nodded. "Like what?"

"I'm sorry?" Lucas responded.

"What words should you have chosen?"

"Like—dandelions."

Dandelions? What does that mean? Nichelle noticed Ronnie smirked to suppress a laugh. It was clearly an inside joke, but when did the two of them get close enough to have inside jokes? What in the hell was going on here?

"Okay, let's get together another time when you've had a moment to prepare the numbers. We'll discuss our plan of action going forward then," Ronnie said, ending her inquisition. It didn't make sense. Why would she press an issue and all of a sudden stop? Nichelle needed to know what was going on between the two of them. As Lucas walked out of the office, she stopped him.

"Can I speak to you for a moment?"

"Sure, I can give you a minute."

The two walked into her office, where Lucas closed the door. "What in the hell was that?" Nichelle asked argumentatively.

"What was what?"

"You and Ronnie have jokes now? I didn't realize you had gotten so close over the last few weeks."

"She's a great woman. I enjoy her presence."

Nichelle's eyes widened. She couldn't believe her ears. "Oh, my god, are the two of you dating?"

"To be brutally honest, it's none of your damn business, Neecie."

"Look, I know I was wrong about the way I handled things, but I'm a good person. Ronnie is someone you just can't trust."

"From where I sit, that sounds like the pot calling the kettle black," Lucas said. "Let me let you in on a little secret, Nichelle—who I see and how I spend my time isn't your concern." Lucas began to leave, but Nichelle positioned herself between him and the door. She put her hands out in an attempt to stop him from taking another step. "Lucas, you can't be serious. Please stay away from her! What I did was wrong, but you're about to make a huge mistake. I care about you, and I can't let you do that."

Lucas leaned in and whispered in her ear. "If you truly cared, we wouldn't be here. So do us both a favor and mind your business. Which is Donovan—right?"

He walked out of the room. Nichelle was going after him, but decided against it. The meeting had led into lunchtime, and the hallways would be busy with employees on their way to get a bite. She decided to stay in and eat a salad. Lucas had to be trying to get under her skin. There was no way he would be in a relationship with a creature like Ronnie. She was the queen of manipulation, but he was smart enough to see through any façade. Yet, at the same time, she had never actually seen Ronnie do anything but be forthcoming and blunt. That's not always taken the right way, particularly for women of color in the workplace. The more she thought about it, the more she saw her objections as her mind playing tricks on her. She needed to give Ronnie the benefit of the doubt, at least for this working relationship to have any success. She finished her salad and went to Ronnie's office around the corner. Ronnie was alone, replying to emails when she approached.

"Is now a good time?"

"Sure, Nichelle, what's up?"

"I just wanted to go over the meeting. I was covering for Lucas. I'm not sure what he had going on this weekend or why he couldn't get his work done."

Ronnie walked away from her desk toward one of the windows in her office. Not making eye contact she responded, "Yes, it was pretty obvious you were covering. Whatever he has going on in his personal life, he's going to need to pull it together if he's going to succeed on this project. I don't tolerate anyone putting me or the company in a compromising position."

The words eased Nichelle's thoughts. Maybe this was all in her head. She'd been spending so much time with Donovan that maybe she'd grown suspicious of everyone.

"Since we're on the subject, I suggest you both keep your personal issues to a minimum. While it's none of my business what the two of you have going on, the company isn't paying you to sort out your drama here."

It was the confirmation Nichelle needed. There was nothing going on between Lucas and Ronnie. "Of course, but let me just say that Lucas and I haven't—"

"Just a moment."

Ronnie put one hand in the air to pause Nichelle's statement. The phone rang and Ronnie walked over to answer it as she put the call on speaker.

"This is Ronnie."

"Ms. Duvalle, this is the front desk. You have a delivery."

"Really? From who? Never mind, I'm on my way." She hung up the phone and looked back at Nichelle. "We can finish this on the way, but we'll have to walk and talk."

"I think we're done. Thanks for listening."

"Anytime. That's what a teammate does." Ronnie smiled and walked toward the front door. As they walked into the hallway, Nichelle decided to snoop to figure out who was sending something to Ronnie.

"You know what? I have to get some coffee from downstairs. I'll walk with you," she said.

"Sounds good." Ronnie responded as the pair headed to the main lobby on the 21st floor. Upon arrival, Nichelle noticed the florist waiting at the desk was the same florist Lucas used to deliver flowers to her upon occasion. A heavy knot grew in the pit of her stomach. *This isn't happening!* It was foolish to think only one person could use a certain florist in town—utter nonsense even—but to the same office? It had to be Lucas. Nichelle quietly slipped away toward the elevator banks. Before she got two steps away, the man behind the front desk told the florist, "That's Veronica Duvalle there."

The florist turned toward her. "Can you sign here? I have one dozen dandelions for you."

CHAPTER 21
REVENGE

Donovan knew word would travel fast after he visited Trouble. It was only a matter of time before someone would be looking for him. That someone would be Carlos. The past few weeks Donovan had been on edge more than normal, but after the last time he entered Nichelle's home and made a fool of himself by searching her bathroom and closet, he realized his nerves were getting the better of him. Truth be told, he wasn't sure what to expect. For all intents and purposes, Rico had Donovan's money when Rico got locked up, and there was no reason to think he had shared this information with Carlos other than the fact Trouble mentioned Rico had been hanging around him more. Trouble knew how to keep a secret and would never betray him, or so he thought, right up until he set him up. Now he wasn't so certain, With the exception of getting Nichelle back in his life, there were no certainties. Word on the street traveled fast, and if Carlos made a move, it would expose what he knew or didn't know about the money. But for $437,000, Donovan wasn't willing to wait around. The cash was his way out of this life, for both him and his Babygirl.

Donovan knew Carlos Ruiz from the neighborhood. He was a smalltime crook-turned-drug dealer who was moving up the ranks fast, a little too fast not to be working for anyone. This made Donovan suspicious because drugs required startup money, and lots of it. To move the amount of drugs Carlos was moving, you needed the kind of money Rico had. He wasn't a really tough guy by any standard. In fact, he was probably a bigger coward than K.T. But power can make anyone tough, and Carlos was gaining power.

Of course, all this was of no consequence to Donovan. He didn't care what Carlos did or was doing, he just wanted what was owed to him. If that meant having to go through Carlos to get his money, then that's what he was going to do. That was why it was time to pay Carlos a visit. Days earlier, he was sure he had heard something or someone move in Nichelle's closet and hadn't ruled out that to be factual. If Carlos sent someone to spy on or kill him, both he and Nichelle were in danger.

Finding out where Carlos lived was easy. In fact, considering his profession, it was almost too easy. Since his meteoric rise in Houston's drug game, he made sure everyone knew what kind of car he was driving. A King Ranch, crème-colored Ford pickup with the license plate "EL HEFE." Donovan just needed to follow him. For several days he followed the car at night. One time he felt the car was on to him, so he switched up his routine and began paying Uber drivers to get around, pretending he wanted to visit an old friend but wasn't sure of the address. If finding out where Carlos lived was the hard part, casing Carlos's home was child's play. He was cautious but not as cautious as a bank was. He had an eight-camera system that covered many of his entrances and exits, but there was no redundant power. Killing the power to all the cameras was as simple as shutting down the circuit breaker the cameras' hard drive was plugged into. That would effectively disable all the cameras. The circuit breaker was outside with no camera fixed on its location. After all, protecting the entrances and exits was the priority—why would the circuit breaker ever need to be monitored?

Donovan knew Carlos lived with his mother, a 5 foot 1, silver-haired Hispanic lady named Gloria, While Donovan knew of her, he didn't actually didn't know her and didn't care to, but he was hoping she'd be home as he broke into her place. He needed the leverage. He went to the desk in Carlos's office and noticed a drawer with a key lock. He tried to pick the lock and realized prison had made him a bit rusty. *Getting soft, D,* he thought to himself while struggling with a lock that would've taken him no time in the past. *Fuck this! Just shoot the fucking lock open*, he thought in frustration, until he realized he not only needed to work on his skills, but he wasn't entirely ready to create a commotion.

After a few more minutes, he finally popped the lock. His reward—eight thousand in cash. *I'll take this,* he thought to himself, satisfied that he was able to overcome the rust time away had placed on his skills. Suddenly, he heard a voice.

"Carlos, is that you, mijo?"

Donovan slid behind the door and pulled out his gun. When the lady walked into the room, he waited for her to get all the way in. She immediately noticed the open drawer. Sensing her panic, he stepped from behind the door and pointed the gun into the small of her back. "You must be Gloria. I need you to come with me."

"Who are you"

"I could lie to you and say I'm a friend of your son's, but we both know that's not true. What is true is that I'm not here to hurt you. I just need you to be cool while I talk to your son, and then I'll be out of both of your lives."

The woman hesitated. She wanted to scream for help. Having robbed several banks, Donovan knew this was her natural reaction.

"Gloria—that's your name, right? Listen, if I wanted to hurt you in any way, I would have already done so. I don't. The only thing I want is to have a conversation with your son. Honestly, I don't even want to hurt him. Now, I know you're afraid, but I need you to believe me because one way or another, I'm going to have this talk."

This skill—the ability to calm down a nervous person with a gun to their body—wasn't rusty at all. The gray-haired woman relented.

Donovan escorted her downstairs before reaching into his bag and pulling out a vest that appeared to have a bomb attached to it.

"Wh... what is that?"

"This is the hard part of our day. Your son is going to come in and probably be upset, right? From what I know of him, he's not a rational man. I need to make sure I get out of here safely. I'm going to put this on you, and I promise I'll take it off when I'm done."

Streams began to roll down her cheek. Donovan compassionately walked over and wiped away a few tears with a tissue.

"Gloria, you have to calm down. I don't want you to work yourself up. Let me get you some water, and then I'm going to move you, okay?"

She nodded. He placed the vest over her body and then tied her to the door. After that, he got her a glass of water and made sure she finished it, taking in every last bit of the sleeping agent he slipped in before he handed it to her.

"Okay, now I need you to go sit in my car, please. All this unpleasantness will be over soon, I promise," he said, nudging the gun in her back. She complied willingly, Donovan knew how to get his hostages to comply. Even in his robberies, he was very pleasant to everyone. His plan was set—she was unconscious by the time Donovan buckled her in his car parked about a block away. Quickly starting the car, he pulled into Carlos's driveway and pulled into the garage. Climbing out of the driver's seat, he found a black folding chair, placed it behind his car, and lit a cigarette. All he had to do was sit and wait.

An hour passed as he thought about his choices; the lengths he was going through to find his money. Cash that was owed to him for time served. Questions regarding his $437,000. His answers were about to come to him as Carlos arrived home. As the garage door opened, Donovan leaned back in the chair. Carlos got out of his car and walked into the garage, a gun in his hand.

"Donovan, what the fuck you doing in my home puta?"

"Carlos Ruiz, so you're supposed to be a bigtime drug dealer now."

"A lot can happen in three years, ese."

"So I keep seeing."

Carlos looked at Donovan, never moving his eyes off him. There was a seriousness about the man and Donovan respected it, but that's where the respect ended. Carlos was a scum-laced tadpole climbing his way up an ever grimier cesspool to the top of a pile of sewage. He was not the kind of guy you wanted to deal with under normal circumstances, but missing $437,000 wasn't a normal circumstance, and if Carlos was involved, neither was the death of his friend Rico.

"So what brings you here, D? We have no business."

"If that were true, you wouldn't have that gun pointed at me."

"Homes, you're in my home in my garage with my mother upstairs. I should kill you right now."

"You could do that, but you don't know what I'm holding."

Carlos looked at a light beeping on a remote Donovan was holding.

"See, in the pen you learn a lot of things, namely who to make friends with and who not to cross. My celly was a bomb maker—loved blowing shit up. He got out about two weeks ago, so I took him out to eat. I told him I was going to need something special in case I ran across this asshole with an itchy trigger finger. He told me guys with itchy trigger fingers shoot first and ask questions later, so tape this to your hand and put the bomb on something they care about in case he shoots anyway. How do you say 'your mother' in Spanish? Oh, that's right—tu madre."

Carlos' skin began to turn red as the blood rushed to his head. "¡Pinche maricon! You put your hands on my mother!"

"Now before you do anything really stupid, if I release this trigger, we're all dead. Boom. So do me a favor and put down the gun. Your mother is fine as long as I have your attention."

Carlos looked at the car and pointed the pistol at Donovan.

"Is this for revenge?"

"All I want is a simple conversation. Put down the gun and we can talk."

Carlos looked at the car again and could see a beeping light flashing in synchronization with the remote in Donovan's hand. He looked back at Donovan, put the gun on the ground, and slid it over to Donovan.

"Okay, just don't hurt my mother."

Donovan stood up, grabbed the gun, and pointed it toward his new hostage.

"Any knives on you, 'Los? I know you Spanish boys like that kind of thing."

Carlos took his knife and slid it over to Donovan, who picked up the knife.

"Now we can talk."

"Whatever you want, just let my mother go, please."

"Not just yet."

Donovan hit Carlos in the back of the head with the pistol, rendering him unconscious. He took his limp body and put it in the trunk of his car, restraining his hands and feet and taping his mouth in case he woke up. He walked over to the front of the car and sat in the driver's seat. He looked at Gloria, still unconscious from the cocktail and said, "Lady, we're going on a road trip."

Backing the car out of the driveway, he made the thirty-minute trip to a part of Houston known as "Dead End." Thirty minutes in the wrong direction of town. The entire way he was listening to Al Green and Johnny Taylor. When he got to Dead End, he continued to drive down a dark, empty, back road that eventually turned into a dirt road surrounded by trees and grass. There weren't any residential or commercial buildings for what felt like miles. The area was an oasis of filth, perfect for a scumbag like Carlos.

Donovan pulled the car up to two holes that appeared freshly dug. He parked the car and stepped out. The rancid smell of waste and decay consumed his lungs as he went to the trunk, pulling Carlos's still unconscious body from it. He dragged his body to one of the holes and dropped him next to it. He then went over to the passenger door and opened it. Gloria had woken up, and though groggy, she was wide-eyed with fear and confusion.

"Gloria, step out the car please."

The lady obliged. Tears now rolled from her face. The light was still flashing on the vest Donovan had connected to her. He made her stand next to the second hole. He then went down to grab a bottle of water he had in the car and poured it on Carlos to wake him up. When he came to, he was screaming through his gag.

"I'm not sure what you're saying, Carlos, but I gotta tell you we're in the middle of nowhere, homeboy. I spent all day yesterday out here digging these holes. You know that shit is much easier in the movies. They just take a shovel and in no time they got a hole. It's nowhere near that easy. Hell, I was thinking about sleeping in and doing all this shit tomorrow, but no time like the present, right?"

Donovan walked over to the hole and looked into Carlos's eyes. The would-be drug kingpin appeared half angry, half afraid.

"I want to lay some ground rules before I remove your gag. See, I knew you lived with your mother—that's why there are two holes. You and I are going to talk, you feel me? Now, I told your sweet mother over there I didn't want to hurt her, and I mean that, so, if I have to use both these holes, that's your choice 'cause I don't like to be lied to, 'Los. So don't lie. Do you feel me?"

Donovan took the gag off and stood back up.

"You're dead, ese. You're fucking dead!"

"We're all dead. Some of us just get there before the others, homeboy."

"I'm not saying shit, puto, until you take that bomb off my mother."

Donovan looked at the vest he had on Gloria and began to laugh out loud.

"Damn, homie, you're gonna kick yourself if you live through this. You know my cellmate I was telling you about earlier? Well, he was a bomb maker, but that's not a bomb. I just had him hook up something to look like a bomb because I know you're not really that smart. It's amazing what you can do with plaster, a Casio watch. and some walkie talkies. But this gun that you gave me, see, that's real. Now, I think your mother is a wonderful lady, but I'll put every bullet in this clip in her if you don't start talking. So I'm going to say this again, and you better look at me real carefully. Where in the fuck is my money?"

"Money? What are you talking about?"

Donovan stood up and pointed the gun at the drug dealer's mother

"No, wait. Okay, okay, your money. I have your money. Please, just listen. This is how it happened. Rico came to me one day said he came into some money and wanted to do some business, so I said I knew a guy who could get us a kilo for eighteen grand. He said we could get two kilos. He gave me the money, and we started up. I didn't know he got the money from you, I swear."

Donovan took out one of this Camel cigarettes, lit it, and took a deep drag. It was apparent Carlos wasn't up to speed on where Donovan's fortune went. In fact, Rico's cut could have easily covered the thirty-six grand Carlos was referring to.

"So you're saying all you got from Rico was 36 grand?"

"Yes, I swear on my life. Look, if it's cash you're looking for, I can pay back the money. I just need a little time. I have eight thousand at home."

Donovan took another drag.

"You had. I took that already. If you live through this, you need to invest in a wall safe, 'Los. So what was the split between you and Rico?"

"He was a silent partner. It was a 50/50 split."

"But then he got locked up for drug possession."

Carlos' eyes shifted downward. Donovan took another drag of his cigarette. He was convinced that Carlos knew nothing about his money, but he was certainly hiding something. He thought about Carlos' choice of words earlier—*Is this about revenge?*

"So you got him locked up for drug possession, and then when he got on the inside, you had him killed because the only thing better than a silent partner is a dead partner."

Carlos didn't say a word. He didn't have to—his eyes gave away the truth. Donovan's best friend was set up by his would-be partner.

"How much did the hit cost, 'Los?"

"Ten grand."

Donovan took a deep drag and finished off the cigarette. He pulled out another one and lit it. Blowing the smoke in the air as if to gain clarity. He could tell his silence was bothering Carlos.

"Hey, ese, how did you know about this? I didn't tell no one but the guy who did it."

"I didn't. You just confirmed it. See 'Los, I knew you were ruthless, but like I said before, you really not that smart. I'm not even sure how you came up with this plan, but it doesn't matter. I never really liked you. I always told Rico you were a shitbag of a person and believe it or not he would defend you. I guess his loyalty cost him in the end."

"Why are you doing this, ese? Is this about power? Okay, you're the man. You can have the drug operation. Just let me live, please. Let me and my mother live."

"I'm not a drug dealer, I'm a crook. And as far as you living, we're way past that, man. You need to make peace with whatever god you serve because you're about to meet him."

Carlos began to cry. His tears mixed with the sweat from the apprehension. The chill of the night dried his tears as quickly as he produced them. "Donovan, please, I'm begging you. Let me and my mother go. We'll leave the city, and we won't come back."

Donovan thought about his words. He told Nichelle he had turned over a new leaf, and he had, but he also knew from the moment he walked into Trouble's house this moment would come. He also knew that if he let Carlos walk away right now, he and Nichelle would never be safe. This was as much for her protection as it was about his money. Carlos had to die.

"I'm going to be straight with you. You're not leaving here. That's just business. But I'm gonna do you a favor. Your mother, I know that's personal for you. You love her. She's probably one of the only people in the world who ever cared for you right?"

Carlos nodded in agreement, still sobbing.

"She seems like a good woman. Probably should've never been mixed up in this bullshit. You'd do anything for family. She doesn't deserve to suffer."

Donovan walked over to Carlos's mother and put the gun to her head.

"Rico was my family. Neither did he."

Pop!

Her body fell limp into the grave. Carlos screamed, consumed with grief, sobbing uncontrollably.

"Let that pain soak in, Carlos. I want the last thing you remember is how powerless you were to protect someone you love. The way I sobbed when I found out about Rico. He was the closest thing to family I had, and you took that from me. All because of two fucking kilos. So yeah, me killing you, that's business, but your mom, that was about revenge, you fucking piece of shit! By the way, here's the favor I'm going to do you."

Pop! Pop! Pop!

His body went still. There was silence in the air. Donovan pulled out his penis and urinated on the corpse. When he was finished, he kicked the body into the grave and shoveled the dirt on top of the graves.

"For Rico."

CHAPTER 22
RESTROOM

"I can't believe he killed them both!"

Lucas looked at her and smiled. "It's not like he really had a choice, Veronica. It's an action movie."

"Well, that movie was too melancholic for my taste. You can consider my debt to you paid, sir—making me sit through that nonsense."

He chuckled, thinking about the night she lost to him confusing a song sung by The Jackson 5 with another group. "Consider your debt paid in full. But be serious—are you telling me you didn't enjoy that movie at all?"

Ronnie rolled her eyes. "I enjoyed the company I kept, but the movie not so much. A New York cop out for revenge. Stop me when I get to the part that isn't cliché."

"That's what's so good about the movie! Come on, they killed everyone he loved, and now he has to avenge their loss."

"Baby, they killed a parrot and his boss he hadn't talked to in over ten years! That doesn't mean shoot up the entire city with no regard. Can we quit talking about this? We're already late for dinner as it is."

"Where are we going?"

"The Jasmine Rose."

"Oh."

Lucas was startled by her response. It was one of the most exclusive seafood restaurants in Houston. He paused to process her words, and then examined their clothing. Ronnie was wearing Jones New York black denim with a charcoal turtleneck. He was even more casual as he wore Ralph Laruen blue jeans with a black sweater and his favorite pair of Nike Cross trainers, silver and black Bo Jackson tennis shoes. This was all fine considering they were going to the movies, but for a restaurant as nice as what Ronnie had planned, he wanted to at least change his shoes.

"Baby, aren't we a little underdressed to go to a place this nice?"

"I'm not sure. I've never been. But honestly, what's the point of having I-don't-give-a-fuck money if you can't ever do things and not give a fuck?"

Her response only made him tenser.

"Wait... I thought this place doesn't take reservations."

"They don't. Douglass has been there waiting on a table for us for the last couple of hours, and he just sent me a text saying our table will be ready in about ten minutes, so we need to hurry before they give our table away."

"Douglass Villarreal? Your employee? Are you serious?"

Ronnie looked at him with a blank expression as if to say, *Aren't I always?*

"Ronnie, you can't do that."

"Do what?"

"Use your employee's time to suit your personal needs."

"Lucas, honey, Douglass gets paid handsomely for situations just like this. Besides, it's not like he minds."

"How do you know if he minds or not?"

"He'd find another job."

Lucas looked at her with amazement, slightly annoyed by her tone.

"You're unbelievable, you know that?"

"Baby, as much as I would love to hear your Boy Scout holier-than-thou routine, can we talk about this after dinner?"

He was silent. Her words stung slightly, and agitated him more. They arrived at the restaurant in the area of town near Upper Kirby, just a few blocks from where they saw the movie. It was a pleasant surprise, albeit ill-conceived. Lucas parked the car in front of the restaurant and handed the key to the valet, then walked around to meet Ronnie whose door was opened by another valet. Still slightly annoyed by her actions, he nonetheless escorted her to the front door, scanning to see if anyone leaving the restaurant was dressed similar to either of them. He didn't want to stand out. Not in his ensemble. His apprehension was confirmed when he read a sign at the front door: *Tennis shoes are not permitted.*

"We can't go in," he said as he pointed to the sign.

"Well, that's stupid. What size do you wear?" Ronnie said, never breaking stride.

"Twelve and a half"

"Can you wear a twelve?"

"Going to be a tough fit, but I..."

"Great."

They proceeded into the restaurant. As they opened the doors, it was easy to see why the restaurant was so exclusive. The interior was a step above any restaurant he had ever been to. A velvet Persian rug spanned the entire lobby. The bar, stocked with only top-shelf liquor, was made of a crème marble. The dim lighting and fresh scent of candlewood and vanilla musk only added to the seclusion. The seats at the bar to the left were all leather and black. There was also a wall-sized painting of Poseidon with his trident emerging from the water—it was truly a sight to see. Lucas was gazing at the picture when the hostesses interrupted him.

"Hi, sir. I'm sorry, but there are no tennis shoes allowed. I'm afraid—"

"We're handling that right now," Ronnie interjected as she waved for Douglass to come over.

"Doug you have our table?"

"Yes. In fact—"

"Give us your shoes."

"My... shoes?"

"Lucas can't go in with tennis shoes on, and since you wear a size twelve, we need those Cole Haans right now."

Shocked by her words, Lucas jumped in. "I'm sorry. What?"

"Is this really that hard to follow? You're going to wear Doug's shoes, and he's going to wear yours."

"The hell he is! These are 1991 Bo Jackson vintage cross trainers! You can't be serious! I don't ever wear these!"

"Okay, fine, take it down a notch. Doug, give us your shoes and take Mr. Kimble's shoes to the car. The valet should have the key."

Doug removed his shoes and gave them to Lucas, who was stunned at what was happening, even as he slid off his own shoes handed them over. Taking possession of the black penny loafers from Doug, he wanted to tell him to put on his Bo Jackson tennis shoes, but he had searched long and hard for that particular pair. Truth be told, he didn't want to let them out of his sight, but he knew if Ronnie could command Doug to give up his shoes without hesitation there was no way the young man would let anything happen to the sneakers. Unsure of what to say in this scenario, Lucas finally responded. "Doug, Veronica, we don't have to do this."

"It's already been done," she replied in a matter-of-fact tone as if this was an everyday occurrence.

"I'm happy to do this, Mr. Kimble," Doug added.

"But it's cold outside, and he's baref—"

"He'll be fine. Douglass, here is the valet ticket. Put the shoes in the back seat and leave the valet ticket with the hostess when you're done. Miss, we're ready to be seated now."

Lucas made eye contact with the hostess who was clearly suppressing her reaction. With a forced smile, she replied, "Right this way."

As they walked to their table, the hostess began to explain the restaurant. "The difference between The Jasmine Rose and other restaurants is that everything we serve is caught no more than eighteen hours prior to serving. Enough time to clean and marinate every fish and prepare a menu, which changes daily depending on what is caught the day before."

"That's interesting," Ronnie replied, although Lucas completely disengaged as the conversation went on. While impressed by the custom soft-brown leather seats, the deep-mahogany oak tables, and the soft vanilla candles at each table, he was still a bit uneasy with what had just happened to Doug. He didn't know him well, but he wasn't comfortable with the fact he was a willing participant in emasculating him. He double-checked the front door only to see Doug walk back in with the valet ticket and put it down on the marble hostess table. This was definitely the low point of an otherwise enjoyable day. As they were seated, his thoughts were interrupted by Ronnie calling his name. "Lucas?"

"Huh?"

"What would you like for an appetizer?"

"Oh... I haven't really looked."

"So why don't you look now?"

"Is that an order?"

"No, baby, what in the ... are you still irritated by the Doug thing?"

He paused and unfolded his napkin and looked at the white cloth on the table before resuming eye contact.

"I take it that's a yes."

"It's not just that. Don't you care what people think about you?"

"Don't you think you care too much? Here we are in one of the finest restaurants in Houston, and you were concerned about some underling's feelings and being underdressed, when, in fact, he's been through far worse, you're with the most beautiful woman in this restaurant and we look like everyone else in here—rich. You care about what people think about you; what people think about me. What people think about you for thinking about what people think about me. It's all really exhausting. See, the thing with you is you keep looking for some sort of approval, and that keeps you conservative, which is excellent for an auditor, but out here, in our lives not as attractive. I know there is something in you clawing to get out. Something draws you to me."

Listening to her words only upset him more. There was a truth hidden inside him that he didn't want to face. Maybe he did care too much about what other people thought. Maybe he should care less, but that wasn't what was truly bothering him. Her words gave birth to the creeping fact that maybe he was drawn to her for the reasons he just noticed. Ronnie took what she wanted out of life, and a part of him enjoyed watching her work. As much as he was agitated by the fact she had just made an adult go home barefoot, he also wanted to be in this restaurant with her right now. In spite of himself, he was glad to switch shoes and keep his own in the process. A tiny perk from power, yet admitting this to himself only angered him more.

"Excuse me, I'm going to the bathroom."

"Lucas!"

Ignoring her he got up and walked off quickly, never looking back. The sign for the restrooms was visible, though still a decent distance from their table. He walked toward the room, opened the solid wood door, and headed inside. The marble floor was the same color crème as the bar hostess table. There were also the same vanilla candles permeating the air. He didn't need to use the restroom—he just wanted to clear his head. Unfortunately, Ronnie didn't get the message.

"Now that was just rude, Lucas. If you wanted to end the conversation, we could have, but don't be a goddamn pussy about it."

"What the hell, Veronica? This is the men's restroom!"

"So let me get this straight ... I can suck it, sit on it, and you can put it inside me, but watching you piss with it is where you draw the line?"

"You know—"

"I wasn't finished. This is exactly what I'm talking about. You and your rules ... they're not even your rules. They're other people's rules you choose to live by. Doug had to go home barefoot. So the fuck what? He got in his fifty-thousand-dollar car and drove to his two-hundred-thousand-dollar home. He won't die, I can promise you. But you, you're already mourning his loss."

"That isn't the point."

"What's the point, then?"

"You don't respect other people."

"Like you do? So I should just let people trample all over me and do what they want out of respect for them? The same way, even though you knew something was wrong, you didn't bother Nichelle out of respect? Tell me, how did that work out for you?"

"That was low Veronica."

"It was honest. Life is a gladiator sport; you either kill or be killed."

"Is that right?"

"That is right, and I'm motherfucking Spartacus. So the last thing I will ever worry about is another person's hurt feelings."

"I don't need to listen to this."

He tried to walk out of the restroom, but Ronnie stood in his way. When he tried to move around her, she stood still.

"What are you going to do, Lucas?" she said looking at him coyly. His temper and manhood began to firm looking into her eyes. She noticed it and placed her hand on his crotch area, stroking him tenderly through this pants.

"Your little gladiator is getting a kick out of this, isn't he? You nasty little boy, you. Tell me, what are you going to do?"

She squeezed his rod, now firming harder. He grabbed her by the throat, squeezing it tightly until her eyes began to water. She began to gasp for air.

"You want to know what I'm going to do?"

She nodded as she squeezed his throbbing cock.

He pressed her against the wall and released her throat.

"I'm going to shut you up."

The two kissed passionately. Lucas was clawing at her gray turtleneck when she took her top off. He pulled her into the spacious empty stall and locked the door. While she was still rubbing his cock through his pants, the two resumed their intense kisses. Lucas soon locked his lips around her areola, aggressively biting her nipple. She returned the favor to his neck as he unbuttoned her pants. He turned her around and pulled down her pants. She wasn't wearing any panties. Bending her over, he pulled his own pants down. Fully erect, he eagerly entered her. With brute force, he plunged inside her with his full might. She was moist with anticipation, saturating his rod with her essence.

"Oh, baby."

She moaned in a frenzied state. He didn't seem to care as he continued to pound her relentlessly from behind. Wrapping one hand around her left breast and another around her throat, he pushed into her as firmly as possible. "Yes!" she exalted through the infrequent breaths he would give her, releasing her throat to gasp for air. His eye fixated on her golden-brown skin as her buttocks rippled from the force of his thrusts. It made him want her more. He tightened his grip around her neck. His punishment was her pleasure. Fluid leaked onto the marble floor as she came intensely. Savagely, he continued to pound her G-spot from behind. He grabbed her by her sandy colored locks and pulled her up while still stroking her. She stood as he continued to give her more pleasure. Releasing her throat, he slowly rubbed her left cheek and slapped her hard. He pulled out of her and turned her around forced her onto the floor. He inserted his rod between her full rouge lips and pushed it in relentlessly. She received him with no hesitation as he returned the flavor of her orgasm onto her palate. Pressing her head against his member, she continued to receive him. After several violent strokes, he pulled out of her and lifted her in the air. Sliding back inside her, he forced her naked body on top of his. She bounced on his rock hard dick as he kissed her, gripping her buttocks tightly, the pain intense as he dug his hand into her skin. He pressed her against the wall and put a hand over her mouth as he entered her again and again with unrestrained passion. He could hear her muffled groans and he stroked her, unsure if it was a yelp of pleasure or pain. He didn't care. He was consumed with this moment. He desired nothing more than to release his built-up aggression into her core. He thought about her words as he pushed harder inside her.

"Am I still a pussy now?" he asked as he pressed her head against the wall. She looked in his eyes and said something he could understand through his hand against her mouth.

"Answer me! Am I a pussy now?" he released his hand as she gasped for air and finally spoke.

"Dandelions."

CHAPTER 23
REDEMPTION

"You got a sec?" Milton asked as Ronnie headed out for the day.

"Sure, Milton. What's going on?"

"I just wanted to look at some of the data you sent over."

Ronnie knew there was more to the president's impromptu visit, but decided to play along. "I've been meaning to talk to you about it, so this is actually perfect. Let's walk and talk."

"I have to admit I was a bit skeptical you guys would be able to work together, but it looks like you're handling business like you always do."

"I wouldn't let water cooler gossip keep you up at night. Regardless of what may be said, the job is priority one."

"Indeed." He responded. Ronnie could tell he was impressed by her demeanor, but she wasn't sure if that was all he was impressed by.

"If you look at the numbers, we not only found effective ways to reduce our production and technology costs, but collaboratively, we've been able to increase our marketing efforts. Our final presentation isn't for some time, but we're well into implementing a critical, cost-effective, revenue-generating process that hasn't been considered before," Ronnie told Milton as he looked over the rough numbers as they walked down the hall.

"I have to admit, your team is doing impressive work. You're doing impressive work, and it's catching the eyes of the right people."

"Thanks, Milton. We've been working hard."

"It appears so. Listen, if you want to get together, I have a suite at the Four Seasons. We can talk more in detail about your progress."

She knew 'talk in detail' meant sex, and she wasn't the least bit interested. "No, I'm going to pass on this invite."

"So, what? A rain check?"

"A *no* check, Milton."

Stunned, he stood silently, after a brief pause he looked at her and asked, "You're serious? Is this why you've been wearing turtlenecks all week?"

She grinned—he was right. The weather had noticeably changed over the course of the week, yet she still had at least two more days to wear collared shirts to cover her escapade in the bathroom at The Jasmine Rose. "I guess it's only fair we talk about this. As of now, I'm turning in my resignation for the position of sidepiece. I've met someone."

Milton hesitated to respond, but after a long quiet spell asked, "Lucas?"

Ronnie could tell Milton was jealous. It looked like she found another way to control him. "Not that it's any of your business, but yes, Lucas."

"Ronnie, you can't be serious."

"I'm pretty serious; it's pretty serious."

There was another long quiet spell. *How long is this goddamn hallway?* she wondered, desperately trying to end this conversation. Eventually, Milton relented. "Well, it's good you found someone. I just hope this doesn't affect your chances of promotion."

Ronnie stopped her stride. "Let's be perfectly clear: my chances of promotion and me raining hellfire down on your world are symbiotic. If I don't get my promotion this time, I will tell your wife every sordid detail she needs to know to in order to have a two-hundred-million-dollar divorce settlement, but you won't be able to pay her a fucking red cent after your trust fund is cut in half because I went to every media outlet and share my *heartbreaking* story of 'a young girl just trying to do what the boss says' with them and the stock price gets downgraded. It's not a threat—it's a guarantee. If you think you have any leverage in this situation, you're terribly mistaken. For the sake of your trust fund, don't make that mistake again."

Ronnie smiled as Milton squirmed. "Still want to fuck me?"

Milton glared at her. "One day you'll make a mistake. People like you always do. And all your cunning, sex appeal, and strategy will mean nothing. You think you can build something with a guy like Lucas, but you can't build anything but a house of cards. You'll be alone, and nothing will be able to save you. It's the only way things end for the kind of person you are."

"And what kind of person am I?"

"You're power hungry. You think you're happy right now? You think getting the senior vice president title will be enough? It won't be. It will never be enough, and you'll make compromise after compromise for success until you look back and realize you're on a path with no return ticket. There's no love at the end of this path. No joy—only misery and regret."

Ronnie grinned and placed a hand on his back. "I'm sorry. It's hard to take you seriously when you just tried to get me into your bedroom. If it makes you feel any better, it was a touching intervention. You know, you really should start a blog. Call it *Words of Wisdom from the CEO*. For your first post, *How to Wipe Your Tears While Wearing a Thirty-Five-Thousand-Dollar Hublot on Your Wrist*."

"Go to hell, Ronnie."

"I just told you I'm not coming to your hotel room."

Milton was clearly frustrated by her comment, and she enjoyed every moment she could get to rattle his cage. She had been promised the promotion months ago when she reduced Kendra to a pile of estrogen, and now, as Milton stormed off in his own direction Ronnie decided to call Kendra. It wasn't long ago the two were competitors, but since Kendra now thought they were friends, she had inadvertently become a voice for Ronnie to bounce thoughts off of. She picked up her phone and located the contact. After reaching her car, she started the motor, paired the phone with her Bluetooth, and called her former rival.

"Hello?"

"Girlfriend, how's Virginia treating you?"

"What's up, girl? I thought you forgot about me out here. You know this place is slow. I miss the big city Ronnie. Uhg! How's life?"

"It's pretty good actually. Work is work, but beyond that, things are fine."

"Good to hear. So where are you heading now—the gym?"

"No..."

"Guadalajara?"

"I haven't been there in a while actually."

"Well, girl if you aren't going home or to the gym, what is making a workaholic like you lea— you're about to get some!"

"Kendra!"

"Oh, girl, I knew it! I mean, you always sound like a pent-up bitch, no offense, but I hear it in your voice. You getting that good dick!"

"It's not even like that, Kendra."

"So you not getting good dick?"

"I—"

"Tell the truth and shame the devil, girl."

Ronnie squirmed to answer the question as she got on the highway. "Okay, yes, but it's not like that."

Kendra screamed with excitement, drowning out the sounds of the highway

"I knew it! Is this the same guy you were seeing the last night I was in town?"

"Not in the least." Ronnie replied, smirking at the irony in her question. *No, that was your man.*

"No, this one is ... he's different. I mean, he's the real deal. Smart and funny and considerate, and he really isn't into a lot of bullshit, you know?"

"Girl, I think you're in love."

"Love? Me? Please."

The idea was foreign, but Kendra persisted. "We've been on the phone for twenty minutes now and you haven't mentioned work one time, which, considering who I'm talking to, I thought was impossible."

Ronnie was silent. She sat in the car as she processed her friend's words. "You think this is love?"

"Here's a test. Say his name or think about him, and if you start to smile, you're in love."

Lucas, she thought, and the smile came naturally. She couldn't believe it. For the first time, she understood the meaning of Kendra's words.

"Girl, I'm going to let you go. I must go in here and talk to this man."

"Put it on him, girlfriend."

"Kendra, stop it." Ronnie retorted.

"Bye, girl."

SHE WALKED INTO HIS HOME. HE ALREADY HAD A GLASS OF WINE prepared and was working on the chicken cordon bleu for dinner tonight. He was sexy even when he wasn't trying to be.

"Veronica, that glass is for you. I would ask how work was, but I was there with you, so let's just get to the part where we kiss."

He walked over and gently placed his lips on hers, and welcomed her. She had desired his touch all day. It was the only thing she looked forward to—weekends of love and passion. The kiss continued to build until she caught herself and pulled away.

"Veronica, I need to say something to you. About the other day in the restroom—"

"Oh, please, what's the point of having a safe word if we never get to use it?"

She could visibly see the wave of relief rush over him. She knew it had been bothering him. She wanted it to. She enjoyed the sex immensely that day, and the only reason she asked him to stop was to see if he could regain control. They were making a lot of noise, and she had been dying to try that place out. In a chain restaurant or someplace uninspired, she probably would've kept going, but she hadn't had a chance to eat there yet.

"There's hardly much you can do to me to make me turn away from you, baby."

"What about the bruises?"

"It just means we're doing it right. Nothing a little MAC and a turtleneck can't fix."

She watched him grin and he leaned in and kissed her. It was gentle like his touch, typically at least. She thought about Kendra's words. This was love.

"Lucas, baby, I need to say something."

"Go ahead," he said, taking a sip of wine from a glass sitting next to them. After walking back to the kitchen, he continued to chop onions.

"You know Milton Burrows?"

"The president of your company? Sure, what about him?"

"Well—I slept with him... on several occasions. Not since we've been together, but from time to time. Before I met you, we would hook up."

"I see." His tone indicated he was deep in thought.

"There's more."

"Okay, I'm listening."

"I think I love you. I should've said it earlier, but I'm a pretty fucked-up person."

Lucas was silent. She wanted him to say something, anything, to stop the festering insecurity in the pit of her stomach. For the first time since she could remember, she was nervous/scared/afraid of what that meant. Caring for someone meant being honest and exposed, and all because the ruse she intended to play got the better of her. She hadn't anticipated actually caring about him, but it was a slippery slope to loving him.

"Is this thing with Milton still going on?"

"No, I just wanted you to know everything, so there were no surprises."

Lucas stopped chopping onions and walked over to her. "This may come as a surprise to you, but before I met you, I was sleeping with someone at the company, too. Her name is Nichelle? You know her?"

Ronnie laughed as he pulled her in close to his chest to kiss her on her forehead.

"Look, sweetheart, it doesn't matter who you were with or what happened before the day we met each other. You are the only thing that matters *now*." He clutched her hands and looked deep into her saltwater green eyes. "Protect us, fight for us, and that's all I will ever care about."

A weight was lifted off her shoulders. For the first time in her life, she felt safe, and it wasn't because of her efforts. This man had come in and transformed the way she viewed the world. The very air had more significance because of how he elevated her. This was love. It was her first encounter with the word, and she enjoyed it.

"Can I help you with anything?"

Lucas chuckled, "Oh, no, I will handle the cooking duties. You just sit there and look delicious because I plan on having dessert all night long." He kissed her on her forehead again and went back into the kitchen.

Looking at him, she smiled. *This is love*. She walked over to him and held him as he chopped another onion. "Lucas."

"Yea baby?"

"Let's go see how far we get until someone has to say dandelions."

CHAPTER 24
READY

Nichelle was preparing for the final preliminary meeting before the presentation. Until now, most of their work had been done via email. Things with Donovan were going great, but she was sore at seeing Lucas and Ronnie together, and so she did most of her work outside the office to avoid meeting with either of them. There were several questions Lucas continued to insist would go over better in a meeting, but she was reluctant to participate. There was a lot riding on this job—first and foremost gaining the boards respect. There were key decisions to make about reducing costs, and the three of them needed to strike a chord between running a successful department and pleasing the executives. She took it seriously. In fact, it was the only thing she and Ronnie had in common, aside from sleeping with Lucas at some point. She also knew that Ronnie had no allegiance to her, so Nichelle made sure to read every email and respond back with thorough follow-up questions.

As she stood outside the door to the meeting room, she noticed Ronnie sitting on one of the office desks, twirling her hair and talking to Lucas. *She is so desperate all the time*, Nichelle thought, but seeing how it made Nichelle physically sick made Ronnie do it all the more.

Anything to keep Nichelle off her game. Getting there slightly early, she decided to eavesdrop on their conversation.

"What are you working on, Mr. Kimble?"

"The final pieces to the preliminary presentation of our audit analysis." Lucas got up to grab a cup of water, kissing Ronnie on the cheek as he passed. Nichelle watched as she sat down at his computer. *I'm going to be sick* she thought, looking at their affection.

"Lucas, babe, why are there two versions of this file?"

"Well, I always run two models. Sometimes a company is hell-bent on reducing its workforce, so I have to prepare a spare in case there's no other way to meet their efficiency expectations."

Ronnie opened the second version of the file. The numbers startled her. "It says here we could cut our spending by twenty-six percent if we lay off the lower ten percent of our workforce. That's huge!"

"It is, but unnecessary babe. Your firm was only looking for a fifteen percent savings. We can hit that easily with the adjustments in technology and software we've been discussing."

"Couldn't we do both?"

He closed the laptop as she salivated over the numbers.

"Veronica, this isn't a pretty part of my job. When I went into this field, I had no idea layoffs would ever be a part of the job."

"Well you're a veteran in this field now so why would that bother you?"

"When I was a kid, my mom got laid off. We struggled a lot after that. I saw my dad work odd jobs and take second shifts to cover her lost income. I never saw my parents fight until they were at each other's necks about finances. It took its toll, and they almost split up. I think companies stop being human when you put people out on the street for profit. I do my very best to make sure no other kid or family never has to go through that kind of emotional stress. It's a part of my job to be prepared and create the model, but as far as I'm concerned, this file doesn't exist."

I can't believe he actually shared that with her. They must be getting really serious. He deserves so much better than this cunt-ass.

She continued to watch as Ronnie sat and listened to him and looked at him with compassion. Finally responding, "Aww, baby, you're such a Captain Save-a-Ho."

"I'm sorry I have a soul," he fired back defensively. Ronnie stood up and straddled him on his chair. "Captain, save me, I'm drowning in all this moisture."

Oh, hell, no! Tell me this bitch isn't going to try to fuck him at work! Enough was enough. She decided to make herself known.

"Ahem."

"Captain, your duty calls," Ronnie said aloud. Nichelle knew what she was insinuating but didn't want to let on to the fact she had been eavesdropping for some time.

"Nichelle, glad you could make it," Lucas said as she walked into the room.

"Cool. Do we want to get started?" she said in cold fashion, taking a seat as Lucas prepared to run through the PowerPoint presentation he sent everyone yesterday.

"Sure thing. The strategy at RainHouse & Arms is simple—help improve your company's output while reducing your cost. The best way to do this is to implement a new accounting system which reduces your overhead, as well as updating your servers for all your processes. It will take some time, but in the coming months, you will notice a dramatic shift in cost."

Nichelle saw him put these types of presentations together before, but she had never seen him in action. It was an exercise in professionalism. Each one of his points was thorough, highlighting the pros and cons of moving forward with a given idea. The math all made perfect sense. She began to feel a sense of loneliness as she recalled the weekends he plowed away at these types of assignments after they made love. She thought to herself, *Surely Ronnie and he do the same thing.* She tried to shake the thought, but it angered her to know that her rival pounced on this man each night while they worked on this presentation, likely laughing at her in the process.

"I have an issue with these numbers," she blurted out. She, in fact, had no issue, but the she wanted to pick a fight.

"Sure, Nichelle. What is it?"

"They don't seem accurate. They seem to be put together without any oversight."

Lucas glanced at Ronnie while Nichelle spoke. "I think the numbers are fine," Ronnie interjected.

"I wasn't talking to you, Ronnie. I was talking to our auditor, or can you not separate your work from your personal life?"

"Excuse me?"

"You heard me correctly. These numbers seem like they lack attention to detail. Quite frankly it's sloppy work."

Ronnie shifted in her chair. "I'll ignore that insult on your close personal friend's work ethic, although I will say that of all the auditors to come through this firm, this is the most detailed and analytical presentation I've ever seen in my life!"

"Just proves how low your expectations are!" Nichelle fired back.

Ronnie stood up, walking toward Nichelle. "Why you little gutterball bitch!"

Standing up, Nichelle retorted, "Look at that! A low-class, trifling, gutterball bitch gets a little money and wants to look down on her own kind. What are you now, Ronnie? A high-dollar whore? Or does sleeping your way to the top make you forget all the time you spent on your knees at the bottom?"

"Guys, stop this now! We have to work." Lucas said.

Nichelle ignored his request. "You're both the problem, and your secret meetings are the issue!"

"Nichelle, we've tried to include you in every aspect of this process, but you didn't want to participate—"

"Don't defend this, Lucas. This clearly has nothing to do with this presentation, or even our team. Nichelle is trying out for her starring role as the victim in a relationship she brought to an end."

"Bitch, the next time you say something to me, I won't be the only victim!"

Ronnie smiled. "So the prom queen has teeth. I'm impressed. I wish all your adoring fans could hear the sewage spewing from that cum dumpster you call a mouth."

"Guys, that's enough! I'm not even sure what's happening here!" Lucas chimed in.

Nichelle screamed back. "I am the only one worried about the success of this project!"

"Worried? Are you serious right now? What do you have riding on it, Nichelle? You're the prom queen. You're the victim if anything goes wrong. You're—"

Nichelle watched as Ronnie struggled to finish her sentence. She couldn't. Instead, she raced to a nearby trashcan and vomited her insides out for several minutes. Nichelle looked at her. *I should shove this hoe's face in her own vomit. It's the least she deserves.* She looked at Lucas kneeling down beside her. *Fuck, do the right thing.* She walked over and grabbed a bottled water while Lucas attended to her. The silver pin in her hair banged against the trashcan, nearly unraveling her long locks. Nichelle leaned in and stopped the hair from falling into the trashcan. *This is my good deed for the day lord.* When the spell was over, Ronnie took some water, found a napkin, and dabbed her face. Lucas tied the trash bag and placed it inside another trash bin.

"I apologize to everyone. I'm not sure why that just happened. I must have eaten something that didn't agree with me." Standing to her feet she looked at Nichelle. "You think you have a lot riding on this? The board won't promote anyone past the level we're at right now if this isn't successful. I've been working my ass off to make sure things are in order. I have everything riding on this. You don't have to believe me—you don't even have to work with me—but stay out of my way if you can't help me."

Nichelle heard the words and realized she wasn't, in fact, mad at the actual work. Despite being a wretched bitch, Ronnie was the best at her job. In another life, she could learn a lot from her.

"Look, Nichelle, if you don't trust me, present your own numbers. You can even run the presentation. I won't say anything. The last thing I need is to get up on stage and throw up in front of everyone," Ronnie said in a very defenseless tone.

"I think that would be a good idea," Lucas chimed in. "We're all trying to do what's best for the company. I worked really hard to avoid laying off any employees, but if you think there is another place to reduce—"

"No, your numbers are fine," she responded. He did, in fact, accomplish his task without losing one job. That was more than enough to satisfy the board of directors. Was she letting her personal situation get the better of her? She wanted to apologize, but decided the best course of action was just to agree with everyone and get out of the meeting. "I will lead the presentation and thank both of you. If I have any questions, I'll make sure I talk to you before then."

The meeting let out, and Nichelle gathered up her stuff. "Hey, Nichelle, can I talk to you for a moment?" She paused. Ronnie was waiting on her. "I'm leaving early today. Can we talk later?"

"It will only be a moment."

After the scene she caused in the meeting, Nichelle felt a bit guilty, and so she relented. It seemed like the least she could do. If she didn't finish her work today, it wouldn't be the first time she took it home. "Sure. What's up?"

"You won't ever like me. I understand that, and I understand why. Honestly, I'm not your biggest fan either, but I respect your work. I respect what you do for this company, and I believe that's why we're both here."

"Okay, is that all?"

"No, that's not all. He'll never say it, and I don't want to get into it with you, but I'm sure you hurt Lucas just now. You should talk to him, not accuse him. In spite of everything, I know he cares about you."

The words were alarming. Ronnie was being supportive, a side Nichelle had yet to see from her. The hairs on the back of her neck stood at attention, warning her to be wary. "What are you trying to do, Ronnie?" She was tired of all these mixed signals.

Ronnie was silent. After a moment, she began, "I'm trying to grow, Nichelle. Everyone has this perception of me, and I probably earned it, but I'm tired of being labeled. I want all of us to succeed. Kendra, despite what you may think, is a good friend of mine. We fought, but that became exhausting. What we both just did in there was embarrassing. I'm tired of fighting with sisters when there are so few of us in the corporate world. So for what it's worth, I want to apologize for disrespecting you."

Nichelle stared at her. Still somewhat untrusting, Ronnie's words slowly brought her to a level of respect and understanding. Ronnie continued.

"Look, just host the damned meeting. Both Lucas and I will be there. I think this is a great opportunity for you to shine, and hopefully this will be the first step in us burying the hatchet."

"Okay, fine, I'll do it," Nichelle said, but her tone was softer than before. For the first time, she believed in Ronnie Duvalle, though a small part of her wondered if she was setting her up to fail.

CHAPTER 25
REFLECTING

It had been about three and a half months, and Donovan was no closer to finding his fortune now than when he first got out of prison. It was disheartening to know he had sacrificed so much of his time to finding his money but was flat broke. He had already burned through the cash he took from Trouble and most of the money he had taken from Carlos. After what happened, he decided he should walk as clean as possible and spent most of his days hustling for small change by his standards. Nothing big enough to get him locked up again, but enough through backroom gambling or selling bootleg items to get by and keep Rocky in his doggie hotel. It was a living, but it wasn't anywhere near what he was looking for. It bothered him considerably that he would need to ask Nichelle for a little cash from time to time. It wasn't something he was proud of, but it was better than being broke, and it was damn sure better than going back to jail. For a while he tried to find a job, finally settling on getting a CDL license to drive trucks. That life was for suckers, but it was the only legit life he could think of without his startup money. He wanted to open a small auto repair shop, working as a mechanic. He didn't really need the experience. He had long ago learned how to work on cars when he was a teenager, and even though it was a forgone conclusion he had stolen Trouble's car, he kept it finely maintained.

Donovan didn't want this life for him or Nichelle. It was all he had been thinking about of late. Where in the hell could his money be? Almost half a million dollars vanished. That's not the kind of money that disappears easily. But as of now, the only person who knew where it could be had taken that secret to the grave.

Sitting in the house and listening to Al Green's *Simply Beautiful*, a record his father played all the time when he needed to think, made Donovan realize he was missing something in his quest for his fortune. Still, he couldn't think of what it was. Maybe he should give all this up. He had Nichelle—his sapphire; God's caramel creation; the woman he wanted to build a family with. They had survived everything life had thrown at them. It wasn't always pretty, and it wasn't even always theirs, but when the smoke cleared, they always stood together. Babygirl was his ride or die. And he had no intention of dying anytime soon. It was time to *live* to the fullest, and in no way did that involve driving big rigs.

The song ended, and Donovan played it again on the iPod. He stood up and walked over to the bathroom mirror. He had gone to jail for this money. Looking at his reflection, he told himself, "You're a hustler, D. That's what you do. Shit, man, if you can't get your money, go back out and make some more."

Donovan picked up his keys and walked out the door. He drove about forty-five minutes down the road and parked his BMW. From there, he walked four blocks down an old suburban road. There was a car in the driveway, a light-blue 1979 Chevy Nova. It was the perfect car to pull off a heist when you had no partners—good trunk space; a quick in and out. He had an idea which bank to hit before he could recruit a crew again. As he descended upon the car, his phone rang. The caller ID displayed *Incoming Call Babygirl*

Fuck! He answered the phone.

"What's up, ma?"

"What are you doing?"

"Just talking a walk. What are you doing?"

"Just disappointed. I came home for a quickie this afternoon, but you were gone."

"Word. Is that right?"

"You know I wanted that stallion. Boy, where are you. Are you close?"

"I'm a bit out the way right now, ma."

"Damn it, D! I need you."

Donovan grinned. It wasn't the time or place since he was standing on the street of a car he was about to steal, but the fact she said 'I need you,' did something to him,

"Are you going back to work anytime soon?"

"I only have my lunch break, but if you plan on fucking me all afternoon, I can make arrangements."

"Babygirl, you know I want to, but I gotta get my bread up."

The phone was silent. He wasn't sure what was happening at the moment.

"Babygirl? Are you there?"

"I am. I just sent you a text."

Donovan took the phone away from his ear and looked at the photo she sent. Nichelle was dressed in a white, Victoria's Secret see-through lace bra-and-panty set and white high heels. Looking at it instantly made the bulge in his pants begin to rise.

"Damn, girl, I guess I can make other plans," he said after looking at the picture. He looked at the blue Chevy Nova, then back at the picture.

"Donovan, don't do nothing stupid. Come home to momma," she pleaded.

It was all he needed to hear. He retraced his steps back to his vehicle. "Babygirl, you always know when to step in, you know that?"

"Why do you say that?"

"Real talk?"

"Yes, please."

"'Cause I think I was about to do something really stupid."

The phone was silent for several seconds. "It's all going to be okay, D. I just want you to know that, in case you didn't."

"As long as I got you, ma, it's always going to be okay."

Donovan opened the car door and sat in his BMW, thinking about what he was about to do. "Babygirl, I'm in the car. I'll see you when I get there."

"Donovan, I—"

"What is it?"

"I know you're thinking we don't have to talk, but I just want to be on the phone with you until you're here."

He was silent. She wasn't checking up on him. She really meant she just wanted his presence. It was something she did back when they were together—the first time. She knew him. He wasn't the best communicator, but if he wanted to talk, she wanted to be there to listen.

"Cool."

As he drove, she silently held the phone. He thought about the crime he almost committed, a felony that would violate his parole. He thought about his best friend, Rico, and what he did with the money before he died. He thought about the woman who, despite knowing all there was to know about him, silently held the phone waiting for him to come back to her. Was it worth the money? Was it worth the time he had lost? Maybe he was looking at this the wrong way. Maybe he wasn't being grateful enough for his freedom.

"Babygirl."

"I'm here."

"You know all I got in this world to my name is my word, right?"

"Doesn't the saying go, 'All I have is my word and my balls'?"

"You got jokes right now, but I'm serious. All I got is my word. I don't have any money, and if I do things the right way, nobody's gonna hire a felon, so it's gonna take—"

"Donovan, I'm not with you for money. I got money. And you got me, so you got more than just your word, baby."

"I'm a man, Babygirl. I can't take money from any chick—"

"Let me stop you right here, D. I'm not just any chick—I'm your ride or die. True, I forgot that for a second, but I'm with you."

He was silent again. She loved him, and he realized it. He parked the car outside her place. When he got to the door, he opened it. She was standing in the hallway in the same attire she had on in the picture, but with a glass of Jack Daniels as an accessory.

"You something else, you know that, Nichelle?"

"I'm whatever you want me to be all afternoon."

Donovan kissed her. The kiss was something more passionate than he had given her in a while. She received him as he began to rub her breasts. Stimulated by the sheer sexual nature of her outfit, he slowly worked his lips from her mouth down to the side of her neck. Nichelle began to take off her outfit.

"Leave it on" he requested. He wanted to remember her this way, in white looking like the angel he needed to save him from himself. He continued to kiss her, moving down her neck, slowly revealing her breast through the sheer outfit. His lips, typically fierce and penetrating were much more gentle, made her quiver. He took both of his hands and placed them around her waist, lifting her straight in the air.

"Oh, my. Damn," she said aloud.

He rested her thick caramel thighs on top of his shoulders as he opened the crotch area of her outfit. He gently placed his lips around her clitoris. She grabbed the back of his head as he applied generous moisture to her already stimulated vagina. He continued to kiss her, first delicately, and then more deliberately as his pace quickened. She clutched the back of his head tightly as she moaned in euphoria. "Oh, my god, Donovan!" she screamed, her octave much higher than her speaking voice. She was cumming ferociously, the sheer power of him holding her in the air against the wall with his lips locked on her center forced a powerful orgasm inside her. The sensation was too much as the fluid leaked from her body onto his chin and down to the floor. He didn't stop —he kept her in the air, slowing his tongue just long enough for the pleasure to leave her body and make room for more arousal. He continued wrapping his mouth around her core, her clitoris at full attention as he repeatedly flicked it with his tongue. He inhaled her, and she moaned much louder than the last time. "Oh, my god!" she yelled, slapping the back of his head with her hand. Trapping her clit inside his mouth, he began to exercise it viciously. Her orgasm flowed, saturating his shirt and his chest as he allowed the mixture of saliva and nectar to slip from his mouth. The second orgasm was too much, and her body went limp. He lowered her from his massive shoulders and held her in his arms as he walked toward the bedroom. He could tell she was exhausted as she panted in recovery, spent from the unexpected pleasure he had given her. She struggled to talk. "That... was soo... where did you..."

"When you're in prison, you think about pussy a lot. Been wanting to do that for a while."

"Oh, my god, I can't... that was incred—"

"I'm glad you like it." She was already half asleep by the time he placed her on the bed, her body was still pulsating aftershocks from the last orgasm. There would be no round three.

He thought about the Chevy Nova sitting in the driveway. How unprepared he was to rob a bank, and how that affected his chances of having what he always wanted. He thought about all he had in Nichelle. Was it enough just to be here now? Could she truly be happy with him if he never had the money? He had always taken care of her, and she was used to that whether she recognized it or not. Had she really turned the corner, and material things didn't matter? Could she be satisfied without having the nicest things in life? Could he be happy with himself if he couldn't give them to her? He stood up to grab a pack of his cigarettes he had in the living room. As he took a step he felt a sharp pain. *Fuck!* He stepped on something but had no idea what. Glancing down he noticed the edge of a Prada shoe, one of the four pairs he had bought her. Lifting the shoe in the air he inspected it and looked back at his woman, now in a deep slumber.

This woman deserves the best. I'm going to give it to her one way or another.

CHAPTER 26
RELATIVES

"Who doesn't know that K-Ci remade this song?"

"I thought it was an original."

"It's Bobby Womack, baby."

"Damn it!"

Lucas sat watching his woman splash bubbles in his face. It was *Soaking Saturday,* the day they spent running a hot bath and guessing what song was an original versus what song was remade. It had been a part of their weekly ritual ever since the Jill Scott concert. Lucas had an extensive library of songs that had been remade. During the week, he'd put together a playlist, and as they sat in the tub either at his house or hers, they would play the game. Often Ronnie found the songs he introduced her more appealing than the remakes she knew. Sometimes she would actually know the song and the remake, but that was infrequent. She wasn't really big into music, or so she thought, until he introduced that world to her. At times, the events of the week would find their way into this moment, but not often. Since they were both early birds, watching the sunrise through the double-paned glass window was an added bonus to their quality time on Saturday mornings. Lucas enjoyed sitting until the water got room temperature, and just as he prepared to get out of the tub, Ronnie said, "Shit, we're out of towels."

"We?" he responded.

"Well I practically live here on the weekends. I'm sure *we* is the proper usage."

That statement satisfied his psyche. *We* sounded nice coming from her lips. As they both stepped out of the tub nude, he kissed her on her neck.

"Well, since you live here you know where the dryer is. Bring me back a towel, too," he said as he slapped her on her rear.

"Careful—you know I like that freaky shit."

As she walked off, he walked into the bedroom and found one last towel he hadn't put up from the last time he washed and dried off. He then pulled out his boxers from the drawer and slid them on. He decided to place new sheets on the bed and wait on a towel. He was almost done making the bed when he heard a scream.

Running to the living room, he saw his parents standing in front of Ronnie. *Oh, shit not today.*

"Lucas, you didn't tell me the goddamn cleaning service was coming over this morning!"

The woman in the living room, Lucas's mother, responded. "Honey, if I were the maid, the first thing I would do is wash your mouth out with soap."

"Well, I wo—"

"Veronica, please don't bait her," Lucas interjected, cutting his lover off from making a grave mistake.

"Bait whom?" she responded, still confused by his non-responsiveness to the intruders.

"I'd like you to meet my parents, Walter and Natalie," Lucas said.

"I'd prefer to meet you with your clothes on," Natalie quipped.

"As would I," Ronnie agreed.

"I don't mind," Walter said, still relishing the woman he just saw naked.

"Dad!" Lucas interjected, as he shuffled Ronnie back into the bedroom to put on some clothing.

The pair got dressed before they came back in, with Lucas proudly holding Ronnie's hand. "Baby ... please say as little as possible."

It was a warning he hoped she would heed as they reentered the living room where Natalie was intensely whispering to Walter. Walter waved toward Lucas and Ronnie to let Natalie know they were no longer alone. Lucas knew his parents well enough to know Natalie was judging him for dating a new woman he hadn't told them about.

"So, who is your friend?" Natalie asked.

"I already told you, Ma—this is Veronica."

"And does Nichelle know about this friend?"

"She doesn't need to know."

"I would beg to differ."

"No offense, Ma, then we'll agree to disagree." Natalie cut her eyes at her son. Then directly examined Ronnie from head to toe, darting back to her son she resumed the inquisition.

"Why wouldn't your girlfriend need to know about a fully naked woman roaming around your house?"

"Because Nichelle isn't my girlfriend. We're not together anymore." Lucas rolled his eyes. He knew his mother's reaction would be one of sheer shock and panic. *And now she's going to try to put us back together again,* he thought to himself.

"And since when did this change of events take place? Luke, you're my baby boy. Why wouldn't you come to me? I could've called her and we could've put your relationship back together."

"Natalie, leave the boy alone. They've been apart for some time now." Walter was providing cover fire for his son's quest to escape this conversation. There was little relief, though, as Natalie turned her investigation toward her husband.

"So, wait, Walter, you knew about this?"

"I did."

"Then why wouldn't you tell me?" she said as she pinched her husband, who winced in pain.

"Ouch! Because it was Luke's business to tell. Our vows are for better or worse, not for better, worse, and to be in the know at all times. If he wanted to tell you, you would know."

She looked back at her son. He could tell she was hurt by the secret he kept from her.

"So you told your father but couldn't find the time to tell your mother?"

"It's not like that, Ma. You're overreacting."

"And all your siblings?" His silence was all the confirmation Natalie needed. He thought to himself And *now comes the part where she tells me how she brought me into this world. 5...4...3...2...*

"You know, I was done having children when you came along. I guess carrying you for nine-and-a- half months to bring you into this world doesn't give you access to what's going on in your children's lives."

"Ma—"

"No, it's okay. Really. I just don't know why everyone in this family insists on trying to keep me outside the loop when all I try to do is love and support you all."

"Natalie, he didn't tell you because you meddle. All the time."

"I do not meddle. I can't believe—"

Lucas chimed in. He knew it wasn't his dad's battle to fight. He needed to tell his mother the truth. "I got this, Dad. Ma, you remember that Thanksgiving when Shanice found out David was cheating on her?"

Natalie's mouth dropped. "That was an extenuating circumstance, and you know it! I was—"

"Let me finish. We were all watching the Cowboys game, and you wouldn't leave Shanice alone until she told you where David was. She broke down and told you everything. And when she finally did, it wasn't enough. You decided to go over to her house and took the knife Dad carved the turkey with to carve out a piece of David. We all missed the game to make sure you didn't go to jail for assault with a deadly weapon. That's the day all the kids made a pact to keep you out of our lives. You overreact and you meddle. It's just the way you are."

"So now it comes to light, after all I do to keep this family close. Well, I'm glad my children are finally close, even if it's because all you want to do is conspire against your mother."

Lucas's dad interrupted her rant. "Natalie, the boy is right. You don't know how to stay out of anybody's business. You're overreacting right now."

There was a calming silence as Mrs. Kimble finally sat quietly. Lucas noticed Ronnie fighting the urge to laugh, which his mother detected. *Oh, Lord* he thought. As he began to gesture to move his mother out the door, she spoke.

"Do all your friends feel comfortable walking around naked in your home?"

Lucas could hear the "in-question" building. Every question from here on out would create a domino effect. The right to remain silent worked in court, but it had no place in Natalie Kimble's justice system.

"She was washing her clothes, Ma. She was literally going to get them when you startled her. And what are you guys doing over here anyway?"

His best defense was to deflect blame as much as possible. He looked at his dad for guidance, but it appeared his dad had resumed undressing Ronnie with his eyes. The old man was happily married, but he wasn't shy about looking at attractive women.

"We came over because we hadn't heard from you in a while, and I wanted to see how my baby boy has been. Now I see you've been ... busy," Natalie said sarcastically, giving Ronnie the once over.

"So, Veronica—"

"You can call me Ronnie. Everyone else does."

"Well, if everyone else calls you Ronnie, why does my son call you Veronica?"

"I'm not sure. He has a weird aversion to nicknames. Probably something he picked up in childhood."

Lucas began to feel like a gasoline-soaked log about to be lit on fire. This wouldn't end well if he didn't step in. "Anyone want anything to eat or drink? Dad? Ma?"

"I'm fine, son," his mother said.

"I got everything I need," his father said with a grin. Walter knew, like Lucas, the fireworks were about to take off and he didn't want to miss one bit of it. He winked at Lucas as he sat back to see where the conversation went next.

"So, Veronica," Natalie continued, "why are you at my son's home washing clothes? Is your washing machine broken, or is there more to your relationship?"

"Nope. That's all there is, Mom," said Lucas, jumping in. "I'm helping a friend wash her clothes. Now she's going to fold them, and we don't want to bore you, so you guys can leave."

"Now you know I didn't raise you to be rude. I asked the lady a question, so please be courteous and let her answer it."

Lucas glared over at Ronnie, his wide eyes reiterating, *Please say as little as possible.*

"So, Veronica, is there more to your relationship?"

"We share a vagina."

It was the sum of all his fears. Lucas buried his head in between his palms.

"In fact, he just got finished giving me his input before you came. Well, *I came* before you arrived. I'm surprised you couldn't hear me from the driveway. Must be good insulation on these walls. So I guess the extent of our relationship is—fuck buddies?"

Lucas was now in full-blown panic. He looked to his father for advice, but Walter was

laughing hysterically on the couch opposite him. He looked at his mother, who was in total disbelief over what she just heard. Clearly at a loss for words, he decided the best thing to do was shuffle them out of the house before the scenario got really ugly.

"Okay, Mom, Dad, it's nice to see you again. Please get up and leave. Now, Dad?" He looked at his father, who was still smiling.

"Oh, my Lord! 'Do not profane your daughter by making her a harlot, so that the land will not fall to harlotry and the land become full of lewdness!' Leviticus 19:29. Proverbs 2.16: 'To deliver you from the strange woman/from the adulteress who flatters with her words;' Proverbs 7:25: 'Do not let your heart turn aside to her ways/Do not stray into her paths.'" When Natalie began rattling off Bible verses, Lucas knew she was not only offended, but would tell the entire family what happened today.

"Mom, she's not a harlot, she's a friend. Now, can you please leave?"

"A man who loves wisdom makes his father glad/But he who keeps company with harlots wastes his wealth!" she responded.

"Come on, Natalie, we're leaving," his father said, ushering his wife toward the door.

"If you think this discussion is over, it's only just begun. I want both of you to know that!" she yelled as she walked out the door.

"It was very nice to meet both of you," Ronnie said politely as she stood up to wave while Walter and Lucas jointly hauled an angry Natalie Kimble through the door. When Lucas was finally able to lock the door, he turned his attention to Ronnie.

"Your parents are nice," she said as she walked to the kitchen table.

"What in the hell is the matter with you?" he said in frustration.

"What? Did I do something?"

"When we left the bedroom, did you not hear me tell you to say as little as possible?"

"I did. *We share a vagina*—by my count, that's only four words." She counted in the air as she talked.

"Damn it, Veronica, you have no idea the chain reaction you just started!"

Ronnie wrapped her arms around his mid-section. "Sweetheart, I'm going to tell you something: your mother has five kids. She knows what fucking is. If a woman with five children can't use context clues to figure out what a butt-naked lady is doing at her son's house on a Saturday morning, she has bigger issues than you think." Ronnie kissed him on the nose as she squeezed him tighter.

"You didn't have to put it out there so bluntly."

"I didn't want to insult her intelligence. She's clearly a smart woman looking for the truth. I just gave her what she wanted."

She kissed him again as she moved her arms up and down his chest and mid-section.

"She's going to think you're a slut now."

"I thought I was a harlot?"

"It's the same thing."

"That's nice. I really like the word harlot. Gives it an Old World feel. I can be your harlot, Mr. Kimble," Ronnie said playfully. Her arms reached down to his crotch, making Lucas relax.

"You want to prove my mother right?" he asked.

"Shhhhh," she responded as she turned his body to face hers. She got on her knees and pulled down his pants.

"What are you doing, fuck buddy?" he asked with a smile to match his father's.

"I'm about to suck your dick so good, by the time I'm done you won't even remember your mother was here—harlot style."

CHAPTER 27
RIGHT THERE

Ronnie was on her knees, Lucas's blue cotton T-shirt clinging against her frame as her nipples pushed the shirt outward. She wanted to please her lover, who was already fully erect at the idea of her being a harlot. She went to pull down his sweatpants when he stopped her.

"I have a better idea," Lucas said, bringing her to her feet. "Go to the bedroom and lay down. I have some work on the presentation I need to knock out real quick, and then you can show me how a harlot deep throats."

Ronnie grinned. "Are you sure you want to do this? Not to brag, but my head game is quite strong. I'm a harlot, after all. We don't wait around for dick; dick wants us."

"My dick wants you. I just have to finish the file."

"No fun, Mr. Kimble, no fun at all," she said pouting. He kissed her on the cheek and she returned to the Cal King-sized bed in his room. The bed was comfortable—too comfortable. Lucas had lots of pillows, but she never noticed the quality of these pillows. The soft coolness of the blanket combined with the pillow's tenderness made it perfect for sleeping. *A quick nap won't hurt,* she thought as she watched an episode *of Law & Order*. Ronnie hardly, if ever, watched TV, but since spending her days and nights with Lucas, she'd become accustomed to having background noise. It wasn't long before she was in a deep, mid-morning slumber. Through her sleep, she heard her phone ringing and moved to grab it, only to find she was incapable of doing so.

She woke up to find her arms and feet restrained. Each limb was bound by a leather strap tied to one of his bedposts. Lying on the 1200-thread count Egyptian cotton sheets, she was totally naked. "Lucas!" she yelled, looking for him. The bronze curtains, normally open to let in daylight, were closed, leaving the room entirely dark. There were candles lit on the nightstands next to the bed. "Lucas!" she yelled again, waiting no more than a second before he entered the room. The flickering candles captured his chiseled frame. He was naked and fully erect. Seeing his chocolate skin shimmer as he walked over to her made her moist. "What's the meaning of this?" she demanded.

He ignored her question and climbed onto the bed, stroking his growing manhood as he looked at her body. "I notice you like giving orders. You're in charge at work. You micromanage every aspect of your personal life down to the olives in your salad, and it got me thinking—what if you weren't in control?" She began to speak, but as she did, he took a scarf and tied it around her mouth. The remnants of what were words were left unspoken as he continued. "I got the idea from you, you know. That time when we first had sex, you wanted me to choke you or talk dirty to you, but even with that, you controlled it all. How hard to squeeze; how dirty to talk—you even came up with our safe word." Her legs tensed up as he ran his hand up her thigh, then back down. He looked at her naked flesh, all of it now exposed to the candlelight. "Today, Veronica, you have no control. You can't tell me what you want because you can't talk. Today, I'm going to give you all that I want you to have." The tone of his voice made her vagina saturate with her sweet nectar. At that moment, he decided to taste her. Euphoria swept through her body with each flick of his tongue. She wanted to grab his head and press it deeper, fighting against the restraints, but soon gave up and gave in, her helplessness building her moisture. He slowly teased her with his tongue, darting it inside her vagina until he pulled it out and placed both of his lips firmly around her clitoris. He sucked on the most sensitive area of her clit with his mouth while licking it ferociously with his tongue. Veronica let out a muffled scream of ecstasy as she came unexpectedly. It was the fastest she had ever cum. Her clit was sensitive to the touch, but she was unable to protest as he pressed his tongue against her again, licking the inner parts of her thighs and moving his mouth back on top of her clitoris and extracting ecstasy from her swollen vagina. It was the second of three orgasms he gave her orally. After she could no longer handle his lips on her, Lucas wiped his mouth and climbed on top of her. Still fully erect, he placed his hand behind the back of her neck as she caught her breath. He held her neck as he forced her to look at him enter her. He slowly penetrated her, deep into her core, his width shoving the softened walls of her body apart like a security guard at a nightclub. She had no choice but to receive every inch of his cock. He took his time, deliberately sliding into her inch by inch as he forced her to look at him enter. "How do you feel?" he asked rhetorically, her green eyes betraying her. She loved the way she was feeling, her body unable to process the sensations fast enough as he slowly, deliberately penetrated her spirit. And each time she rolled her eyes into the back of her head as she took him in. He tightened his grip around her neck, forcing her to look at him again. He was halfway into her as she moaned through the gag around her cheeks. By the time he was fully inside her, she came once more. The fluid spilled from her body like an old faucet. Her toes curled and she orgasmed with one single stroke of his rod. It was beyond what anyone had ever made her feel. She had given her power to him, and he was using it to please her in ways she thought unimaginable. "Right there," he said as he finally placed all of him inside her. "Today, this is where I'm going to live."

The orgasms came in waves. He was pleasing her and punishing her with each stroke of his dense pole, its thickness and firmness relentlessly gliding in and out of her in rhythmic fashion. Never before had she released so much ecstasy in any encounter. Her hands and feet were marked due to her repeated fights with the restraints each time she came. The gag over her mouth was wet with saliva; her body saturated by sweat from her body clenching and unclenching after every orgasm. He had almost reached his own climax when he removed the gag from her mouth. Her mouth was still open, simultaneously gasping for air and moaning from pleasure when he silenced her by sliding his member between her lips. Her saliva, mixed with her own sweet nectar, made him glide in with ease. Standing over her, he began to stroke her orally the same way he had vaginally. She wrapped her tongue around him as he continued, his firm dick pushing deeper into her mouth. With each stroke, he swelled until he released his own sweetness into her throat. He was so deep inside her, his hot semen slid down her throat with ease. She received him wholly, not leaving a drop of saliva or semen to waste. Satisfied, he pulled out of her orifice and crumpled next to her, visibly weakened by the ecstasy they had just shared. It was the first time she could catch her breath since this escapade began. It was the most intense sexual encounter she had ever experienced.

He looked at her with penetrating eyes and released her arm from the leather strap nearest him. Next, he did the foot nearest him. He was fading fast, the orgasm having taken all the life out of him. She undid the other two straps. Still naked, she crawled underneath his chest. The two of them, the harlot and her master, lay in each other's arms for the duration of the day, naked in a comatose-like sleep.

CHAPTER 28
RING

The next morning, Lucas left home early, heading to his parents' house. Ronnie was going to stay home and out of sight due to the fiasco with his mother. Nonetheless, he needed to talk to his father. He hit the doorbell, but there was no answer. There was also no sign of his father's Toyota Tacoma sitting in his parents' cobblestone driveway. He hit the doorbell again and heard a voice say, "Nobody's home unless you're leaving money."

Lucas chuckled and turned around to hug his father standing there in overalls and white T-shirt, the scent of yardwork beginning to build under his armpits. "Hey, Pop, how are you? Where's the truck?"

"I'm good, son. Just washed it yesterday. I didn't know if it was going to rain today, so I decided to use the garage for once. What's going on?"

Lucas scanned the area and asked, "Is Mom home?"

"Uh-oh. Now I know something's going on. You know it's Sunday. She's at church all day, which gives me some time to do this yardwork and watch some football."

Lucas took that as an invitation to help out in the yard before catching a game. "How much more do you have to go?" he asked.

Walter looked around the already cut yard. "I only got the flowerbed left," Walter replied.

"Cool. I'll get my gear out the garage." Yard work was Walter's one enjoyment. Lucas had tried for years to get him to hire a lawn service, even offering to pay for it himself, but Walter took great pride in his yard. He always said that it was one of the more difficult jobs a man would ever have to do in life. "If you can cut the yard on a hot summer day in Houston, you can do anything," Walter always told his children. Lucas hated cutting the grass, but enjoyed spending time with his dad. It was a bonding mechanism. His father would give him great advice, and today he was in need of great advice. The two spent hours pulling weeds out of the flowerbed. Not really speaking, just murmuring words about who's the best running back in the NFL, and who would win the NBA championship this year. It was their typical small talk. His dad was one of the few people in the world he could talk to with such ease.

By time the two finished, it was the peak of day, right in time for halftime of the first game. Walter and Lucas walked inside the house and were both hit by the chill of the air conditioner. They dripped with sweat and decided to take off their shirts and grab a beer while watching the game. "Boy, you look like I used to when I was your age," Walter said, complimenting his son on his physique.

"I just hope I look like you at your age."

"You gotta stay out in that yard, son. That's all the exercise you need."

Lucas walked into the living room of his parents' home, the hardwood floors polished, the scent of Old English lingering in the air. His mother must have just cleaned the floor this morning. There were innumerable pictures of him and his siblings on the walls. Lucas walked over to the one that had all of them.

"You and Mom did really good for yourselves. Was there ever a time you doubted it would work?"

Walter realized they were getting to the reason for his son's impromptu visit and decided to choose his words carefully in order to keep the dialogue as open as possible. "Well, let's see... There was the day I said I do, then the day your brother was born, then the day your sister was born, then the day your twin brother and sister were born, and certainly the day you were born," the shirtless man said as he grabbed his son by the neck and shook him in a playful manner. "Dad, you play too much!" Lucas said somewhat tense, shrugging his shoulders to shed his father's hand from his neck.

His father chuckled and said, "Okay, Luke, I guess this is serious. I'll be right back."

Lucas nodded and sat down on the couch in front of the 65-inch LCD television and turned on the game. The Texans were down to the Colts by three touchdowns going into the half.

"What's the score?" his father called out as he walked back into the living room with two cold beers in his hand and joined his son on the couch.

"You don't want to know," Lucas responded, taking one of the beers from his father.

Upon looking at the screen, Walter's face soured. "Bunch of bums!" They both took sips of their Dos Equis beer. "So what's this about, Luke?" his father said, cutting through the small talk to ensure his son didn't bury the topic because the game was on.

Lucas took another sip of beer before putting it on the glass coffee table in front of him. "Boy, use a coaster! You know your mother would kill you and me!"

Lucas slipped a coaster under his beer, then turned to his dad. "I'm in love with Veronica, Dad."

Walter took a sip of beer and leaned back against his couch as the sweat began to evaporate from his body. "Seems like the other day you were in love with Nichelle."

"I know, and I've been thinking about that. I was really angry at Nichelle when things happened the way they did between us, but now I see that maybe she was just in my life to prepare me for the person I'm supposed to be with."

Walter looked at the sincerity in his son's eyes as he took his third sip from the bottle. "Luke, you know I'm going to support you no matter what you decide, and I know you didn't come all this way just to tell me you love this girl, so what's really going on? You want me to smooth things over with your mother? 'Cause you're a grown man. What you do, or who you do it with in your house, is your business.

And I'm not gonna lie, Luke—if you don't want your company wearing clothes, I'll never complain."

Lucas laughed. "No, Dad, it's not like that at all, although if you could do that with Mom that would be most helpful. The other day we were walking, heading to the Miller Outdoor Theater to hear the Motown revival, and they played all these classic songs. You know, the songs we grew up listening to in this house. And I looked over to her and I thought to myself, *I never want to feel this way about another person again*. I mean. I only want to feel like this with *this* woman in front of me for the rest of my life. And she's all kinds of wrong for me, Dad. Everyone else thinks she's this person who can't be trusted. You have to watch your back around her. But she's always had my back. From the moment we met, she's always had my interest at heart."

Walter put his hand on his cleanly shaven chin as if to think. "Well, I'll say this—you know she didn't leave the best impression on your mother, but I like her. She has fire and you need some of that in your life, so if you're looking for validation from us, it's going to be a split. The real question is what you want from her."

"I want her to be my wife."

Silence filled the air. Walter knew his son was being sincere. Walter stood up, walked over to the wall, and pulled down a picture. He came back and handed it to Lucas. It was a picture of him as a young man holding his bride to be. Lucas examined the picture as his father sat back down.

"You asked me if I ever had any doubts."

"Yeah." Lucas responded unsure of what the picture had to do with anything.

"Well you're looking at one. You see the night this picture was taken, I didn't know if I wanted to be in a relationship at all. Your mother had just come back from college, and I was about to head off to grad school. It seemed like our relationship wasn't going to work. Timing, you know?" Walter took another sip of beer as he sat down and continued his thought. "We were young and there were plenty of ladies out there, and I wasn't sure what I wanted. Grad school was a two-year commitment in Louisiana, and your mother had just started working here as a paralegal. I thought it was best to break up and go our separate ways, but your mother said something to me that night. She asked me if I loved her. I said sure I do. Then she asked me if you're so willing to work so damn hard for everything else in your life, why wouldn't you be willing to work for us? Why wouldn't you put the kind of fight you put into getting your degree and starting your career into our relationship?" Walter leaned over in his son's direction and looked him in the eye. "That moment was when I knew I was going to marry this woman. I bought a ring the very next week, and we worked like hell at this life we built. It wasn't always easy—you know that firsthand. The time she got laid off, we had a real hard time. But we had food on the table every day and clean clothes on our backs. So, to answer your question, did I have doubts? Hell, yes. On all the occasions I told you I did earlier. I wasn't joking. But do I have any regrets?" Walter took the picture out of his son's hand, examined himself and his bride, and began to smile. Lucas watched his father get caught up in his own thoughts as he gazed at the picture. After some time, he came back to their conversation and looked at Lucas. "No, son, I don't. My advice to you is this: if you can't see yourself living without her, then don't."

Lucas leaned over and gave his father, a man wise beyond his years, a hug. "Thanks, Pops. That is exactly what I needed to hear."

His father nodded and said, "You've always been a good kid. You're going to do the right thing for you. I have no doubt about that."

As Lucas walked out of the house, he processed his father's words. Ronnie was still at his home, probably about to leave to get ready for the big meeting tomorrow. He picked up the phone to dial Ronnie's number. "Hey, baby, what's going on?"

"I'm just walking out of your place. How are the parents?"

"They're doing pretty good, I have to admit."

"I'm surprised your mother hasn't strapped you down and given you holy water through an I.V."

"She might have, but she's at church—harlot."

"If she only knew her son speaks in tongues."

"Veronica."

"Tell the truth and shame the devil. Hey, I'm going to stay at my place tonight. You want to have dinner?"

"I still have a few errands to run, but I called to ask you a favor."

"Sure, what is it?"

"I want you to get on my laptop and grab the file for the presentation."

"Okay. What for?"

"Well, do you think you and Nichelle can handle the meeting tomorrow? I would never ask under normal circumstances, but the numbers run themselves."

"OK, you mind telling me why you're flaking out on the most important meeting of this project?"

"I will I promise, but for right now just know that I... have something I need to do."

—Buy a ring? You can do that after work!

—She is going to get the wrong file and make Nichelle look bad!

CHAPTER 29
RUTHLESS

Monday morning arrived, and Ronnie was ready for her meeting. It was what the entire last few months had been about, and she was ready to finally earn the title she so desperately craved. All her efforts led to this time; her time. She found love along the way, and while that was great, this was, beyond the shadow of a doubt, her moment. The moment the board recognized her importance to the firm. Under normal circumstances, getting dressed for the occasion would've taken time, but not today. Getting dressed was actually a breeze because she had picked out the outfit for this occasion two weeks ago. She woke up and put on her playlist *Sr. Vice President Duvalle vs. The Motherfuckers at Burrows Industries,* a name she had been working on for some time. Everything was going to go according to plan. She rapped to the first song, *Motivation* by T.I., as if she were getting ready for a title fight. "Haters get on your job! Motivation!" As she belted the lyrics, she put on her tailored black Chanel pants and her crème Chanel blouse to match her crème-and-black-tweed belted Chanel coat. The red bottom on her four-inch Christian Louboutin black heels were the only accent to her ensemble. She checked herself once more. "Flawless," she said as she walked out the door. The meeting wouldn't start until noon, but she had tons of things to do before it began. She wanted to fire off several emails and make sure she was prepared for the follow-up when Milton and several select executives welcomed her into their little boys' club. It was finally all coming together. She was halfway to her car when her battle with nausea kicked in. She stopped in the middle of the atrium. *Hold it together, Duvalle. This is your moment. You can do this!* She took several deep breaths, pulling in oxygen as she cleared her mind and settled her stomach.

Now composed, she proceeded to her car. She had just unlocked the vehicle when she lost it. She spewed last night's veal Marsala onto the pavement, some of which made its way onto her coat. "No, no, no, no, no!" she screamed, wiping her mouth. She opened the car and found some paper napkins she had in the back seat and examined her coat. Wiping off what she could, she let out a scream as her attempts were unsuccessful. She took off her coat and sat in the car. "Okay, Duvalle, think—think, damn it!" She turned the car on and connected her phone via Bluetooth. "Call Douglass," she said, reversing out of her parking lot.

"Burrows Industries. This is Doug."

"Douglass, I need you to leave the office immediately!"

"Ronnie? What's wrong? Is everything okay?"

"Meet me at Tip Top Cleaners now!"

She hung up the phone and drove over to the cleaners, six blocks from her home. Parking her car, she jumped out hastily and walked into the building and waved down one of the workers. A short, middle-aged Korean woman wearing a green knit sweater and gray sweatpants greeted her.

"Excuse me, miss, I have an emergency! I had an accident, and I ruined my coat. I need someone to take a look at this ASAP!"

The woman inspected the coat and took her phone number. She quietly walked over to the counter and wrote out a receipt.

"This will be available tomorrow at four."

"Unacceptable. I need this within the hour!"

The woman shook her head vigorously. "We cannot do. Tomorrow at four."

"Listen to me—I need this coat cleaned in the next hour. If you can't make that happen

find me someone who can. In fact, let me talk to the manager right now! I need your manager right now!"

Ronnie could tell the woman was put off by her demeanor and apparently began cursing at her in Korean. Shortly afterwards, a middle-aged Korean man wearing a gray Rice University sweater and gray sweatpants surfaced. Ronnie walked over to him. At this time, Douglass walked into the cleaners. Ronnie snapped her fingers as if to beckon her employee to stand next to her.

"Ronnie, what's going on?" Douglass asked.

"Douglass, I need you to get them to work on my coat. Today is colossal. I need my coat for the meeting today!"

Douglass looked at the coat and noticed the blotted stain against the crème.

"Ewww, what happened, Ron—"

"Damn it, Douglass, who cares what happened? I need this coat for the meeting, and I need it now!"

"Of course. I'm sorry, Ronnie, but if you don't mind me saying so, you live right next to the office. Couldn't you go home and change?"

"Would you tell Michelangelo while he was creating David to just start over? No, because he was creating a goddamn masterpiece! This is my day, and nothing will ruin it! Stay here and don't leave until they give you back the coat clean. I don't care if you have to get back there and help them scrub, have this coat to me by noon!"

She walked out without waiting for a response. She picked up the phone and made an appointment with her primary physician who was only fifteen minutes away. She wanted to know why this was happening. The doctor was able to fit her in within the hour, so she headed directly there. When she arrived, there was only one patient ahead of her. She started feeling queasy again when the nurse called her to the back. She made it to the bathroom in time to save the rest of her outfit before heading into the waiting room. When the doctor arrived, she was slightly agitated.

"Dr. Radford, thank God. I think I need something for anxiety."

"How are you, Ronnie? Explain to me what's going on."

"For the last couple of weeks, at indiscriminate times, I've been getting headaches, and more importantly, I have gotten queasy. I puked right before you came in."

The doctor checked her vitals and looked her once over.

"When was your last cycle?"

Ronnie, stunned by the question, stumbled to answer. "I—I'm not sure. I think... um—"

"You're showing signs of pregnancy. It's the only reason I ask."

"That's impossible. I have an IUD."

"How long have you had it?"

"Since forever. College. They last a decade."

"I see. How old were you when you got to college?"

"Eighteen."

"And how old are you now?"

"I'm twenty-eig..."

There was a silence. Ronnie had taken the process for granted for so long, birth control was an afterthought. She wasn't sure how to respond.

"Let's just run a pregnancy test to rule it out then."

"Doctor, we're wasting time. I have a very important meeting today."

"And I want to make sure you're perfectly healthy. It's just a quick test to help diagnose what's going on. If there is nothing there, we'll move on."

"Fine, let's get this over with."

Ronnie got up and went to the bathroom to take the test. She came back confident that this was just a formality. After four minutes, the doctor came back into the room.

"Congratulations. What you're having is morning sickness. You're pregnant."

Ronnie sat silent, stunned by his words. She couldn't hear him say anything after that. *Pregnant? What was happening?* She came back to reality when the doctor waved his hand to grab her attention.

"We need to remove the IUD so you won't have any issues with the pregnancy."

Silently, she removed her clothing and allowed the doctor to remove the IUD. She knew her world would change today, but she never imagined it would change like this. She remained in a daze as the doctor prescribed prenatal pills to her and scheduled a follow-up visit, along with several brochures about pregnancy. She walked out of the doctor's office and quietly sat in her car. The phone rang, bringing her back to reality.

"Hi Ronnie, it's Douglass. The coat is ready."

"Good job, Douglass. Bring it to the office. I'm on my way."

She looked at the time. It was already noon. She had been sitting in the parking lot for over an hour. She hurried over to the office and retrieved the coat from Douglass. Putting the coat on removed some of her current thoughts, but not enough to get through the meeting. She asked Douglass to give her a moment while she returned to sit in her car.

"You can do this, Duvalle. Today is your day." She repeated the phrase several times to gain the momentum she had before the day started. She got out of the car and walked into the office. Upon walking through the double-paned glass doors, she realized she hadn't eaten all day. By losing last night's meal, she was famished. She walked to the café, where she wanted to get something heavy, but decided to go with a chicken Caesar salad. From there, it was off to the 21st floor and her office to eat. It was almost time to present the last several months' worth of work. She finished her salad and went into the conference room to prepare for the biggest moment of her professional career.

When the meeting began, Ronnie put the presentation on the projection screen. Months of hard work were now coming to a head as she finally set aside her differences with Nichelle. "Before we begin, I want to apologize to you all that Mr. Kimble, from RainHouse & Arms, could not be in attendance because there was an emergency at their own firm. We've been in contact, and I assure you everything is fine, but for now, may I introduce to you one of our newest and most diligent vice presidents, Ms. Nichelle Myers." Applause erupted as Nichelle took the stage. Ronnie walked past her and said, "You got this, girl. Good luck."

Nichelle smiled, feeling the newfound love from Ronnie, who sat down next to several of the senior executives. The stage was unnecessary for such a small audience. Ronnie often thought Milton requested this room so he could undress whoever was speaking, male or female, with his eyes. The presentation seemingly lasted much longer than she wanted to be there. She constantly checked the time to make sure things weren't running over, but Nichelle was a natural. She systematically relayed the information, and there was generally positive feedback.

"As you can see, the final numbers indicate we can save 14.39 percent of our finances globally by investing in technology and thus reducing our overhead for the systems we are currently using." Nichelle presented the numbers as Ronnie and Milton and three of the executives looked on. Milton nodded in agreement.

"Excellent work, Nichelle. How soon can we get this started?" Milton asked.

"We can start within two weeks," Nichelle replied. "We have already started the process by talking to vendors. We just need final approval from the board."

Milton smiled and said, "The numbers make sense. I don't see a way we could do any better."

He looked at Ronnie, who was visibly quiet. "Ronnie, you're more quiet than normal. Something you want to share with the class?"

Ronnie looked around the room and said, "I'm sorry, Milton. I've tried my best to be a team player, but I can't sit here and be quiet while we're not doing what's best for the company." Surprise fell upon everyone's face, particularly Milton's and Nichelle's. "What do you mean?" Milton asked.

"Yeah, Ronnie, what do you mean?" Nichelle said sarcastically.

Ronnie got up and walked up to the podium. "I don't want to be crass. I've really tried to be a team player, and so out of respect for all the hard work that Nichelle and the RainHouse & Arms firm has done, I didn't want to present what I'm about to say."

Ronnie glanced at Nichelle, who was outraged and confused at the same time. "Please, Ronnie, if you have anything contrary to these numbers, now's the time to speak," Milton urged.

Ronnie took out a USB flash drive and plugged it into the

computer running the presentation. "Not so much contrary to the numbers, but an enhancement." She clicked on a PowerPoint presentation to open it. "I've independently worked on the numbers for the final quarter, and while we save close to fifteen percent doing what my peer recommends, by severing the lowest ten percent of our employees, we can create a net savings of 26.39 percent in time for the price-to-earnings ratio. Most of these jobs can be backfilled to effectively send the best message to Wall Street regarding our strength and bottom line. This is the solution I would take."

The room was silent. Ronnie looked at Milton, who nodded to indicate the title was hers. She continued with her presentation. "Now, I understand it may not be the most popular, and in no way is this a reflection on Nichelle's inexperience, or RainHouse & Arms' work. If anyone is to blame, it should be me for giving her too much responsibility too soon. They are both exemplary in my opinion, but the numbers speak for themselves. We'll save nearly double by reducing our workforce to maximize our potential."

Nichelle's mouth dropped, but Milton stood up. "You're right, Ronnie. The numbers speak for themselves. While both arguments are valid, I think we should proceed with your recommendation in order to make sure we hit the bottom line."

"Good. I've already taken the liberty of creating a shortlist of names of employees and salaries that need to be shed in order for us to hit the numbers."

Miltion interjected. "Ronnie, one name that stands out to me is Douglass Villarreal. Are you sure you want your guy's name on this list?"

"He's a great employee, Milton, but sacrifices must be made. To show my commitment to this company, I made hard choices. He was one of them."

Nichelle interjected emphatically. "Mr. Burrows! Sir, can we reconsider? This seems a bit excessive."

Milton looked at Ronnie, who was shaking her head dismissively. He turned back to Nichelle. "I applaud your compassion, but this is what's best for the company, Nichelle. You'll learn this as you get more experience. I have no doubt of that. Great work, everyone."

As the three executives were walking out, Milton walked past Ronnie. "Good catch, Ms. Duvalle."

Ronnie noticed Nichelle hadn't moved from her chair while the room was clearing out. "Something you need?" Ronnie asked.

Nichelle stood up and chuckled mockingly. "Does Lucas know about this little maneuver you just pulled?"

"Know about it? He prepared the document! This is his data. There are no secrets between me and my man, Nichelle."

Nichelle paced the floor, agitated by Ronnie's comments. "You know, when I first got this job, I already knew you were a viper. I tried to warn Lucas so many times not to deal with you—just keep it professional—yet you slithered your way into his bed and infected him with your poison. He didn't even have the balls to be here to sell me out personally." She walked closer to her as she tried to suppress her anger. "You had me convinced, Ronnie. For once I thought you were actually going to do the right thing. You said all the right words, put up the right amount of resistance, and I have to admit I never saw it coming. Not only do I look like an idiot with the board, but you were working on this alternate plan the whole damn time while looking like the strong leader every one of those jackasses who just left the room thinks you are."

"Now, now, now, Nichelle—potty mouth. We must control our feelings."

Nichelle grabbed her belongings and was about to storm out when Ronnie asked the question that had been on her mind for some time. "Is this about me beating you today, or is this about Lucas?"

"It's about the *people,* Ronnie. I don't know what or how, but the Lucas I knew would never go for this. I know that for a fact! I can't believe you sacrificed all those people's jobs just to get a foot up in this company."

"Let's be very clear, Nichelle—Lucas is my man now. You can't know anything for a fact about my man. Whatever you two used to have is no longer relevant."

Nichelle pushed a chair out of her way and walked toward Ronnie. "Your man? You grimy bitch! You slither and scrape your way to my sloppy seconds, then boast like you haven't gotten ahead in life by laying on your back? I know the real you, Ronnie!"

"You know what your problem is, Nichelle? You're still a victim even at this level. You want to blame everyone for the choices you made. Yes, I'm with Lucas, and he loves it. Did I take him away from you? No, you pushed him out of your life. All men are dogs, Nichelle, and if you don't feed your dog, you can't be surprised when he's in the neighbor's trash looking for food."

Nichelle's eyes cut like a dagger as she glared at Ronnie, moving ever closer to her. "And that's all you'll ever be, Ronnie: trash, basura, garbage wrapped in a Chanel suit." Nichelle turned around and walked away before she did something she regretted. As she was walking out the door. Ronnie's voice pierced her eardrums.

"That may be true, Nichelle, but now you no longer have a dog."

CHAPTER 30
RESPONSIBLE

"I can't let it go just yet. It's a lot of fucking money," Donovan muttered to himself as he drove down Bellfort. As much as Nichelle's words impacted him, almost half a million dollars was hard to let go, and he wasn't planning on doing it anytime soon. He needed answers, with Trouble and K.T. not being smart or bold enough, and Carlos not having a clue, any leads on finding his money died with Rico. He had to pay a visit to Rico's mom. It was the only other place outside of the usual hiding spots he could think that the money could be. Donovan pulled up and turned off the car. He wondered again if this was worth it. He finally had Nichelle again, and he could probably take his time and rebuild his life the right way. There were no more reasons to look over his shoulder. No more ghosts. He was a free man; there was no price on that. He turned the ignition back on, put the car in drive, and kept his foot on the brake. After all they had been through as a couple, it was finally an opportunity for them to write the next chapter of their life with no secrets, no agendas, nothing between them. He could finally treat her the way she deserved to be treated, the way he always wanted to. Of course, that was why he wanted the money in the first place—to treat her the way he always wanted to. She was with him for who he was—there was no question about that—but whether he wanted to admit it or not, something attracted her to a man like Lucas. He was clearly successful, and $437,000 was a step in the right direction for his own success. He parked the car and turned it off. He got out and walked to Ms. Carol's house with a shrug of his shoulders. He was right the first time. It was a lot of fucking money.

Carol Vasquez, or "Ms. Carol" as everyone knew her, was a tall, lean black woman with jet-black curly hair. She had married Armando Vasquez in the early '90s, but he was killed in a liquor store robbery gone wrong. She was a nurse at the medical center who hadn't taken a day off work in all the time Donovan knew her. A creature of routine, she would be at home tonight catching up on all the daytime TV she recorded during the week, binge watching her favorite soap opera, *Days of Our Lives*. Rico used to watch this as a child, and Donovan thought it was the most feminine thing he had ever seen him do, always teasing him about it. By the time they got to high school, both boys were fans. One of the silver linings about being locked up was he could keep up with the storyline. Several inmates watched the show, but he was one who actually enjoyed it. It brought back memories of better days with Rico and Ms. Carol.

Light from the TV illuminated the living room. "Some things never change," he said as he proceeded toward the door. The house was about thirty-five years old. A light-blue Hardie plank covered the exterior, and the same burglar bars that protected all the homes in South Acres protected this one. Donovan knocked on the door and waited.

"Who is it?" the voice on the other side of the door asked.

"It's D, Ms. Carol."

The door opened, and a tall, dark-ginger woman opened the door with a smile on her face that lit up the night. "Donovan, baby! It's so good to see you!"

Donovan walked into the home and hugged his friend's mother as she relished seeing him after all these years. She was starting to age noticeably; Donovan attributed it to the loss of both her husband and son through similar circumstances. A tear formed in his right tear duct. It was the first time since he'd been home that anyone greeted him this way. He fought his emotions back into a corner as he held on to his friend's mother a bit longer. "It's good to see you, too, Ms. Carol. How are you?"

"I'm blessed and highly favored child. I'm even better now that you're here," she responded, still holding on to the boy she knew was now a man. The two separated, and Ms. Carol kissed him on the cheek as he walked into the house. "I just got home. I was watching my soaps."

"*Days of Our Lives*?" Donovan responded.

"You know it! Come sit down! I ate a big lunch today, but I got some beef in the fridge. I can make you some tacos or a hamburger. Which one do you want?"

Even though he wasn't hungry, Donovan knew refusing her would be a wasted effort. "I'll take some tacos, Ms. Carol."

She was already in the kitchen chopping an onion to prepare either meal. Donovan examined the place. There wasn't a lot of change since he last saw it. The furniture was still the same. The house was clean but cluttered, more than usual to his recollection. Aside from a 50-inch television, there was nothing noticeably new in the home or anything to indicate Ms. Carol had any money outside of what she earned as a nurse.

"How long have you been out?" she asked.

"A few months. I would've been by sooner, but I know you have a strict schedule, and I had a lot to take care of."

"As long as you see me, that's all that matters." The aroma of onions, bell peppers, chili powder, and ground beef filled the home. Donovan forgot how good her tacos were and suddenly began to develop an appetite. The tacos were done in no time, and she brought him a plate of food and a glass of tea. "Here you go, D!" she said, placing the food in front of him as he sat in the La-Z-Boy next to hers.

"Thank you, Ms. Carol," he responded. He noticed her graying hair and frailty as she took a seat to relax. She was always a slender woman, but she was noticeably smaller, almost sickly. He began to feel guilty for not checking on her sooner. He was so fixated on getting his money and getting his life back, he never stopped to think about how Ms. Carol was dealing with Rico's death.

"You doing okay? I heard what happened to Rico. I'm so sorry."

The smile on her face evaporated with those words. "I've had good days and bad days. Work helps, and seeing you really helps. God is going to provide because he always does," she responded.

Donovan nodded in agreement as he bit into a piping-hot taco. She turned up the volume to the TV. Her smile regained some of its form. He realized that the woman in front of him was an inch away from broken. He wondered why Rico hadn't given his mother any money from his own profit from the robbery.

"Ms. Carol, I gotta be honest. I know Rico may have come into some funds before he went away. Did he try to help you out?"

She hit pause on the DVR. "Now, boy, you know better than to interrupt my soaps!" She fussed as she put down the remote to look at him. "You know, growing up, you and Rico were always good boys who made bad decisions. But you were the smart one I knew once you were gone it was just a matter of time before he did something to get himself hurt. One night he came in here and he had the receipt to the mortgage on this home in his hand. It was paid for. I slapped him and asked him where he got the money for this. He told me he made a lot of money off of music, but I knew he was lying. He sat right there in that chair you're sitting in. 'Momma, you won't have to work—I made it big now.' I looked him in the eye and I told him I didn't want no parts of anything he was doing. It wasn't of God. I told him, like I'm going to tell you right now, you need to stop all this foolishness. People work too hard, and life is too hard. You bring pain on the ones that love you. I just try to live a simple life. I got a house free and clear, but I lost my baby. So I keep working so people in that hospital never have to lose theirs."

It was bittersweet knowing Rico took care of Ms. Carol's mortgage. Since he could remember, it was always something she talked about as a burden. No longer having the bill, but losing her son, he knew the tradeoff wasn't worth it. "Promise me you'll stay out of trouble, Donovan. I can't lose you, too."

He reached for her hand and held it tightly. "I'm always going to be here for you, Ms. C." He looked at the woman who was like a mother to him—she had lost her son and her husband to crime, and he was the last connection she had to either of them. He was certain this was another dead end to his quest. There was no way she had the money, and even if she did, she would've given it to him or the church. He decided to drop the matter and enjoy her company as they watched their third episode of *Days of Our Lives* together. When the final episode went off, Donovan went to the kitchen and cleaned the dishes as Ms. Carol fell asleep. He swept the floor and wiped down the counters. As he finished, he went into the master bedroom and turned on the television. Ms. Carol could only sleep to the sound of the TV, so he wanted to make sure she would go right back to sleep when he left.

"Hey, Ms. Carol, I'm about to leave. I just wanted to let you know so you can lock the door."

She stood and yawned as she extended her arms for one final embrace. "Okay, sweetheart, it was good to see you. Don't go too long without checking in on me. You know us old folks need to hear from you from time to time."

He nodded and kissed her on the cheek. "Yes, ma'am, will do."

She opened the door to let him out. "Are you staying with that girl of yours?"

"I'm sorry?"

"That girlfriend you had. I thought she was your girlfriend."

"I'm not sure who you're talking about," Donovan said.

"Nice brown-skinned girl. Rico brought her around here about a year after you went away."

"He did?"

"Yeah, he wanted me to move out to Third Ward in that neighborhood she lives in. Said it was closer to work, and we'd be neighbors. I told him I was fine right here. Besides, why would I stay out there when they jacked up the prices the way they have? I can drive just fine."

Donovan looked blankly into Ms. Carol's face.

"Donovan, are you okay, honey?"

"Yes, ma'am, I'm... fine."

"You don't look fine honey. Are you sure?"

"I will be. I just need to go have a talk. Have a good night, Ms. Carol."

Donovan kissed her on the cheek and walked out the door before she could say anything else. He took out one of his cigarettes, lit it, and took a deep drag. He exhaled the fumes buried in his chest. "Time to go have a serious fucking talk."

She spent his money to buy the condo! That bitch knew the money was gone!

CHAPTER 31
RAMIFICATIONS

"Lucas, you need to give me a call right now. I don't know what you and your girlfriend are pulling, but this isn't what we talked about!" Nichelle barked into the phone as she walked out of the building completely flustered by the events that had just taken place. It was no surprise that Ronnie would take any opportunity to embarrass her—especially if it meant making herself look good—even at the cost of hundreds of jobs. It was a classic Ronnie Duvalle maneuver, but to have Lucas run the numbers and agree to laying off so many people was something she never thought would happen. Nichelle was completely aware that Lucas had gone out of his way in the past to save jobs in order to keep people employed. She knew the story of his mother getting laid off all too well—it was one of the things they had in common. She even heard him tell Ronnie this wasn't what he wanted to do when she overheard them talking. Was all of it a ruse to make her look bad? Was this his ultimate way to even the odds with her for hurting him the way she did? She wondered if he knew what was happening. *He had to—he crunched the numbers!* Ronnie was good, but creating an algorithm that complex wasn't her strength. Was he so angry at her that he would stoop this low in order to hurt her? She picked up the phone and called him again. His voicemail picked up.

"Lucas, this is Nichelle. We need to talk. Call me. Bye." She hung up and opened her car door. She threw her purse in the passenger seat and sat there in frustration, until her thoughts were disrupted by a knock on her window.

"Nichelle, are you okay?" Ms. Patrice was leaving for the day, but thought she'd better check on an obviously distraught coworker.

"I'm fine, Ms. Patrice. Thanks for asking."

"Okay, because I thought I saw you talking to yourself, and you know that's kind of crazy."

Hi pot, I'm kettle, Nichelle thought to herself. Suddenly, she realized Ms. Patrice would be on the layoff list. She was a hard-working woman, good at her job, but her personality made her difficult to work with. It was almost unavoidable. Her heart saddened. "It's just been a long day, Ms. Patrice. Are you doing okay?"

Nichelle knew what was coming next, but she didn't mind. Where a simple yes or no would have done, Ms. Patrice launched into one of her long dialogues about everything from why they don't have tea in the breakroom to the fact that the company should give the employees the option to work on Mondays. It was as random as she had always been. An hour passed and Nichelle never interrupted her. She knew it would be one of the last times she would be able to hear Ms. Patrice complain. Deep down she knew the lady was misunderstood. She was older than all her coworkers—a relic who just wanted to fit in.

"Okay, Ms. Patrice. I have to go now, but you have a good night," she said, finally cutting her off before the old lady gained her second wind.

"Okay, honey, I'm about to go to get my hair done. I can't miss my appointment."

It was a well-discussed fact that most people thought Ms. Patrice rolled out of bed and came to work, yet she always talked about going to get her hair done. It normally looked worse the next day than it did before she went to the beauty shop. Nichelle tried to suppress her laughter as she thought about what the woman's head would look like tomorrow.

"I'm sure it will look great," Nichelle said, trying to be encouraging and polite while ending the conversation. She started up her car and drove off. As she continued toward home, she realized she wanted a stiff drink and a stiff dick. She wanted to unwind. No, she needed to unwind. Replaying the meeting in her head, she was severely embarrassed and still in disbelief that Lucas could play a hand in blindsiding her like this. She picked up the phone to call him again, but decided against it. Right now she wanted a buzz and sex. Good sex, angry sex—the kind of sex Donovan could give her—but a buzz would have to come first. She decided to drive to Lucky's, a bar near her home. She walked in and was relieved to see her favorite bartender, Juan, was working. "What's up, Juanito!" she said as she walked in.

He saw her and nodded back. "¿Que pasa, chica?"

"Nada, papi," she replied in their usual banter. By the time she got to her seat, he had a drink poured for her. *Teriyaki Tea*, a variant on a Long Island iced tea without the usual liquors, rum, tequila, vodka triple sec, and Coke. Juan replaced the Coke and triple sec with Midori and Sprite. It only took two for her to have a buzz, but after the day she was having, she decided to play it by ear. By her fourth one, she was certain she wasn't driving home. The bar was within walking distance of her home—five minutes typically, so she had no issue leaving her car at the bar overnight. Ronnie put herself in a position to not only embarrass her, but to become senior vice president, which would mean she would now be reporting to her nemesis, a fate she could hardly conceive of let alone tolerate.

"Fuck!" she said aloud as she took a sip of what would be her fifth drink. Juan, typically light-hearted and playful, seemed to pay more attention to her than normal. The most she had ever had was three of these before she switched to water, yet she was well into drink number five. Noticing this, she decided to close out her tab. She didn't want to be judged, and besides, she had a bottle of wine at home. She could use that to throw herself her own personal pity party. "Lucas Kimble ain't shit!" she said aloud.

"Señorita, you good to get home?" Juan asked as she headed to the door.

"I'm fine, papi. I'm right down the street. I'm probably going to walk."

"Okay, have a safe night."

She paid her tab and walked out the door. She spied her car, and against her better judgment and earlier plan, got behind the wheel to drive home. It was pretty late and expecting a hangover in the morning, she didn't want to walk over here in the bright daylight. "Fuck it," she said as she started the car and drove home using the best concentration available to her. She pulled out into the street, which was empty, and began to drive. There were only two lights between her home and the bar, neither of which were ever red, until tonight. The first light was red. She decided to reach for her phone and make another call to Lucas when she slipped and dropped the phone. Since she was stopped at the light, she unbuckled her seatbelt to grab the phone. Fumbling with it, she was finally able to retrieve. As she looked up, a police squad car had pulled up in the next lane. *You have got to be fucking kidding me.* The liquor was heavy on her breath. Getting pulled over would certainly mean jail, and with the day she was having, seemed unavoidable. Slowly she pretended to try not to notice him and call Lucas. She glanced over to notice the cop was looking directly at her. *Why won't this fucking light change?* She instantly regretted the decision to drink in the first place.

"Whoop!" the cop's siren went off. She jumped in her seat, afraid he was about to pull up behind her and give her a ticket. Or worse. However, to her great relief, he drove through the light, heading off, leaving her with her regret. *You got to do better, Chelle,* she thought, thankful for the reprieve. When the light finally did change, she was able to make it home without hurting herself or others. In less than two minutes, she reached her driveway, where she noticed Donovan's car sitting outside. *Perfect.*

Donovan greeted her at the door with a rum and Coke in his hand. *Even better*, she thought as she took the glass out of his hand. "You have no idea what I've been through today." She walked in and guzzled the cocktail. "That bitch Ronnie pretty much made me look like a fool in front of everyone. To make matters worse, I'm sure Lucas helped her because she's a lazy, stupid, trifling bitch." Donovan stayed silent as she continued her monologue.

"I know you don't ever care to hear about Lucas, but he isn't the kind of guy who would double-cross someone. I know she had to have had her claws in him for him to sign off on this," she went on. "They're probably going to lay off hundreds of people and then promote the ho for doing it." Nichelle took off her earrings and shoes and began to pour both of them another drink—bourbon this time. She handed him his drink and downed her bourbon without bothering to toast.

"That's enough work for one day. You know what I need?" she asked without waiting for a response. "I need this dick!" she said as she walked over and pulled at his belt. She got the belt loose before he pushed her hands away. "Donovan, I'm not in the mood to play. I want you, and I want you right now."

"You want me, huh?"

"Yes, so quit playing."

"Okay, I'll give you what you want if you answer me this one question."

"Damn it, D! Okay, what is it? I'm horny!"

Donovan downed his bourbon like a shot and put the glass on the counter. "Where in the fuck is my money?"

CHAPTER 32
THE REVELATION, PART ONE

"I don't know what you're talking about," she replied. It was a lie, and they both knew it.

"Babygirl, almost five hundred thousand dollars of my money. Where is it?"

"Donovan, I—"

Before she could respond, he put his fist through a wall. "Be very careful about your next words, Nichelle. I know Rico would never spend my money. And I now know you and his mother knew about the money before he was killed. He hid it with a loved one for sure. And since my momma don't have it, and his momma don't have it, I'm going to ask again—where in the fuck is my money?" His temper flared to the point of explosiveness. Nichelle had seen him like this in the streets before, but he had never once been this upset with her.

"I...I spent it."

Donovan's eyes widened as if a train were about to hit him. "You did what?" he asked in disbelief.

"I spent the money, Donovan," she reiterated.

"How much of it did you spend?"

"All of it."

Bam! He threw his fist into the wall again. "You spent four hundred and thirty-seven thousand dollars of money I sat in jail for? Motherfucker!" he screamed as he pounded the wall again. Bam! "And what did you spend it on, Babygirl? Just what in the fuck did you spend my money on?"

She didn't answer him. She didn't have to answer—it was all around him. He started looking at the home she bought and how nice everything was. The new prices of the neighborhood. The black Audi in the parking lot. And not once had she complained about her student loans. That was a conversation they had weekly before he was locked up. It all came into clarity. The money he went to jail for—the money he killed for—the money he set aside for both of them to start over and have a new life—she had already taken advantage of. It was the final indicator she indeed had moved on with her life. He took out a pack of Camels and shifted it to find a cigarette to put in his mouth while she sat against the wall silently.

"So this is what four hundred thousand dollars looks like," he said aloud in a half chuckle as he lit the cigarette and took a deep drag. "I mean this would be comical if it wasn't my fucking life!" He turned to her and said, "Same old selfish-ass Babygirl." He noticed both her hands were behind her back, so he walked a little closer and said, "What are you hiding now?" Before he could take another step, he knew the answer. Electricity filled his body. While he was ranting, she found her Taser in case she had to subdue him.

"Motherfucker!" he yelled, his body in agonizing pain as she put him down. He grabbed her by the neck and shoved her as hard as he could to get the Taser out of her hand and turn it off. There was a loud shattering of glass as she crash-landed through her coffee table. "What in the hell is wrong with you?" he screamed while Nichelle's adrenaline took over. She scrambled to the counter where she had been keeping a gun since Donovan returned. He raced to cut her off, his body slowed by the voltage that had coursed through his system.

"Get out!" she screamed at the top of her lungs. She turned around to point the gun at him, only to find he was already standing over her clutching her wrists.

"A gun, Nichelle?" He knocked it out of her hand, then slapped her across the face. "Do you have any idea what you're doing right now?

That money was supposed to build a life for both of us. That money was my freedom. I was out the game!" He slapped her again. This time, blood trickled from her nose. "This was my ticket out of this life. This was *our* ticket! I did the time, and you spent every goddamn dime!" He grabbed her forcefully by her neck again. "This is why you stopped accepting my calls, stopped writing me back, stopped seeing me?" he asked, releasing her neck.

"Yes, okay," she replied after gasping air into her lungs. "Fuck, I couldn't look you in the eyes anymore. At first I thought to myself you didn't do anything wrong so I waited, but when I got all that money, I felt betrayed. You lied to me, and so you got whatever you deserved. I was going to pay you back if you found out, but you weren't supposed to get out so soon."

The rage exploded in him as he put his fist through the wall again and again, glass shattering as picture frames hit the floor. "If you were going to pay me back, how much do you have?"

"Four thousand."

Donovan looked her in the eyes blankly, emotionless, processing her words for several moments. He turned around and walked over to the gun and picked it up and then came back and lifted Nichelle off the ground, pressing her against the wall with his weight against her. He took the gun and held it in the air. "Nichelle, I want you to listen to me very carefully. You need to take this motherfucking gun and keep it with you at all times because I'm about to snap. The only reason you're still breathing is I'm never going to jail again. So I'm going to leave now. If I walk back through that door at any time tonight, shoot me—and you better not miss." He pressed the gun firmly into her hand. "Because if you don't, I'm going to kill you. Do you feel what I'm saying right now?"

She nodded as he released her body, leaving the gun in her sweaty, strained palm. As he made his way to the door, he stopped and turned back. Looking through her he said, "One last thing—if the cops think I had anything to do with this, you already know what time it is."

She understood him perfectly. At this point, he had lost everything waiting for him on the outside. The money was important, but what he was now able to accept was much more chilling—the girl he loved evolved into a woman he hated. He lost her the night Rico gave her his share of the money. The only thing he had left was his freedom, and he would kill for that.

As he walked out the door, she looked for her cellphone, clutching the pistol in her trembling hand. A constant stream of tears rolled from her face. She located the phone through the shattered glass on the floor where the coffee table once was. Eyeing the long crack in the screen, she quickly unraveled in the corner of her condo. She slumped to the floor and sobbed openly, head between her knees. Her phone screen shimmered when her tears hit the crack. She took several deep breaths to compose herself. As she picked up the phone, she sorted through her contacts. The *Place Emergency Call* feature stood out. She remembered Donovan's words, and so she continued scrolling through her phone, finally pressing "Call". As the phone rang, she began to lose composure. It didn't get any easier when the voice on the other end said, "Hello?"

"Hello," she said, choking back tears. "I need your help."

CHAPTER 33
THE REVELATION, PART TWO

"So I take it the meeting was a success," Lucas said as he walked into the living room, kissing his lover on the cheek.

"Better than expected. How was your day away?"

"I can't complain. It was ... rewarding," Lucas responded. "So the Board is okay with 14.3 percent?"

"They loved it. I'm a shoo-in for senior vice president."

"Good," Lucas said, starting to get nervous.

"Are you alright?" Ronnie asked, noticing his behavior.

"I'm cool, baby. I just wanted to see you ... no, I had to see you today. I mean tonight."

"Are you sure you're okay, Lucas? You're acting odder than normal," Ronnie asked for the second time.

"Baby, I'm fine," he said unconvincingly.

"Then what couldn't wait until tomorrow? You know I'm getting feedback from the presentation tomorrow, so I still need to be sharp."

Lucas pulled his lover in for a kiss. "I just wanted to wish you luck —not that you need it."

"We did great work together, making my promotion a formality at this point. I can't imagine your firm not doing the same." He leaned in for a kiss to congratulate her, but she pushed him away. "You're not spending the night," she said coyly. "I have to be focused."

He grinned, knowing "You're not spending the night" was all but an invitation to stay the night with her. He had gotten to know her so well that when she said things, she typically wanted the opposite. "Okay, well, I'll just stay a little while if that's alright with you," he responded, knowing that's exactly how the next step in their song and dance was supposed to go. He looked at her in her satin nightgown, freshly showered from leaving the gym. The scent of *Bond Number Nine Park Avenue South* lingered in the air. She had no intention of going to sleep anytime soon. Nor did he. The night was so young, and there was so much to talk about. He walked over to the kitchen and poured himself a glass of Johnny Walker Black. He drained the glass in two gulps and poured himself another.

"Lucas, I'm going to ask for the third time—"

"I'm fine, Veronica. I'm just ... I'm just unwinding." He knew she knew better, so he walked over to the side of the couch and sat down. She was still examining him, trying to decipher the truth between his words and his actions. His nervous excitement made it apparent he wasn't himself. He had this planned out in his head, but it was unraveling in front of him. He wanted Ronnie to be his wife, and he wanted to have her on her terms as long as the one condition of the rest of their lives could be fulfilled. He wanted to tell her that right now without planning and calculation, but it wasn't his nature—he planned and calculated everything, especially his words. He had written his proposal word for word right after he picked up the ring. He kept the note inside the box in case he forgot what he wanted to say. But beyond that, so she would never forget, he wanted her to know how she made him feel. How he always felt when they were together. He knew she had to feel the same way. No one loves as intimately as they did without bearing any emotion. It wasn't possible for anyone with a soul. He wanted to propose tomorrow after her promotion, but in the off-chance she did not get the promotion, he couldn't take the risk. He didn't want to compete with disappointment. The emotional conflict would be too great. No, it had to be tonight. It had to be now.

He laid down on the couch, knocking over her purse. He realized the liquor was now

starting to relax his inhibition. He put the contents of her oversized handbag back where they belonged while Ronnie made herself a glass of wine. "You're hiding something, Lucas. You're not very good at keeping secrets, so you might as well tell me now."

"I'm not as good as you apparently," he retorted. The remark caught her off-guard since she had been prepping herself to have sex with him the entire time he was in her home, even when he accidently knocked over her purse over and placed the belongings back. She then turned around and there lay the pregnancy test, one of several she had taken after the meeting.

"Lucas, it is ... well, it's a pregnancy test. I'm with child." She took a gulp of wine.

"You're having a baby, and you're drinking?" he said jumping off of the couch, feeling an entirely new set of emotions.

"All rise for Judge Mental" she replied. "Yes, I have a glass of wine in my hand, not a heroin needle. It's been a long week, and I deserve this glass of wine."

"Why? Because you don't plan on keeping the baby?" Ronnie sat silently as Lucas continued. "I think you thought I was asking you about the pregnancy test, which I'll admit is still a shock, no question, but I was asking you about this."

He lifted a paper for her appointment to Planned Parenthood. Ronnie's face went flush, her eyes wide, looking at the paper, then back at him. "What the hell, Veronica?"

"Lucas, don't go there." She walked closer to him with her glass of wine, taking another sip before putting it down. "You want to know the truth?"

"Yes, the truth," he responded, as if he expected her to lie without encouragement.

"To tell you the truth, I worked damn hard, too damn hard to get where I am. I've worked eighteen-hour days, done unspeakable things, busted my ass more than anyone, and tomorrow it's all coming together, so I'll be damned if some kid gets in the way of a lifetime worth of work, Lucas, Yes, I'm going to Planned Parenthood. I do not intend to keep this child."

"Veronica you can't—"

"Yes I can," she fired off before silence fell over the room.

"Don't I have a say?"

"No, you don't have a say, Lucas! Believe it or not, it's my body! It's my uterus. It's my egg. The only thing you did was carelessly put us in this situation to begin with, so this is how I'm going to handle your mistake!"

The words stung like a thousand wasps all hitting him in his heart at the same time. His eyes no longer told the story of excitement, just pain. Ronnie looked at him, the man she could now say she loved, for whatever she knew about the word, and recognized his hurt, it was similar to the look in his eyes on the first day they met.

"Lucas, I never wanted children. I just want to be CEO. I want money, power, and on occasion, sex. That's..."

"Veronica," he interrupted, "you never wanted love—you told me that yourself. Do you remember?" Her eyes locked on his, confirming she did. "And yet here we are in love with one another, and don't tell me that you don't love me because I know you do. Everyone told me you were all kinds of wrong for me. I had just gotten out of a situation where I was blindsided, and then you almost proved them right. But you know what? I fought for this, I fought for *us*. Every time someone told me why we shouldn't be together, warned me about what kind of person you are, when you told me love wasn't an option, I kept going because I knew deep inside there was something special, something life-changing, happening between us." Lucas walked over to Ronnie and held her hand. As he placed their interlocked fingers on her stomach, he looked passionately into her deep green eyes. "That life-changing moment, our love, is inside you right now, and I'm asking you ... no, I am begging you to *please* reconsider. You want to be CEO, fine. I will quit my job and raise this baby. I will fight for us always. I'll do anything and everything it takes to make you happy. You know that. You can have it all—even things you don't want."

His phone objected to his train of thought. Lucas looked at the caller ID.

"Well, aren't you going to answer it?" Ronnie said, looking for a break in the emotion. Realizing she needed one, he placed a kiss on her neck and picked up the phone.

"Hello?"

"Hello? I need your help," the voice on the other end said.

"Nichelle, it's not a good time."

"Lucas... please, I... I don't know who else to call."

He had not talked to her in some time, but she was clearly distraught, sobbing through the phone. Ronnie, who could hear her from several feet away, leaned in and listened intently.

"Calm down. Tell me what's wrong."

"I'm scared. There was a fight, and I... I just don't know."

"Wait, what? Are you okay? Tell me what happened."

"I know this is crazy after all I've done, but you're the only one I feel I can talk to. I need to see you."

Lucas looked at the phone and looked at Ronnie, who, in turn, rolled her eyes in disgust. He put the phone on mute and said to Ronnie, "She would've never called if it wasn't serious. Not where things stand with us now."

Ronnie, who was clearly against the idea, felt this was the lesser of two evils. She could either continue a conversation she did not want to have with him, or have him play hero to his ex-girlfriend. She decided the latter gave her the best escape from her own predicament for the night. "There's a ho that needs to be saved Captain, duty calls," she responded, agreeing reluctantly to let him go. He picked up the conversation. "I'm on my way. I'll be there shortly."

As he hung up, he pulled Ronnie in closely, kissed her on her lips, and said, "I love you with all my heart, soul, body, and essence. The only reason I'm leaving is because it seemed like a matter of life and death. Just please promise me we'll be able to talk about this before you make any decisions."

"Lucas, I'm sure she's just being the victim again. You shouldn't give in to that woman."

"I don't think it's that kind of situation."

"You don't think, or you don't know? She's a liar, you know. You know firsthand you can't trust anything that comes out of that woman's mouth. She's pathological."

"I just heard the most important news of my life. I don't want to leave, Veronica, but I have to."

"We should talk about the meeting today. I—"

"We can talk about everything when I get back, but most importantly our child. Please keep an open mind to what I have to say."

She couldn't resist his sincerity. As much as she loved him and wanted no parts of raising a child, she agreed to his request. He kissed her one more time, and as he walked toward the door, he said, "I'm always going to fight for us, Veronica. Never doubt that."

And then he was gone.

CHAPTER 34
REGRETS, PART ONE

Ronnie had just avoided a conversation with Lucas she never planned on having because she never planned on telling him *I'm carrying your child*. It was a simple strategy really, in fact it only had two steps:

1. Avoid him like the plague after the procedure.
2. Claim she was sick or too busy with work.

In short, do what Nichelle did, only better. Yet, for some reason, he was not only aware she was pregnant, he wanted her to *keep* said child. "How could you fuck this up, Duvalle?" she said aloud. The audaciousness of his request was jarring, only outdone by the mere fact she was now cohabitating her body. She walked over to the kitchen table and picked up the glass of wine she had been nursing—a glass that would've normally been her third by now. And yet, she was only halfway through her first. What was going on? Was Lucas in her head? She looked at the glass and took a giant gulp. She had fought tooth and nail to become senior vice president; scratched and clawed her way to the top of the mountain. Now there was no one in the way. She earned this drink. And no boyfriend, no ex-girlfriend, and no fetus were going to get in the way of relishing her accomplishments. She finished the glass and began to pour another, as if willing herself to become intoxicated. "Such bullshit," she muttered to herself. All of it was bullshit—meeting the man she'd finally open up to; his ex-girlfriend not being able to handle her own issues; the pregnancy. She didn't subscribe to any of it. She recalled the time she told Lucas, *"Love, the happily ever after kind, is bullshit to me,"* and she was happy with that. Happy with her professional life, her sex life, her mate. Could she once again find an unexpected joy? Could parenthood do that for her?

"I'm not going to be anyone's baby momma," she said aloud. The conversation she was having with herself was beginning to take legs. She thought about raising this child on her own. How many times had she been abandoned as a child by her mother, her stepfather, and her sister? And how many times did she have to find a way to make things work? She would just do the same thing to her child. She might not want to, but she knew she would. She'd always place work above her child. She was no good as a person. Certainly not good enough to be a mother.

But Lucas was a *great* man, by any standard, and he'd be a phenomenal father. He wouldn't allow her to raise their child alone. He just offered to quit his job for the sake of her career. He meant those words. Could she truly have it all? Was it worth finding out? What made this man so certain that everything, even the unseen and the unknown, was going to work out? What made him say, "I'll always fight for us, Veronica?"

Questions flooded her mind as she poured herself another glass of wine. When she put down the bottle, she rested her palms on the countertop and stared at the glass. She was utterly disinterested in drinking it, and she couldn't understand why. She didn't want to understand why. She decided to pick up the phone and call Lucas. She grabbed her cell and called him, but the phone went straight to voicemail. She called again. Still no answer. Ronnie thought about how hurt Lucas was before he left. Maybe he was avoiding her. Maybe his sudden *need* to see Nichelle was his way out of her home, even out of her life. It sounded silly, but the thought kept growing like a rampant weed. She recalled how hurt he was when he first met her, and how she, for all intents and purposes, took him from Nichelle because he was vulnerable. The same hurt was in his eyes as he walked out the door tonight. Did she just "return to sender" her lover?

"Lucas would never," she said, but she knew that was untrue. The fact is, Lucas *would* leave his lover if he felt betrayed, or if he needed comfort. She was a living witness to that. She also knew it was just a matter of time before he knew about her actual betrayal at work. *What am I doing? Why am I so damn determined to undo every shred of happiness I've discovered over the last few months? When am I going to learn to be happy?* Was this quest for power more important than the joy of love she was discovering? Ronnie picked up the glass of wine and poured it into the sink. She walked into the bedroom to put on something to wear outside, then searched for Nichelle's address on her phone. She created a route on her phone before concentrating on what to wear. There was a pink Under Armour sports top and matching gray-and-pink-outlined spandex bottom. It was the outfit she was going to wear to the gym before she decided on wearing the black spandex pants and green sports bra. She slid out of her nightgown and put on the outfit to show her physique, in case there was any question what Lucas would be walking away from. As she got fully dressed, she looked at her profile in the mirror. Impressed by her posterior, she nonetheless felt the need to adjust her sports top to accentuate her breasts. "A baby isn't going to ruin all of this," she said with confidence. She slipped her sneakers on and grabbed her keys and wallet.

Fully dressed, she stopped one last time to consider her actions. Maybe she was overreacting to all of this. She had never been the type of woman to chase a man under any circumstances. Yet here she was about to leave her home to pursue a man whose child she didn't want to carry. She had never been the type of woman to care what anyone thought of her, let alone who she was sharing a bed with. They were all just there for her pleasure—the ones who could please her, that is—and yet she realized at this moment how deep the rabbit hole went for her love for Lucas. She had never been one to fall in love, yet she was now in love, no question about it. His words came back to her. "I'll always fight for us Veronica." Was her pride now getting in the way of doing the same thing? Was she *chasing a man,* or fighting for the first person she'd ever truly loved? The question was rhetorical. She knew the answer. She picked up her phone and located her GPS app and hit *Start Route* on her phone. Her destination was twenty-six minutes away.

CHAPTER 35
REGRETS, PART TWO

As Lucas parked his car outside Nichelle's home, a storm of emotions swirled around him. He looked at his phone. He heard the ring on his drive over, but decided to ignore it. He was trying to process all his thoughts and emotions. Ronnie was pregnant, and he was going to propose tonight. It truly was the life he wanted, but after her outburst, he was sure it wasn't what *she* wanted. As much as it hurt him, he understood the pregnancy was unplanned and their life up to this point was happenstance. He wanted to be objective and consider her point of view, yet all he could truly see was that the woman he wanted to be his wife did not want to carry their child. Whatever the reason, he couldn't see beyond that singular thought. He had better give that some space before he said something he regretted. As he got out the car, his attention turned to his former lover, the person he would've gladly accepted this life with before her indiscretions. Why would she be calling him now, after all that transpired—the lying, cheating, and heartbreak? More importantly, why was he still running to the rescue? Did he still have some residual feelings for her? Was this chapter in his life truly over? The question was a valid one. He had been in love with Nichelle, at least until he found out about her ex-boyfriend. Those feelings were raw for a long time, but it was soon after their breakup that he began dating Ronnie. In fact, this was the first time he was truly able to sit back and see the situation for the whirlwind it was—he needed to see Nichelle. He needed to see if his feelings were genuine or a byproduct of their breakup. He needed closure. As he walked up the steps, he noticed the door to her townhouse wasn't all the way closed. His senses heightened, he realized he could be walking into genuine trouble, particularly if her fight was with Donovan. Donovan let him go before, but warned Lucas never to come back.

He gently creaked the door open. "Nichelle?" he exclaimed. There was no answer. He walked into the home, peering down the hallway. Moving cautiously, he noticed some broken glass in the living room. He retreated quickly to the hallway closet door, opened it slowly, and pulled out the aluminum baseball bat he got her for her protection. He held it behind his back and crept down the hallway. "Nichelle?" he exclaimed again, slowly making his way to the living room. The closer he moved toward the living area, the more debris he noticed. He started to see cracks in the paint of her walls, followed by fist-sized holes. He followed more cracks until they led to a crater of a hole in the wall. As he walked into the living room, he was dismayed by the damage. There was no other way to describe the living room but destroyed. He gripped the bat tighter, bringing it to his side in case of attack. He continued to scan the area for Nichelle, but could see nothing.

Click.

"Don't you fucking move."

The sound of the gun cocking and the commanding tone made him freeze. He slowly turned in the direction of the voice. Sitting in the corner was a badly beaten, bloodied Nichelle, holding a gun pointed at his chest.

"Nichelle, what happened?" Lucas said as he walked closer.

"I said don't move!" she screamed as tears flowed from her face, mixing with the blood from her nose and lip to form a pink drip from her chin. He could tell she was distraught and afraid.

"Nichelle, I'm going to put this bat down and walk over to you, okay? It's going to be okay, I promise you."

"It's never going to be okay!" she shouted. "What... Why..." She couldn't finish her thought. Lucas placed the bat on the floor and slowly made his way to Nichelle in the corner.

"Nichelle, look in my eyes. It's going to be fine, I *promise* you. Just put the gun down, and we will figure this out together." Nichelle looked in his eyes. As she did, a renewed stream of tears flowed down her cheeks. She dropped the gun and slumped in the corner, openly bawling. Lucas walked over to her and put both his arms around her. "It's alright," he repeated, intensifying his hold on her. She melted into his arms, seeking comfort, her blood and tears saturating his shirt. She regained shreds of her composure, attempting to speak though the sobbing.

"How did we get here, Luke? How in the hell did we get here?" He stood, silently processing the events that led to all of this. "I—I... just... want... everything to... go back to ... how it used to be," she said, catching her breath and pressing her head against his chest.

"Donovan did this to you?" It was a question he already knew the answer to; a question he wanted to avoid because he didn't want her to relive it. But he had to fill the silence after her statement.

"I did something terrible, and he found out."

Lucas sat silently, though he wanted to say, *You did something terrible to me, but I didn't put holes in your wall* or *Did you cheat on him, too?* but now wasn't the time or place. "Let me get you some ice for your face. It's going to swell if I don't." He slowly got up and got ice from the ice machine in her fridge. Wrapping it in his already stained shirt, he walked back and placed it on Nichelle's bruised face. She embraced his hand and looked at him as if to say more than thank you. "Tell me what happened," he said.

Nichelle removed the ice from her face, choosing to speak through the pain. "I never told you why Donovan was gone. Truth is, Donovan robbed banks for a living. Him and his partner were pretty good at it, too. The last job went bad and he got caught up on a robbery charge, but no one could prove he did it. They never found the money, so they put charges together they could prove and sentenced him to seven years in prison."

"Okay, I'm with you so far. but what does that have to do with what happened now?"

"They never found the money, but Donovan had it. Before he went to jail, he gave the money to his partner, Rico. They were like brothers, and Donovan trusted him completely. Problem was, Rico got picked up on a separate charge, so before Rico went to prison, he gave me Donovan's share of the cash."

"How much?"

"$437,000," she responded. Lucas's eyes opened wide. "And I spent every penny of it."

"So, let me guess. When Donovan found out you spent the money, this is the end result."

Nichelle nodded. Lucas sat back, surprised by the tale he just heard. A new set of emotions joined the mixed bag he was already juggling. The woman he thought he knew was a complete stranger.

"You must think the worst of me," she said, already thinking the worst of herself.

"I didn't know you then," he responded, "but I believe you've grown. We can't pick our circumstances in life, and we can't always choose who we love. Sometimes those two things wipe out any rational decision we might normally make."

Nichelle climbed to her feet, picking up the ice pack from the floor. "I still love you, Lucas, I know I've done some terrible things, but I hope we can at least talk about a possible future together."

Lucas, dismayed by her words, stood up, too, and held her hand nursing her swollen lips. "Nichelle, I have to be honest with you—I have no interest in rekindling a relationship."

Nichelle was hurt, but not surprised "I think I just needed to hear it from you," she said as he looked into her eyes. "Do you love her?"

"I do," he responded.

"Why?" she retorted. Lucas was silent for a moment, but decided to answer the question.

"Because she's honest, and she's cruel, and she's manipulative, but she's always herself with me." was the gentlest way he could say it. The words still stung Nichelle like a hornet, and Lucas decided it was best to leave the current conversation. "The point is ... she makes me happy."

Nichelle made her way into the hallway. Lucas picked up the gun with one hand and the bat with the other. He walked over to help her put things in order. "I know you two are never going to get along, but the fact is you don't have to. If you care for me like you just said you did, then you need to understand I'm happy right now."

Nichelle sat silently as she nodded. "I'm a good person, Lucas."

"You are, but sometimes good people do bad things."

"So is that why you changed the plan at our meeting?"

"What are you talking about?" he responded. "I didn't change anything. The meeting should've reflected the fourteen percent reduction." His words were cut off by footsteps at the front door. Lucas signaled Nichelle to hide while he investigated. He put the bat down and started toward the hallway with the pistol.

Lucas turned to see what was going on in the hallway. He pointed the gun in the direction of the sound and made out two bodies in the darkness. One of the bodies screamed, "Do not move!" and Lucas yelled back, "Come out of the shadows before I shoot!" The remaining figure screamed, "Gun!"

Two shots rang out, both hitting Lucas in his chest. He flew backwards, smashing his head against a piece of metal from the broken table before hitting the tile floor.

CHAPTER 36
REMORSE

Nichelle screamed in terror, "Lucas!"

Instinctively, she scrambled to the body when the shooters stepped into the light from the hallway. They were police officers, obviously called by one of the neighbors because of the previous disturbance. "Ma'am, don't move! Show me your hands!"

Nichelle lifted her hands in the air. "Officer, I live here!"

"Is there anyone else here? We got a call of a disturbance at this address. Are you okay?"

"You don't understand!" Nichelle screamed anxiously. "This man had nothing to do with it. I called him to help me after the break in!"

The officer assessing the situation put his gun away while his partner checked Lucas for a pulse. "He's still breathing!" he shouted back.

The young Hispanic officer talking to Nichelle got on his radio. "This is Officer Santiago dispatched to Apple Grove Lane. We need a bus here now. Civilian down."

"What did you do?" Nichelle shrieked as she began to cry again.

"Ma'am, I need you to calm down."

But Nichelle refused. "I won't fucking calm down! You just shot an innocent man!"

A noise rose up from the floor. Lucas was trying to talk as blood leaked out of his body. "Call Ver—" he said as he began to fade.

"Lucas!" Nichelle screamed as she pushed her way past the officer in front of her.

"Veron—" He couldn't make out any more than that. Nichelle knew he wanted her to call Ronnie, but she ignored the request.

The paramedics arrived on the scene minutes later and hurried to check his vitals. By now, several other officers were on the scene talking to Santiago and his partner about the shot. "Did you identify yourself?" one of the officers whispered, though Nichelle overheard. "No, he did not! He screamed 'gun' and started to shoot!" she yelled, making sure everyone heard.

"Ma'am, we need you outside," one of the officers demanded.

Nichelle defiantly said, "This is my home, paid for in full. I have more right to be here than any of you, YOU get outside!"

Officer Santiago, the one who pulled the trigger, seemed worried. Nichelle glared at him. "You did not follow protocol, and you're going to cover this up! If he dies, this innocent man's blood is on your hands!"

The paramedics had Lucas stabilized and were rolling him out of the home. Nichelle walked outside with him, into the bright flashing lights of half a dozen police cars. Several of her neighbors were being held back by the police. Nichelle felt numb to the entire experience. Just two hours ago, she was on her way to have sex and a drink for what was seemingly a hard day. Now she was living a nightmare.

"Let me through, damn it!" It was the voice of her nemesis, the absolute last thing she wanted to hear at this moment. She didn't bother to look in her direction because she knew it was only a matter of time before Ronnie got what she wanted. As Nichelle made her way to the ambulance, she heard Ronnie scream, "Lucas! Oh, no, baby! Lucas!"

An officer tried to restrain her, but she was so insistent and emotional he was having a hard time doing such. Ronnie turned to Nichelle with venom in her voice. "What did you do?" Nichelle, still emotionally anxious, yelled back, "Ronnie, shut up!" She turned her attention to the paramedic. "Can I ride with him?"

The paramedic responded, "If you're not family, you can't ride."

Ronnie interjected. "I'm coming with him. I'm his—"

The paramedic cut her off. "Ma'am, he's in critical condition. You can meet us at St. Luke's Hospital."

He slammed the door, and the ambulance took off. Nichelle made her way to her car when Ronnie grabbed her. "What happened?"

Nichelle took a deep breath. As much as she despised Ronnie, she felt she deserved an explanation. "Someone broke into my house. When we started to clean up, we heard a noise and he went to check on it. It was the police, and that one over there shot him without warning." She pointed to Officer Santiago, who was leaving her house.

"You inconsiderate bitch!" Ronnie yelled. "Not bad enough that your own life is a cluster fuck, you have to drag down everyone around you all the time because you don't know how to stand on your own. You're just a parasite. In fact, the first thing I'm going to do when I get this promotion tomorrow is fire you."

Nichelle began to walk away, but Ronnie's words were too much. She turned around and hit Ronnie in the eye with a left hook, followed by several punches to the face before the officers pulled her off Ronnie. Nichelle was enraged as she screamed, "You have some fucking nerve! Lucas is shot and you're talking about your promotion? You've whored your way to the top, and now you act high and mighty because you're sleeping with my ex-man? Fuck you!"

The police restrained both of them, but that didn't stop Ronnie from shouting, "I want her prosecuted for assault."

The police, aware of the situation, decided just to restrain the women until they were able to calm down. Nichelle screamed at the cop, "Get your damn hands off me. I'm going to the hospital." The police officer let her go, but as she walked by Ronnie, who was holding her eye, she said, "You don't have to fire me. Consider that ass-whooping my letter of resignation."

Nichelle was walking to her car when the police officer stopped her. "Ma'am, we have to ask you a few more questions."

Her temper, already boiling over, left no consideration for the police. "If you want to ask me anything, you'll have to do it at the hospital. Thanks to Officer Trigger Happy over there, this may be the last few moments I get to spend with someone I care about. Excuse me." She pushed her way past the officer and got into her car. Once she turned on the engine, she sat back to process the chaos. She noticed the trail of blood that led from her home to the streets. She thought about what she told the police officers: "This may be the last few moments I get to spend with someone I care about." The words hit her hard, like a ton of bricks. She would cry if she wasn't out of tears. She thought about Donovan—why didn't she tell the cops it was him who actually caused all the damage and chaos? She wasn't really afraid for her life. Numb to the pain, she backed her Audi out of its parking spot and headed for St Luke's, all the while praying that Lucas was somehow okay.

The medical center district was not far from her home. She had to only cross 288 as a major highway in order to be on the outskirts. Parking was an entirely different scenario, however. There were so many hospitals, many of which shared parking, that it became a labor to find something reasonably close to St. Luke's. She lucked out as a car was leaving just as she circled the emergency room entrance for the second time. She quickly put on her blinker and waited until they pulled out. As she ran toward the doors, she saw the paramedics who brought Lucas in. She crossed over to them and flagged the one who rode in back. "Excuse me! Excuse me!"

The dark-skinned, long-bearded paramedic responded, "Hey, your boyfriend is going into surgery now. He was breathing on his own."

A weight lifted off of Nichelle's shoulders. "Thank you," she said and turned toward the entrance.

"Look, I know I just met you and all," the paramedic continued, "but I've answered a lot of emergency calls. From my experience, holes in the wall don't come from a break-in. That's personal. If the guy in surgery didn't give you those bruises, you should tell the cops who did. If he did, then let's just say I don't feel bad whatever happens to him."

Nichelle, at her wits end, had no filter for her comments anymore. "What's your name, sir?"

"Greg. Greg Tribbett."

"Well, Mr. Tribbett, I appreciate your two cents, but you should mind your own damn business."

As she stormed off, Greg shouted after her, "I have a daughter."

Nichelle stopped, allowing him to walk over. "You're right, I should mind my business but... it's just that I have a daughter, and if she was in a situation where she was being abused, or couldn't talk to anyone or was afraid, I would hope she could come to me. I know you don't know me, and I should have just kept my mouth shut, but since she's been in my life, I see these kinds of things totally different, you know?"

Nichelle said, "I apologize for snapping. It's just been a stressful day. I really have to go, though. Thank you for your concern."

Greg reached into his pocket. "This is strange, I know, and I am in no way trying to pick you up, but here's my card. If you need to talk, I want to listen."

Nichelle cautiously took the card, totally unsure of this man's motives. "Thanks." she said drily. She turned to walk off, looking back in his direction just to determine what his true motive was. She dismissed the thought as she refocused on finding Lucas's location and information. As she walked through the hospital, she was greeted by a nurse.

"Miss, have a seat. The doctor will be with you shortly." The nurse quickly retrieved an ice pack and handed it to Nichelle.

Realizing the nurse thought she was a patient, Nichelle clarified her situation. "No, I'm here looking for Lucas Kimble."

The nurse responded, "You're not here for yourself?" staring at the swelling on Nichelle's face.

"No," she said, her voice muffled behind the ice pack. "Lucas Kimble was brought in not that long ago. I need a status on him."

The nurse responded, "Are you related to him?"

"Yes, I'm his sister." Nichelle didn't want to lie, but it was hardly the worst sin of the night, and at the rate her day was going, it was the only way she could get close to him. The nurse directed her to the waiting room where the doctor would inform her about the surgery.

As she headed to the waiting room, a voice called out to her, "Ms. Myers!"

She felt like a powder keg when she recognized who it was. She turned around. "What in the hell do you want?"

Officer Santiago stood there, not three feet in front of her. "I wanted to check on Mr. Kimble. Have you heard anything?"

She couldn't tolerate his question. "I don't believe this shit. You shot the man in cold blood, and now you want to see if he's going to live? Why? So in case he somehow survives, you can finish the job?"

"He had a gun, Ms. Myers."

"Yes, for our protection, but you didn't stop to do anything but pull the trigger."

Officer Santiago stepped closer to Nichelle and looked her in the eyes. "It's an unfortunate circumstance. On the force, they teach you to protect yourself, and if you feel threatened, above all else, make sure you come back alive." Santiago paced as if to gather his thoughts. "If he were a bad guy, I'd have no problem blowing him away. But I never signed up to hurt innocent people. I hope to be able to tell him that myself soon."

Nichelle started to cry. Officer Santiago tried to console her until she pushed him away. He stood there waiting until she eventually composed herself. Once she caught her breath, he reached into his pocket. "Look, there's no good way to do this, but I figured he'd want you to have this."

The officer pulled out a Tiffany's box with a bow smeared with blood. Nichelle put her hand out, and Santiago placed it in her palm. "I didn't open it, but I also didn't think it should get caught up in evidence for the next three weeks. The very least I could do is give it to you." Nichelle stood there stunned. She knew Santiago didn't have a clue, nor should he. Lucas was going to propose to Ronnie, possibly this very night.

"When you're up to it, you're going to have to come to the station and answer questions about the break-in."

Santiago's words snapped her back to reality. "Oh, yes, thanks, officer." She was certain he interpreted her tone as disdain for him and not for its true nature—shocked about her ex-lover's intentions. She turned around and walked away, curious about the object now in her possession. She found the nearest restroom and stood in front of the mirror near the sink. She opened the box delicately so she could recreate its bow. Inside the box was a smaller box that contained the ring. She was about to open the lesser box when a note fell out of the top of the larger container. Nichelle picked up and unfolded the note. It was Lucas's proposal. He had never been good with big moments, so it wasn't rare for him to memorize what he was going to say before he presented something so important. Yet, beyond that, Lucas just loved words, more so than the average person. Lucas wrote this on a card that Ronnie could always have. It revealed the true nature of his feelings for her. Nichelle scoffed at herself. In the back of her mind, she truly believed there was a chance for her and Lucas to get back together. They had incredible chemistry while they were an item, and this made her believe that somewhere inside him, if she worked hard enough, he still had feelings for her. Maybe they could recapture what they had. Now she clung to no such hope. The words on the paper clearly and precisely indicated where Lucas stood in regards to his feelings for Ronnie, and in essence, herself. One little note extinguished all hope.

She looked to the bathroom stall, and then back at the note. She hated Ronnie and felt she deserved nothing good in her life. Flushing the ring down the toilet along with the note would be what she deserved. She was cruel, heartless, and devious—everything Lucas said she was in their last talk. Nichelle then thought about the attention to detail he must have paid to purchase that ring for her; the man hours he spent in the store and online and asking questions. She recalled his smile when he did thoughtful things for her. As she daydreamed, she thought of his massages, his consideration, and the way he always wore his heart on his sleeve. You could tell his mood by looking into his eyes. She thought about how happy his eyes looked when he described Ronnie. "If you love me like you say you do, you'll understand."

She looked at the stall once again before packing up the box in its original package and placing it in her purse.

pawn that shit and get
Donovan some money

CHAPTER 37
RECONCILE

After spending her time at Nichelle's home gathering all the information she could about the incident and threatening to call everyone from the chief of police to the mayor, Ronnie eventually settled down and became the solution-oriented person she was paid to be in crisis situations. She called Lucas's parents on the way to the hospital to let them know what she knew. His mother answered the phone. In a calm voice, Veronica said, "Mrs. Kimble, it's Veronica. May I speak to your husband please?"

Lucas's mother responded, "Veronica? Where is Lucas? Why are you calling?"

Ronnie knew this wasn't going to go over well. Lucas's mother was extremely protective of her "Little Luke," and Ronnie was well aware she wasn't very fond of her. Still, she had no time to go back and forth with her. "Natalie, I need you to put Walter on the phone right now." Ronnie's determined tone made the other end of the phone go silent. Ronnie thought Natalie might have hung up, until an older man's voice resumed the conversation.

"Hello, Ronnie?"

"Hi, Walter. Are you sitting down?"

"What's going on? Is everything okay?"

Ronnie took a deep breath, then very systematically relayed what she knew. "No, sir, everything is not okay." When she finished her story, the phone went silent. She could hear Lucas's mother sobbing openly in the background.

"Mr. Kimble?"

"Yes, sweetheart, I'm here. Is he—?"

"He was alive when the ambulance got here. I didn't get to ride with him, but he's at St. Luke's Hospital. I'm on my way there now. They'll only give updates to family, so I'm suggesting you meet me there."

"We're on our way," and with that, the phone went dead.

Ronnie arrived at the hospital and was able to find reasonable parking. When she began to head in to the emergency room, she saw the police cruiser driven by Officer Santiago and his partner. She slapped the hood as she passed, gathering the attention of both officers. When they looked up, she flipped them off as she proceeded into the hospital, mouthing the words, "You will hear from my lawyer." As she entered the hospital, the station nurse stopped her. "Miss, please fill out these forms. The doctor will be with you shortly."

Ronnie, realizing her eye was starting to blacken due to her light complexion, responded, "Oh, no, I'm not seeking medical attention. I'm looking for my brother, Lucas Kimble."

The nurse examined her, shrugged her shoulders, and responded, "He's on the fifth floor, Here's an ice pack. I'll give you two. Give the other one to your sister, will you?"

Ronnie was at first confused by her statement, but then realized Nichelle must also be a *sister* of Lucas in order to be in his waiting area. "Thank you, Maureen," she said after examining the woman's ID badge. Ronnie walked toward the elevator and hit the button. As the door opened, she turned back to the nurse. "Oh, and Maureen—"

"Yes, honey?"

"We may need a doctor on the fifth floor."

As she exited the elevator, she surveyed the floor for the appropriate waiting room. It was too soon to get a status update, so she figured she'd find Nichelle and settle the score. She looked in one area, but couldn't find her. She was taking out her earrings for the upcoming confrontation when she heard her name drily called. "Over here, Ronnie."

Ronnie turned around to find Nichelle sitting in a chair in one of the more empty common areas with a blank expression on her tear-stained face. There were remnants of dried blood under her right nostril, and her bottom lip was swollen and still partially bleeding. Ronnie put her earrings in her purse and said, "Okay, bitch, let's do this."

Nichelle didn't bother to look in her direction. She was watching a rerun of *The King of Queens*. It was the only thing on television, and it appeared she was engrossed in it. Ronnie surmised it was a healthy distraction from the events of the day, but she was still out for blood. She walked over in front of her and hit the power button, squarely looking her in the face. "You want to fight, let's fight. No sucker punches this time."

Nichelle slowly focused in on Ronnie's eyes. "I have no interest in fighting you. You win ... at everything." Nichelle used the remote to turn the TV back on and continued watching as if Ronnie were not there. Ronnie, dissatisfied and somewhat puzzled by the response, turned the TV off again.

"What is that supposed to mean?"

"It means I called human resources. I turned in my resignation effective immediately, and I'm leaving the city. As soon as I know Lucas is okay, I'm gone." Ronnie paused for a moment before she took a seat adjacent to Nichelle as she continued. "I've been trying to keep everything together, but the more I do, the harder it's become. I've just run out of fight. So if you want to hit me back, by all means be my guest. I don't have any fight left in me."

Ronnie sat in silence for a moment, then handed Nichelle the spare ice pack. "I was intimidated by your talent." Ronnie said. "I'm a master at moving things to the right places to get what I want, but people are naturally drawn in by your creativity and responsiveness. You were a threat. Work is all I've ever been good at, so to see you come in and effortlessly make years of my effort get overlooked was too much for me to handle."

"Is that why you started sleeping with Lucas?" she asked directly.

"No," Ronnie responded. "Not that I'm above that. It just wasn't the case here." Ronnie leaned in and looked Nichelle in the eyes, "Truth is, when I met him, I didn't know who he was, but he seemed like a caring person. I guess it was about the time your relationship was ending. He was just unlike any man I'd ever met. Any person I'd ever met. He believes in you." She leaned back in the chair, looking away as if searching for old memories. "I'm not a good person." she said bluntly, "Far from it, actually, but Lucas is. He makes you want to be better on your own, so I can honestly say it had nothing to do with you. It just happened."

As Nichelle listened to Ronnie talk about the man they both loved, Ronnie could see the disgust being forcibly suppressed. Finally, Nichelle said, "We're not friends. You're still a thoughtless, egocentric, mutt-ass bitch as far as my money will take me, and one of these days I'm going to cum at the sheer thought of hitting you in the eye," she uttered, "but whatever you're doing is making Lucas happy, and that's really important to me."

Ronnie started with a sentimental response. "Well, I can appreciate your honesty." Nichelle smirked and reached inside her purse, retrieving the blood-stained Tiffany's box. "He was going to give this to you tonight. I'm not going to lie, I seriously thought about flushing it down the toilet, but enough's enough. With any luck, he's okay and you can pretend you never saw it."

Ronnie looked at the box, her lover's blood dried on the bow and lid. She filled with a deeper love than she thought possible when she opened the box. Once again, the note hit the floor. Veronica picked it up and began to read:

Veronica, from the time I met you until this very moment, I've never felt more alive. I was heading into a dark place when we first met, and I'm not sure how or why fate decided to put you in front of that building at that time, but what I found was a friend. A true friend—not always perfect, but always real. From there, we built something that only you and I can describe. I don't know where tomorrow will lead us, but I do know I want to wake up spending it with you. What I guess I'm trying to say is, "Will you marry me, Ronnie?"

It was the first time he had ever called her by her nickname, a sticking point in their relationship. Lucas, a man of deliberate words, had found a special way to use the one word so many people use when referring to her every day. Yet, in this one moment, it never had such sweetness. Tears began to fill up as she folded the note back and opened the smaller box. A three-carat, brilliant round cut, VVS1clarity, D-colored diamond rested on a platinum band. Ronnie sat there speechless. A sense of guilt overcame her about the last conversation they had before this tragic night. She wanted everything to go as planned; to be stunned by his presentation. She wanted to still be in her home, with him getting ready for tomorrow morning. She set her emotions aside for the time being, feeling Nichelle's unquestionable glare. Never looking up, she placed the ring and the note in her purse. The silence lingered until she finally spoke "I know that was hard. Thank you."

She looked up as Nichelle nodded, finally severing her animosity. The bittersweet moment was interrupted by the arrival of Walter and Natalie Kimble, both charging in like a pair of detectives who had just learned their informant lied to them. Walter looked stressed out to see both of his son's lovers together in the waiting room. He stammered as he asked his question, "Uh ... Ronnie, where is Lucas?"

"I don't know. I think he may still be in—"

Natalie Kimble interrupted. "You don't know? What do you mean you don't know? "Weren't you the one who called to tell us? Why does the nurse downstairs think we have two daughters that were both beaten? How in the hell did all this happen? Somebody needs to tell me what happened and tell me right damn now!" she yelled, taking to the role of bad cop like a fish to water. Both women were shocked to hear this good Christian woman swear, but they thought she could be a natural at it.

"Natalie, calm down," Walter said, playing the role of good cop, as usual.

"I will not calm down, Walter. Our son has been shot, and I want to know why!"

Ronnie's stomach began to turn at the tone of Natalie's questioning. She took a deep breath to respond when Nichelle cut her off. "Mrs. Kimble, Lucas was at my house. There was a... break-in, and I called him to help me. He came. I had my gun out because... of recent criminal activity in the area. So just as a precaution, he took it from me. The police arrived shortly after, and we thought maybe the burglar came back because the cops did not announce themselves. They saw him standing in my hallway with the gun and fired."

Ronnie looked at Mrs. Kimble, her eyes scanning for a solution as the tears welled up.

"Are there any leads? Is the officer who shot my son... is he—" Walter took over the questioning, still using his gentle approach to gather information.

"No," Nichelle replied.

"Well, there has to be justice!" demanded Natalie. "This can't happen to my baby boy. The police are not allowed to just shoot people!"

Ronnie took another deep breath to fight her nausea. "Natalie, right now you and Walter need to talk to the medical staff to find out your son's condition. They haven't been very forthcoming with us. I don't know if there is just nothing to tell yet, or if they just didn't buy the whole sister act, but you're his parents. They have to talk to you."

"She's right, Nat," Walter said.

Ronnie took another breath, trying to focus. "You can... excuse me." She found the nearest trashcan and fell to her knees. She had lost her battle with nausea, spewing the salad she had for lunch and the wine she had for dinner into the trashcan. Walter walked over to the water dispenser sitting in the waiting room and filled it with a cup as Ronnie's insides continued to spill out. She took several deep breaths as she reached for the water. She rose to her feet, finding a napkin in her purse to wipe her lips. She felt partially embarrassed. "I'm sorry about that everyone. I was going to say you can go to the nurse's station and they'll be able to get a doctor for you to provide some kind of update."

She wiped her lips again, still feeling queasy. Natalie and Walter both walked off to the nurses station, but soon returned dejected. "The nurse said they are almost done with the surgery, and the doctor will be out shortly. They are moving us to the ICU Outpatient Waiting Area," Walter said, the anxiety clearly getting the better of him. Ronnie felt she should comfort them in some way, but did not have anything to provide. She and Nichelle quietly gathered their things and walked out of the waiting area into a brightly lit hallway. As Ronnie stood up, the nausea returned with a vengeance. They were halfway down the hall when she took a detour into the bathroom and found the nearest stall. The other half of her lunch, along with some of her breakfast, spewed into the toilet.

"Fuck!" she shouted as her body began to settle itself. She opened the stall and stood in front of the bathroom mirror. She felt somewhat relieved, but looked nearly as awful as she felt. She took some water and refreshed her face. Her eye was starting to bruise deeper, standing out against her golden bronze skin. She considered applying foundation, but decided against it. It wasn't the appropriate time, and considering how harshly Lucas's mother already treated her, applying makeup in the bathroom while her son was on an operating table would likely prove to her she was a harlot. Ronnie did put a few wild hairs into place so as to not look completely disheveled. After giving herself a final onceover, she opened the bathroom door and proceeded down the hall to where the rest of the group was heading. Walter lingered behind long enough to help her find her way to where they were waiting. Feeling the need to apologize again, she began to talk. "I'm so sorry everyone. I—I've been dealing with a bout of food poisoning."

Walter put his arm around her. "It's quite alright, Ronnie. I understand sweetheart." They were all standing in the hallway outside the Intensive Care Unit. Many families were clustered together hoping to gather any good news. One older woman in the corner with her Bible prayed aloud in Spanish for her "mijo," Javier. The sight of everyone made it all too real for Natalie. She broke into tears as Walter abandoned comforting Ronnie to console his wife. Nichelle, who had been all but numb to the situation since explaining it to Lucas's parents, began to pace. Ronnie walked over to her. "Nichelle, it's going to be okay."

Nichelle looked at Ronnie. "He wouldn't be here if it wasn't for me. None of you would. This is entirely my fault. All of it."

Ronnie, convincingly stated, "You didn't pull the trigger, Nichelle." Ronnie could tell Nichelle only thought she was saying this to look good in front of Lucas's parents, but nonetheless, she continued.

"Look, I know I blamed you earlier. I was upset. Hell, I still am, but this isn't your fault. You have to know that."

"Yeah, alright." she responded, still unconvinced. She crossed over to Natalie to put an arm around her. The consolation was cut short when the doctor came out of the steel double doors still in his scrubs. He scanned the room and said aloud, "I'm looking for the family of Lucas Kimble."

CHAPTER 38
RECOVERY

"I'm his father," Walter said as he shook the doctor's hand. "Doctor, please, can you tell us anything?"

The doctor matter of factly described Lucas's condition. "He lost a lot of blood, but he got here pretty quickly. No vital organs were struck by the bullets, so we were able to remove them successfully." Mr. and Mrs. Kimble let out a collective sigh of relief. "However," the doctor continued, silencing their brief moment of relief, "he suffered massive head trauma. There is a contusion on the brain and a crack in his skull. The crack in his skull should heal on its own. It was a slight fracture, but we won't know the side effects, if any, until the swelling from his head trauma goes down."

Confusion set in amongst all four parties present. "What does that mean in plain English, doctor?" Natalie asked.

The doctor looked at everyone. "That's just it. We don't know what it could mean. It could be nothing. But the brain operates, well, everything, so we won't know if he's lost any neurological functions until the swelling comes down and the body recovers on its own. For now, we're keeping him in a medically induced coma."

The entire group was speechless. Ronnie pressed the doctor for more answers.

"Not to be crass, but can you go into further detail? We'd appreciate as much information as you can provide."

The doctor responded, "Vison, hand-eye coordination, speech, motor functions, memory—all these things are controlled by the brain. Right now, he's on assisted breathing, but his lungs seem operational, so he could breathe on his own. We're simply taking every precaution."

"My baby is going to be okay, right?" Natalie asked, looking for reassurance.

"We can't say anything for sure until the swelling goes down. For now, we are going to do everything we can to ensure he makes a speedy recovery. Excuse me, I have to get back to work. The nurse will let you know what room he'll be in."

The doctor walked away. Ronnie, Nichelle, Walter, and Natalie stood in silence, each of them forming their own pathway of tears. Nichelle looked up and said, "I'm sorry, everyone. I'm so very sorry." and began to walk away.

Ronnie looked at Walter, who was torn between going after Nichelle and staying with his wife. She decided to make his choice easy by walking off, flagging her down.

"Nichelle, stop. You're causing a scene. This is not what the Kimbles need right now." Nichelle snapped back, "And what about me? What about what I need?"

Ronnie, stunned by her response, said, "Are you serious? Nichelle, Lucas has been shot. The man is fighting for his life. His parents are devastated. Just what in the hell do you need right now?"

"Don't do this to me. Just tell the Kimbles I'm sorry, but I need a moment."

She walked off, leaving Ronnie standing by herself. "Un-fucking-believable." she muttered as Nichelle walked toward the elevator. When she turned around, Walter was heading toward her. She met him halfway.

"Ronnie, where's Nichelle?"

"She went to grab some fresh air. Did the nurse tell you where he's going to be?"

"Room 1308. Natalie is already walking that way," Walter said. He led Ronnie to the elevator and together they took it up to the thirteenth floor. When they arrived, Natalie was in the room with Lucas, who was on breathing support and unconscious. Neither one of them wanted to interrupt her as she cried and talked to her son. Walter stood at the window looking at his wife.

Ronnie asked, "Are you going to go in there?"

Walter said, "She needs time to process this; time to be alone with him. We all do, but I'll give her that now."

Ronnie stopped and looked at him. "Walter, you've been so strong for everyone. Are you okay?"

"I'm holding up. It's a hell of a day, though, I'll tell you. On one hand, you find out your boy is in the hospital, and on the other, you realize you're going to be a grandfather."

Ronnie's mouth fell wide open. She had all but forgotten about the pregnancy with the series of events. "I didn't know Lucas told you."

"He didn't," Walter responded.

"Then how did—"

"Sweetheart, I have five children and worked in an era where I couldn't afford to take care of myself. If I don't know anything else, I know morning sickness, even if it happens at night."

Ronnie recalled throwing up twice since she had been here and was working on a third time. "Mr. Kimble... Walter... I..." Ronnie stopped herself.

Walter looked at her as if to read what she was thinking. "You're unsure about the pregnancy."

"I was ... I mean ... I am."

The sad look already present on Walter's face grew, similar to the one Lucas had before he left her home earlier that night. His silence was an invitation for her to continue talking, so she proceeded. "Before everything happened tonight, Lucas found out, and I told him I wasn't sure if I was going to keep the baby. Now, well, I just want him to be okay."

Walter, realizing this, began to tell a story. "Two days before the high school state championship game, Lucas had a 103-degree fever. We went to the emergency room and found out he had the flu and had lost about twelve pounds in water weight. Natalie stayed with him the entire night until they put us out. The next day, they released him to us, but they wanted us to come back if his condition worsened. It did. The morning of the championship game, his fever was about 104; his whole body was hot to the touch. It went down, but he was in bad shape. Natalie wanted to go straight to the ER, but he begged and pleaded with us not to because he wanted to see his friends play for the championship because they all worked so hard for it. Natalie reluctantly agreed, so we went to the game. I thought it was odd that when he got in the car he had on a cover and his basketball sneakers, but I didn't pay it no mind. When we got to the game, Lucas took off the cover and the jacket and had on his basketball uniform. Well, you know Natalie had a fit about it. The insanity of this boy, as weak as he was, playing in a game, but I'll never forget what he said next: 'You don't know what this means to me, Momma. You always taught me to fight for what I love and challenge myself. And this is both of those, so why are you standing in my way?' It was one of the first times I ever saw Natalie quiet. He kissed her and walked into the gym. The game wasn't even close. From the moment that boy hit the floor, you would've thought he was in perfect health. Fought for every ball, dove for rebounds, made perfect passes. He had fifty-six points, nine rebounds, thirteen assists, and eight steals. He was the MVP of the game. It was the best game he ever played in his life."

Walter took Ronnie by the hands and looked her in the eyes. "My point is, sweetheart, the boy has always loved a challenge, and he's always fought his hardest for the things he loves the most. Lying in that hospital bed right now, I know he's going to be alright because he's got something to fight for."

Ronnie saw the same sincerity in Walter's eyes that she adored in his son,

"He *loves* you. I don't mean any disrespect by what I'm going to say next, but you seem like a hell of a challenge for any man to want to fight for." They both chuckled as he squeezed her hands endearingly.

"It's all so new to me, Walter. I just don't know how you are all so certain about these things."

"Ronnie, let me explain something to you. In matters of the heart, you can never be certain. It requires two people, and when it's all said and done, you never really know what another person is feeling, or doing, or thinking. All you can do is be certain of your own feelings and have faith that the way you feel is reciprocated by the person you love. You can't second guess life—you just have to live it."

His words gave her chills. She hugged him and he embraced her. "Thank you," she whispered in his ear.

"Anytime, sweetheart. Whatever you decide, I want you to know you can always talk to me."

Their embrace was interrupted by Natalie Kimble walking out of the room, exasperation covering her face. Walter released one arm and invited his wife into their ongoing embrace, to which she quickly sought refuge. "You should go in there and see him if you're up to it," Walter said as Ronnie held on to the two of them.

"Okay," she responded. She untangled herself from the embrace and proceeded through the door.

The lights in the room were dim. There were a multitude of sounds going on, the most notable of which were the heartrate monitor and the breathing machine. Ronnie looked at her lover, hardly recognizable with a bandage wrapped around his skull. It was the first time she had actually seen him since he left her home earlier that night. She walked over to him as he slept. She had so much she wanted to tell him at the moment, none of which he could hear. She ran her hands over his bandages fighting back her emotions. "Lucas, I don't know if you can hear me, but I really wish I could hear your voice right now. I wish we could talk about everything. You're an amazing man, and I'm not sure why you love me the way you do. I'm not sure I ever deserved it. But for the first time since we met, I truly appreciate it. I truly understand how much you care for me." She paused, looking at him lying there unconscious. She began to weep again. "And I wish you could hear how sorry I am for every hurdle I put you through. So many hurdles. I wish you were looking at me right now, Luke, because I would give anything ... *everything* just to know you're going to be okay."

She squeezed his hand, half hoping to get a response, but there was none. Slowly, she leaned in and kissed him on his cheek and whispered in his ear "I love you, Lucas Kimble. Fight for us."

CHAPTER 39
RUNNING

Nichelle looked at her watch. The time was 9:48 in the morning, and the flight she was waiting on would be boarding soon. She sat in Houston's Hobby Airport and ate her orange. She was looking forward to the long flight. She was looking forward to getting out of the city. She was looking forward to sleep. She wanted to wait to find out about Lucas, but from the doctor's report, there wasn't going to be an answer anytime soon. Being here, in this life, where she was clearly no longer wanted, was a burden she no longer wanted to carry. Her iPhone buzzed. She got the notification that the executive meeting had been postponed. She smirked as she shook her head and powered down her phone. She looked at the television and saw another episode of *The King of Queens* was on. *Does this show ever go off TV?* She wondered. It was one of the episodes she saw last night at the hospital. As she looked on, local news broadcaster Michael Mello interrupted the program to discuss an early morning robbery of a bank in Sugarland, a city on the outskirts of Houston. She walked closer to hear the report. "Police indicate the robbery was done by one man who got away with a substantial amount of money in a blue Chevy Nova. Authorities have no leads. The suspect was fully clothed from head to toe in all black and wore sunglasses. No one was harmed. Here is footage of the crime from the video feed in the bank. Again, authorities have no leads. If you have any information on this crime, please contact the police." The grainy camera footage indicated a tall, strapping male. Nichelle sighed with exhaustion and walked away from the TV. There was no doubt who committed the crime.

I have got to get out of this city, she thought, and the sooner the better. The glare from the sun on this perfect day was being blocked by her sunglasses. It was the only thing that had gone right in the past twenty-four hours. She needed it along with makeup to cover the facial bruising she had endured last night. She always loathed people who wore sunglasses inside, but now she was one of them. "Now boarding flight 786 to New York," the flight attendant said on the loud speaker. Nichelle picked up her black Kate Spade carry-on bag and made her way toward gate 4B. She was flying first class, so she knew she would be one of the first people seated and moved past several people slowly forming a line to board. "Now boarding first class and business class," the attendant said. Nichelle proceeded without pause to the flight attendant and handed her a ticket to confirm her seating before heading down the ramp to the belly of the plane. As she entered the aircraft, she located her plush, blue leather seat with ample legroom. Perfect for the three-and-a-half-hour nap she planned on taking. Nichelle put her carry-on in the overhead bin and sat down to buckle herself up. She was followed by a middle-aged white man who had been looking at her posterior as she walked down the ramp. He had the seat next to her and eagerly took it. She noticed in her peripheral vision that he tried to make a hand gesture to assist her with the carry-on, but she moved as if she never noticed. She was in no mood to be jovial. As she slid on her seatbelt, she reached into her carry-on to search for her headphones before he tried to engage her in conversation. She ruffled through her other bag, a black Louis Vuitton Lockit tote, when the gentleman spoke.

"Looks like the plane is going to be packed today."

Fuck. Just slightly too slow to avoid conversation. "Yeah, it looks like it's going to be," she responded as she connected the headphones to her phone.

"Are you heading to New York for business or pleasure?"

"Neither," she said, hoping her short answers would make the man realize she wasn't in the mood to talk, a hint he didn't receive.

"Ah. So if neither, what are you going for?"

She put the headphones in one ear to indicate this conversation would be ending soon. "To escape," she replied. Her short tone almost seemed to have the adverse effect on him.

"You must be related to Snake Plissken."

"I'm sorry. Who?"

"Snake Plissken from the movie *Escape from New York*. Everyone else is trying to escape New York, and you're trying to get there."

Nichelle understood the reference well enough, but gave him a blank look as if to make him feel much older than her in a last-ditch attempt to let the conversation die a natural death. The awkward silence worked as the man began to stammer to recover from the ill-conceived pun, giving her the chance to put in the other earphone. She opened the shutter to the window and looked out of the plane. She could feel the man's eyes still on her, less intense than before, but still on her.

"We're half cousins," she said aloud. The man next to her laughed a very artificial laugh, and she rolled her eyes as she once again felt like she was trying to take the high road.

"My name is Frank," he said, extending his hands.

"Nichelle," she replied.

"What's bringing you to New York?" he asked as he tried to focus his eyes on hers and away from her breasts.

"I'm going to see my brother," she replied.

"Ah. Seeing family is always nice. Are you going to be staying for a while?"

"Yep."

"How long?"

"As long as it takes."

The gentleman was quiet for a moment before resuming his line of questioning. "I don't know you at all, but if you're running from something, it's still going to be here when you get back, you know. That's the one thing I've learned over the course of my life."

"Who says I'm coming back?" Nichelle said as she removed her glasses. She could tell he noticed some of the bruising on her face through the makeup. "My boyfriend did this to me— that's what you're thinking, right? Well, you're right, he did. I probably deserved it. Thing is, I don't know what I deserve. I'm not sure what's going to happen next. I'm scared, tired, and frustrated with my life, and to top it all off, I'm three months pregnant and I don't know who the father is. So if you don't mind, I'm going to sit here in silence and try to forget everything about the city of Houston."

The man was silent for a long while. After some time, he responded, "Does anyone know?"

"I'm sorry?"

"The pregnancy. Does anyone know?"

Nichelle chuckled. "To be honest, you're the first person I've told."

"You should tell the potential fathers—they have a right to know."

Nichelle rolled her eyes "Hmm, let's see Frank. Potential father one is probably about to get himself thrown back in jail, totally unrelated to using my face as a punching bag, by the way, so there's no point in telling him, and potential father two will probably get engaged to my ex-boss when he gets out of his coma. If he gets out of his coma, that is. So, no, telling the potential fathers isn't an option."

The gentleman was about to speak again when the cabin doors closed and the stewardess went over the plane protocol. Nichelle took this opportunity to close her eyes and pretend as if she were dozing off, which worked. The man remained quiet after the stewardess finished her announcements. She thought about Lucas and Donovan, both men she loved despite being emotionally hurt by one and physically hurt by another. A clean start was what she was looking for. She hoped that this flight was the beginning of that start.

CHAPTER 40
THE RETURN: AN EPILOGUE

B*eep, beep, beep...* the noise was a constant annoyance throughout the haze of the last few moments. "Can someone shut off that alarm clock?" he said aloud. Or at least he thought he said it aloud. It was a state of bliss, sleeping the kind of deep sleep where you never know if you're truly awake. The sleep-in-till-noon kind of sleep. *Perry Mason* was on in the background. The sound of Raymond Burr's voice used to put him to sleep when he was a child. He loved the show. As a child, he always wanted to hear what was happening as he dozed off, just like he was trying to do now.

Beep, beep, beep. The alarm again, not ever stopping, It just got louder and louder. Everything was annoying, but he could deal with it all—just not the alarm. "Please turn it off," he insisted. All the sounds continued to build, but the true annoyance was the alarm growing louder and louder with each pulse. *Beep, beep, beep* ... "Can someone please shut off that damn alarm?"

He urged his eyelids to open, but it was as if a flashlight were hitting him directly in his eyes. He couldn't see a thing. Wait, it was a flashlight. There was a man holding it, mouthing words, "Can you understand me?" which was ironic because he couldn't understand him. He couldn't understand what was going on at this very moment. He was as confused as he was annoyed by the beeping alarm. *Beep, beep, beep* ... He turned his head to avoid the light and locate the damned thing ... only to realize it wasn't an alarm at all. He was connected to a heartrate monitor.

"Can you understand me?" insisted the man holding the flashlight. This time he heard him. He fought his eyes back into the light to figure out who the man was. He was a doctor. Nothing made any sense. Why was he at the doctor's office? Why was he connected to a heartrate monitor?

"Mr. Kimble, nod if you can hear me or understand me in anyway." *Kimble ... is that my name?* He was afraid now. Confused and afraid. The light went away. The doctor made direct eye contact with him. "Mr. Kimble, nod if you can hear or understand me, sir." Cautiously, he nodded. "Good, that is great news," said the doctor.

The questions began to form, along with his coherency. "Where—" Lucas tried to form the words "Where am I?" but only the first of the three came out.

The doctor seemingly understood his intended statement and went on to answer him. "Sir, you were in a serious accident. We can get into the details later, but for right now, there are a couple people who have waited a very long time to see you."

As the doctor stepped back, a warm, familiar voice echoed in the distance. "Lucas? Baby, is that you?"

"Mom?" he responded, half sure of his statement. He turned his head and eyed two figures who vaguely resembled his parents. Slowly he was getting his wits about him. "Mom? Dad?" Natalie and Walter Kimble leaned down and hugged their son and began to cry loudly and openly.

"Oh, thank God! I never gave up on you, Lucas," his mother said aloud. With his memory slowly returning to him, he realized that she appeared thinner than the last time he recalled seeing her, although he had trouble remembering exactly when that was.

"My baby boy!" Walter added, looking slightly unkempt.

An avalanche of inquiries were building by the moment. As he held his parents, he decided to start with the question at the top of the list. "Mom, Dad, what happened? How did I get here?"

He sensed his dad's arms pull away. Gently, his mother did the same. They looked at each other with concern. A concern he hadn't seen since ... he couldn't remember when. He couldn't really remember much at all. But he knew they were concerned. He concentrated really hard, trying to capture the moment he saw this concern on his parents' face. Was it high school? "Dad." he said, his confidence wavering, "The last time I was in the hospital was high school, right?"

"Yes Luke."

"We ... I ... I had a ... I was sick!"

"Yes, baby!" his mother exclaimed. "You had pneumonia right before the big—"

"Natalie! Let the boy think!" his father interjected. He looked back at his son and asked, "Luke do you remember what was happening when you were sick then?"

He didn't have a clue, but he didn't want to disappoint them, so he guessed, "I had a ... big dance that night? And I got sick ..."

His mother looked away, panicked by his response. Clearly he was wrong.

"The doctor said this would happen," Walter said, looking at Natalie, trying to be positive.

"What would happen?" Lucas asked, trying to get his father to focus on his question. His dad reestablished eye contact with him, placing his hand on his shoulder assuredly. "Son, you were shot."

Shot! Why was he shot? Who shot him? The avalanche grew along with his strength. He leaned back and tried to move his legs. He didn't recall much, but he did know that in the movies if someone gets shot they almost always lose the ability to walk. He quickly tried to feel sensation in his legs. There was none. He closed his eyes and willed his body to bend his legs. There was no motion. Fear began to flood his system, a fact that did not escape his mother. "What's wrong, baby?"

"My leg, it's not... responding."

He closed his eyes and focused again. As he tried, his mother interjected, "You just need a little help." She grabbed his leg and began to push it.

"I can move my own goddamn leg, Mom!" he lashed out angrily at the top of his lungs. His tone frightened her, and as she dropped his leg, it hit against the metal rail. Hard. The pain he felt immensely satisfied him. He could feel pain in his leg! His leg muscles must just be weak or atrophied. A quiet sigh of relief rushed over him as concluded his quiet test of all of his extremities. "Sorry, Mom. It's just—"

"I understand."

"It doesn't give me the right to talk to you that way."

There was a silence. Looking away from his parents, he located a calendar on the wall. It was November 16th, almost two weeks since the big meeting at work. That singular event returned considerable chunks of his memory back to him. "I remember now. It was a basketball game. Last time I was in a hospital I was supposed to play in a basketball game and got sick. But I asked you both to take me anyway."

"That's right, Lucas," his father said, gesturing for him to go on.

"I scored fifty-six points, nine rebounds and ... twelve, no thirteen assists!"

"Praise the Lord!" Natalie exclaimed.

"Work ... I work for RainHouse & Arms. I was supposed to go back to work for a new assignment on October 25th, so I must've been ... in here since the 23rd. Dad, do you mean to tell me I've been out of it for a month now?"

His dad made eye contact with his mother as she began to look uneasy. "Son, you've been in here for *thirteen* months. You already completed that assignment. Do you remember?"

Lucas became visibly shaken. "I don't believe you. That's not possible."

He glanced back at the calendar on the wall and noticed the date was November 16th, 2016. Reality started to sink in. "I don't understand. Why was I out for so long?"

"Baby, when you got shot— " Natalie couldn't finish the sentence. She was highly emotional, leaving her husband to step in and finish the sentence.

"Son, when you were shot, you fell and hit something really heavy. There was a fracture in your skull and some swelling around your brain, along with cerebral fluid leakage. The doctors were concerned you might not make it. After the first month, there was no visible sign of progress. They wanted to operate, but there was a chance you would heal naturally if uninterrupted. So we decided to let God bring you back to us." His father's words sat in the pit of his stomach like a large bowl of potatoes. "You mean to tell me I've lost over a year of my life?"

"Son, we're just glad you didn't lose the rest of your life."

It was logic he couldn't argue with. From the look in his parents' eyes and the way things sounded, it was a nothing short of a small miracle he woke up at all.

"I'm thankful I'm just ... overwhelmed."

"We called Ronnie, and she'll be here soon."

"Who?"

"Veronica," his mother responded.

Lucas sat up and tried to pull his IV out of his body. "Where is Nichelle?" Lucas demanded. His father tightened his grip on his son's shoulder. "Son, calm down. What's the last thing you remember?"

"I—I don't know. Who is this Veronica? Is she a doctor?"

His parents looked at each other.

"Stop doing that and tell me what's going on! And where is Nichelle?" He removed his father's hand from his shoulder.

"Son!" Walter yelled, beckoning him to relax.

Lucas wasn't fazed by his father's request. "Dad, I have to get out of here!"

"Son, please, just... just calm down."

"Dad, I'm not going to calm down until I find out what the hell happened in the last year of my life."

"Son, it's an incredible story if you're up for it, but maybe, just maybe, you should hear it from Veronica."

THE END

HERE'S A SNEAK PEAK AT THE NEXT NOVEL- SEDUCTION: A MONEY, POWER & SEX STORY

Welcome to the V.A.

"Another beautiful day in Richmond, Virginia. Clear skies with a high of 78. We've had amazing weather, folks." Kendra changed the channel as she held the phone to her ear. By the fourth ring, she was highly annoyed, but still she waited on her friend until the phone picked up.

"If this heffa don't answer the damn phone!" She mumbled softly to herself, but like always, it went to voicemail. She hung up without leaving a message. She simply pushed the 'End' button angrily and tried the phone number again. Same result.

"Hi, you've reached the voicemail of Ronnie Duvalle with Burrows Industries. Please leave a message, and I will promptly return your call."

This time, Kendra accepted the invitation. "Damn it, Ronnie, it's Kendra. I know you're getting my calls. Now, give me a call back this morning. I just want to check on you."

Kendra hung up the phone. Flustered, she put the phone down and looked at the stock price of the company she worked for. It was moving north of fifteen percent in early morning trading, despite rumors of turmoil coming out of the Houston office. *What in the hell is going on?* she thought to herself as she scrolled through the rest of her portfolio. It was always soothing for her to look at her accounts. It reminded her she was doing well. It also distracted her from the other thoughts on her mind. Kendra Daniels was never a person to do well without answers. She wanted answers—no, she *needed* answers—but beyond that, she wanted in on the action. She needed to be in the action; to be in the know. That was paramount to everything else, and the action for this company was in Houston. She looked at the phone as if willing it to ring, but to no avail. She wanted to call again, but didn't want to appear desperate. There was nothing she could do but wait. She opened a draft of an email to send to Ronnie, thinking the woman would respond a bit more expediently that way when the phone rang. She looked at the caller ID: Queen Savage Bitch. She smirked at the name coded in her phone for her former rival turned friend. It was the contact name she saved when they first met each other, and she hadn't bothered to change it because, in many ways, it still fit. It was the first time she thought about it, though, since she'd moved back home to Virginia after taking an unofficial demotion after her disappointing performance in Houston. She picked up the phone and in an accusatory fashion and said, "Girl, I know you saw me calling you. Not cool, Ronnie."

"I'm sorry, Kendra, I didn't know I reported to you. I thought it was still the other way around."

"Bitch, you know we still have the same title."

"For now, but as you can tell by our soaring stock price, that's temporary. You're welcome, by the way. All the money I'm making us is sure to help in your bed-and-breakfast-slash-tour-the-Confederate-monuments business you're undoubtedly working on in that God-forsaken city."

"Ah, Ronnie, still taking your daily dose of vitamin bitch, I see."

"I miss you, too, girl."

It was their usual banter, although it always dug a little deeper than Kendra would like. Ronnie was her friend, and while she respected her skillset, she couldn't help but feel, that on a professional level, she was more qualified than her rival. It was just her competitive nature. Right now, Ronnie had the advantage. She worked in corporate headquarters, and most importantly, was delivering results. A fifteen percent upswing in the stock price meant she was making millions for shareholders, and anyone who can make the shareholders richer would get more chances to do so. Which meant Kendra's days in Virginia would be longer than she wanted. Yet, she was still proud of her friend. At this level, she was aware that there had to be solidarity among women of color—a lesson she learned the hard way while living in Houston roughly six months earlier, competing with Ronnie for the same vice presidential position. While Kendra did all she could to assert herself, and her analytical skills were second to none, Ronnie was supportive. She was the ultimate team player and even covered for Kendra on occasion. That left an impression on Kendra to make sure she never competed with another sister again for a job. At least not in a way they'd tear each other down. It also exposed her insecurities. At the time, she would've done anything to belittle Ronnie, not only because she wanted the title, but because, if she were being truly honest with herself, a part of her just didn't like the woman back then. It wasn't until she was being transferred that she truly gained respect for Ms. Duvalle.

"So, are the rumors true?" Kendra insisted, cutting straight to the original intent of her call.

"The rumors?"

"Bitch, don't play with me! Tell me what is going on down there. I hear there are layoffs coming, and on top of that, the girl who took my place took a leave of absence. What was her name? Nicole?"

"Worthless was her name."

"Ronnie!"

"Nichelle. Her name was Nichelle."

"That's right... Nichelle. Myers, isn't it? Why did she leave?"

"It's such a long, sordid story, Kendra. A lot is going on, but the good news is your 401(k) will look all the better for it."

"So, that's it? Ho, I want details!"

"Kendra, it's a really long story."

"Ronnie, I'm in Richmond, Virginia. This is where time goes to die. Spill it!" She was in no mood for Ronnie's faux coyness. She knew if she were in Houston, the gossip would spill over and she'd know all the dirt—maybe even a useful tidbit or two to help her regain some leverage in the company. But even the rumor mill was slow in Richmond. There wasn't a lot she could do but wait for Ronnie to tell her what was going on.

"Okay, I'll tell you, but some of this stuff is still unfolding, so I don't have the answers to everything."

"God damn it, Duvalle!" Kendra said, frustration saturating her tone.

Ronnie finally got the hint and revealed everything that happened in the past twenty-four hours. "We had a meeting with the board. Rainhouse & Arms, the new audit firm, recommended an upgrade in technology to reach our quarterly projection. They then recommended a ten-percent reduction in workforce to exceed the quarterly fiscal projection. The board loved the idea."

"So, basically, layoffs to make more money."

"Well, in layman's terms, yes."

"Then why did Nichelle need to take a leave of absence?"

"That's much more complicated. She was upset about the workforce reduction, but—"

"Wait," Kendra interjected. "Did you say Rainhouse & Arms? I've heard that name in the news recently. Isn't that where that guy worked who is at the center of the police shooting that all the protests are about in Houston?"

"Yeah."

"Holy shit! Was he working on our account?"

"He was more than that. He's the guy I've been dating."

There was a silence on the phone. Kendra was at a loss for words and wanted her friend to say something, but what she didn't know. She was too overwhelmed by the information she just received.

"Ronnie, why didn't you lead with that?"

"Because the whole thing is a cluster fuck! I don't know. You're asking a lot from me right now."

"Damn, girl, I'm sorry. Lucas is his name, right? I saw it on the news. Is he okay?"

"He's in a comma. It's too soon to say anything, honestly. We're not sure what to make of the circumstances right now. It's really touch and go."

"What in the hell happened?"

There was more silence on the phone. Kendra's mind raced. She was concerned for her friend, but at the same time, her mind was building a stockpile of questions.

"Ronnie?"

"Lucas... he and I were having a... disagreement over something when Nichelle called."

"Hold up," Kendra interjected "This was after work, right? Why would Nichelle call him after work?"

"Because he had recently broken up with Nichelle around the time he got to the company, so they had some ten—"

"Are you fucking kidding me?"

"Stay with me, Kendra."

"This is too much. I need a drink." Kendra got up as she listened to the rest of the story. She also sensed Ronnie needed a moment to sort it all out. Her purple, laced boy shorts clinging against her milk chocolate thighs, she walked into the kitchen to pour a glass of wine. She kept a bottle of Wild Horse Cabernet for occasions like this. She poured the already-open bottle into a glass and went back to the living area where her laptop sat and glanced at the stock price. Up seventeen percent now.

"So... what happened again?" She heard a deep sigh on the other end of the line. The wounds were still fresh from the night before.

" Lucas had recently broken up with Nichelle when we met. I don't usually date men on the job, but he was different."

"I remember you said you loved him, but you failed to include he was Nichelle's ex."

"It never seemed important when we were talking. This all started around the time you were leaving town anyway."

"Right. You were going to meet him the last night we had drinks."

"I think so. I can't remember. At any rate, you had your own issues with your man. Besides, you barely remember the girl's name until now, and their past wasn't any of my business."

"Fair enough. So, how did he get shot?"

"I was about to tell you that before you decided to interrupt me for the umpteenth time."

"Sorry, but you gotta admit, this is pretty far-fetched."

"You get no argument here."

"So... how did he get shot?"

"We were having a disagreement, and Nichelle called him. They had some issues to resolve. He went over to her house, and well..."

"Let me get this straight—he got shot at Nichelle's house?"

For the first time since she knew Ronnie, Kendra sensed her vulnerability. There were echoes of what sounded like muffled sobbing followed by what was obviously a mute. She knew that Ronnie was too proud to actually cry on the phone, but the fact that she was able to let her guard down at all meant this topic was much more sensitive than Kendra had considered. Her friend's lover was in the hospital fighting for his life, and she had been treating the entire event like a soap opera. While she wanted answers, she decided the best thing to do was change the subject.

"So, when do they announce you as the queen of all Burrows Industries?"

Kendra sensed the phone unmute, followed by a sniffle and her friend's cracking voice. "I... um... I'm not sure. We're having a meeting today."

"Well, the stock is up around eighteen and a half percent. I'm sure it has to be soon."

Ronnie chuckled shakily, which made Kendra feel better "Enough of all that, girl. How's life on your end?"

"Oh, you know, the usual. Just looking at floor plans for my Confederate bed 'n' breakfast as you so eloquently put it." The two chuckled at the joke as Kendra continued. "Outside of that, I'm still dealing with Marcus's ass."

"What do you mean?"

"You remember how you thought he would go back to the way he used to be once we left Houston?"

"I do."

"Well, let's just say that plan didn't work out as well as you thought it would. I mean, don't get me wrong, he's wonderful again, but—"

"But what?"

"Something's definitely different. He's different now."

"Well, I didn't know him before, so what do you mean 'different'?"

"I can't really put a label on it, but if I had to say anything, I'd say it feels like he's trying too hard."

"I thought that's what you wanted."

"I wanted my Marcus back. Right now, he's hot and cold. Does that make any sense?"

"Not in the least."

Kendra took a pause. It was hard to put into words what was going on with Marcus, though she wanted to talk about it, if for nothing else than to have a healthy distraction from her newfound awareness of her friend's problems. Marcus trying too hard wasn't as bad as Ronnie's boyfriend getting shot, but it was still her problem and she wanted to get it out in the open. Since she and Marcus moved back home, she'd never actually taken the time to figure out what was bothering her. This was her opportunity to do so. She took a deep sigh and unloaded what had been eating at her for the last few months.

"The thing is, Marcus... he's lazy, unmotivated, and that shows up sometimes in the bedroom. Don't get me wrong. He has the equipment and he knows—well, knew—how to use it, but now he's just looking for a way to be done in the bedroom. Like he's spent his energy all day fucking someone else, and that's when he's not acting like he's God's gift to all women."

"Okay, now we're getting somewhere, Normally I'd say this would be too much information about your boyfriend's... um, package, but I haven't gotten any, and by the looks of things I won't be getting none anytime soon, so I'll indulge. I thought you realized you were just being paranoid when you lived down here."

"I did. Well, at least I thought so at first. I thought we'd get on that plane and life would go back to normal, but it didn't. In fact, it did the exact opposite. It felt like guilt. I mean, it wreaked of guilt. I'm convinced now that something definitely happened in Houston."

"But Houston is your past, Kendra, at least in the sense of this relationship. I have to admit it sounds like you're looking for something, anything, to justify your feelings. You don't have any concrete proof he did something wrong, or is doing anything wrong right now. And most importantly, he's trying. Don't take this the wrong way, girl, but it sounds like you're looking for a reason your career didn't work out here and not anything Marcus actually did."

The words stung, the truth behind them piercing a most vulnerable wall she hadn't bothered to defend since she was talking to her friend.

"Well, that hurt, you blunt motherfucker," she said playfully.

Ronnie laughed at her retort. "I'm sorry, girl. I just think you're worried about the wrong thing. It's not like he's—"

"Intuition."

"Excuse me?"

"Intuition. I know this man's sleeping patterns; I know his scent; I know how he lies, when he lies, why he lies. I pay attention to his eating habits, and consequently know the pattern of his bowel movements. I know when he drinks vodka he's going to pass out before he can get it up, and when he drinks Hennessey, I'm going to be laying in the room with my legs folded up in the air with my titties bouncing against my knees and my big toes touching the headboard until four a.m. I know how the bristles of his mustache feel on my pussy when he gets a fresh haircut. I know this man. In-tu-ition. It's what made me feel something was wrong when we were in Houston, it's what made me feel something isn't right since we got back from Houston, and it is certainly what's making me feel—at this very moment—something is definitely wrong."

Kendra stayed quiet, hoping her friend would fill the void. Anything would've done at the moment. Instead, the silence persisted, which only made Kendra's insecurities grow. She wanted validation from Ronnie, but knew she would get no such reprieve. Marcus, for better or worse, was her rock, her foundation, and she knew that women like Ronnie, women like the one she was pretending to be anyway, thought taking care of a man was a weakness. Yet, Kendra hoped that maybe, in light of Ronnie's own relationship woes, she'd be supportive. The awkwardness grew as no words were exchanged.

Kendra was about to speak when the phone beeped. It was Burrows Industries.

"Hey, Ronnie, are you calling me from work?"

"No."

"Okay, well, hang on, girl, I gotta call you back. This is the Houston office."

"Really? That's odd. What could they possibly want?"

"I'm not sure, but I'll let you know. Let me grab the line, and I'll call you back."

"Okay."

Kendra clicked over just in time to get the line.

"Kendra Daniels."

"Hi, Kendra, this is Milton Burrows. Do you have a moment to speak?"

They gonna offer her to come back!
Back into the fire!

ABOUT THE AUTHOR

Norian Love was born in Los Angeles, California, in 1979. He grew up in Houston, Texas, where he's lived for the last twenty years. While taking a short hiatus from working for Fortune 500 companies as a technology specialist, he rediscovered his passion for writing poetry and released his first book, *Theater of Pain*, which was critically acclaimed. The reception and momentum of this book sparked him to create his eagerly anticipated follow up, *Games of the Heart*, a few years later. The final installment of his poetic trilogy, *The Dawn or the Dusk* has recently been released and is already receiving praise as the best book in the series.

ALSO BY NORIAN LOVE

Memories of Tomorrow Series

Theater of Pain (Book 1)

Games of the Heart (Book 2)

The Dawn or the Dusk (Book 3)

Novels

- Money, Power & Sex: A Love Story

Seduction: A Money .Power & Sex Story

- Autumn: A Love Story

Ronnie: A Money, Power & Sex Story

- Donovan: A Money, Power & Sex Novella

If you enjoyed this book or found it useful, I'd be very grateful if you'd post a short review on Amazon. Your support really does make a difference, and I read all the reviews personally, so I can get your feedback and make this book even better.

If you'd like to leave a review, then all you need to do is click the review link on this book's page on Amazon: Click to Write a Review

Thanks again for your support!

Lucas 5'11 – with Nichelle 3 months
2 Dogs Nightcrawler (Black Lab
Milca
Light brown eyes
Black Mercedes CLK

Nichelle 5'3 impatient, horny, drives Black Audi A5
AKA Donovan's "Baby Girl"

Donovan Brown – smoker Camels – sentenced to 10 years in prison – murder + robbing bank
6'3 240 lbs Age 17 started Only had to do 3; had a pit Rocky
owed $437,000 from bank robberies

Ronnie Duvalle – she slept c marcus! – 3 months. Backstabbing whore!
American Express Centurion Card? ric
28 y 5'6 green eyes not interested in long term relationship
high yella more interested in her career –
BMW X5 SUV youngest up
2nd Fl condo

Kendra with Marcus 6-1; came from VA – being transferred there to Houston
Ronnie knows her only 8 months

Made in the USA
Middletown, DE
21 November 2022